"I won't be here," Dione said calmly.

"You're *my* therapist," Blake snapped, tightening his grip on her wrist.

She gave a sad little laugh. "It's normal to be possessive. For months you've depended on me more than you have on any other person in your life. Your perspective is distorted. Believe me, by the time I've been gone a month, you won't even think about me."

"Do you mean you'd just turn your back on me and walk away?" Blake asked in a disbelieving tone.

Dione flinched, and tears welled in her eyes. "It... it's not that easy for me, either," she quavered. "But I've been through this more times than I can remember. I'm a habit, a crutch, nothing more, and I'm a crutch that you don't even need now. If I left today, you'd do just fine."

"That's not the point." His flesh was suddenly taut over his cheekbones. "*I* still need you."

"Linda Howard knows what readers want, and dares to be different."

—*Affaire de Coeur*

she was there. The woman washed her hands and dried

LINDA HOWARD

Come Lie with Me

MIRA

MIRA

ISBN 1-55166-549-2

COME LIE WITH ME

Copyright © 1984 by Linda Howington.

Visit us at www.mirabooks.com

Printed in U.S.A.

Come Lie with Me

The ocean had a hypnotic effect. Dione gave in to it without a struggle, peacefully watching the turquoise waves roll onto the blindingly white sand. She wasn't an idle person, yet she was content to sit on the deck of her rented beach house, her long, honey-tanned legs stretched out and propped on the railing, doing nothing more than watching the waves and listening to the muted roar of water coming in and going out. The white gulls swooped in and out of her vision, their high-pitched cries adding to the symphony of wind and water. To her right, the huge golden orb of the sun was sinking into the water, turning the sea to flame. It would have made a stunning photograph, yet she was disinclined to leave her seat and get her camera. It had been a glorious day, and she had done nothing more strenuous than celebrate it by walking the beach and swimming in the green-and-blue-streaked Gulf of Mexico. Lord, what a life. It was so sweet, it was almost sinful. This was the perfect vacation.

For two weeks she had wandered the sugar-white sands of Panama City, Florida, blissfully alone and lazy. There wasn't a clock in the beach house, nor had she even wound her watch since she'd arrived, because time didn't matter. No matter what time she woke, she knew that if she was hungry and didn't feel like cooking, there was always a place within walking distance where she could get something to eat. During the summer, the Miracle Strip didn't sleep. It was a twenty-four-hour party that constantly renewed itself from the end of school through the Labor Day weekend. Students and singles looking for a good time found it; families looking for a carefree vacation found it; and tired professional women wanting only a chance to unwind and relax beside the dazzling Gulf found that, too. She felt completely reborn after the past two delicious weeks.

A sailboat, as brightly colored as a butterfly, caught her attention, and she watched it as it lazily tacked toward shore. She was so busy watching the boat that she was unaware of the man approaching the deck until he started up the steps and the vibration of the wooden floor alerted her. Without haste she turned her head, the movement graceful and unalarmed, but her entire body was suddenly coiled and ready for action, despite the fact that she hadn't moved from her relaxed posture.

A tall, gray-haired man stood looking at her, and her first thought was that he didn't belong in this setting. P.C., as the vacation city was known, was a relaxed, informal area. This man was dressed in an impeccable three-piece gray suit, and his feet were shod in supple Italian leather. Dione reflected briefly that his shoes would be full of the loose sand that filtered into everything.

"Miss Kelley?" he inquired politely.

Her slim black brows arched in puzzlement, but she withdrew her feet from the railing and stood, holding out her hand to him. "Yes, I'm Dione Kelley. And you are…?"

"Richard Dylan," he said, taking her hand and shaking it firmly. "I realize that I'm intruding on your vacation, Miss Kelley, but it's very important that I speak with you."

"Please, sit down," Dione invited, indicating a deck chair beside the one she had just vacated. She resumed her former position, stretching out her legs and propping her bare feet on the railing. "Is there something I can do for you?"

"There certainly is," he replied feelingly. "I wrote to you about six weeks ago concerning a patient I'd like you to take on: Blake Remington."

Dione frowned slightly. "I remember. But I answered your letter, Mr. Dylan, before I left on vacation. Haven't you received it?"

"Yes, I have," he admitted. "I came to ask you to reconsider your refusal. There are extenuating circumstances, and his condition is deteriorating rapidly. I'm convinced that you can—"

"I'm not a miracle worker," she interrupted softly. "And I do have other cases lined up. Why should I put Mr. Remington ahead of others who need my services just as badly as he does?"

"Are they dying?" he asked bluntly.

"Is Mr. Remington? From the information you gave me in your letter, the last operation was a success. There are other therapists as well qualified as I am, if there's some reason why Mr. Remington has to have therapy this very moment."

Richard Dylan looked out at the turquoise Gulf, the waves tipped with gold by the sinking sun. "Blake Remington won't live another year," he said, and a bleak expression crossed his strong, austere features. "Not the way he is now. You see, Miss Kelley, he doesn't believe he'll ever walk again, and he's given up. He's deliberately letting himself die. He doesn't eat; he seldom sleeps; he refuses to leave the house.''

Dione sighed. Depression was sometimes the most difficult aspect of her patients' conditions, taking away their energy and determination. She'd seen it so many times before, and she knew that she'd see it again. "Still, Mr. Dylan, another therapist—''

"I don't think so. I've already employed two therapists, and neither of them has lasted a week. Blake refuses to cooperate at all, saying that it's just a waste of time, something to keep him occupied. The doctors tell him that the surgery was a success, but he still can't move his legs, so he just doesn't believe them. Dr. Norwood suggested you. He said that you've had remarkable success with uncooperative patients, and that your methods are extraordinary.''

She smiled wryly. "Of course he said that. Tobias Norwood trained me.''

Richard Dylan smiled briefly in return. "I see. Still, I'm convinced that you're Blake's last chance. If you still feel that your other obligations are more pressing, then come with me to Phoenix and meet Blake. I think that when you see him, you'll understand why I'm so worried.''

Dione hesitated, examining the proposal. Professionally, she was torn between refusing and agreeing. She had other cases, other people who were depending on her; why should this Blake Remington come before them? But on the other hand, he sounded like a challenge to her abilities, and she was one of those high-powered individuals who thrived on challenges, on testing herself to the limit. She was very certain of herself when it came to her chosen profession, and she enjoyed the satisfaction of completing a job and leaving her patient better able to move than before. In the years that she had been working as a private therapist, traveling all over the country to her patients' homes, she had amassed an amazing record of successes.

"He's an extraordinary man," said Mr. Dylan softly. "He's engineered several aeronautical systems that are widely used now. He designs his own planes, has flown as a test pilot on some top-secret planes for the government, climbs mountains, races yachts, goes deep-sea diving. He's a man who was at home on land, on the sea, or in the air, and now he's chained to a wheelchair and it's killing him."

"Which one of his interests was he pursuing when he had his accident?" Dione asked.

"Mountain climbing. The rope above him snagged on a rock, and his movements sawed the rope in two. He fell forty-five feet to a ledge, bounced off it, then rolled or fell another two hundred feet. That's almost the distance of a football field, but the snow must have cushioned him enough to save his life. He's said more than once that if he'd fallen off that mountain during the summer, he wouldn't have to spend his life as a cripple now."

"Tell me about his injuries," Dione said thoughtfully.

He rose to his feet. "I can do better than that. I have his file, complete with X rays, in my car. Dr. Norwood suggested that I bring it."

"He's a sly fox, that one," she murmured as Mr. Dylan disappeared around the deck. Tobias Norwood knew exactly how to intrigue her, how to set a particular case before her. Already she was interested, just as he had meant her to be. She'd make up her mind after seeing the X rays and reading the case history. If she didn't think she could help Blake Remington, she wouldn't put him through the stress of therapy.

In just a moment Mr. Dylan returned with a thick, manila envelope in his grasp. He released it into Dione's outthrust hand and waited expectantly. Instead of opening it, she tapped her fingernails against the envelope.

"Let me study this tonight, Mr. Dylan," she said firmly. "I can't just glance over it and make a decision. I'll let you know in the morning."

A flicker of impatience crossed his face; then he quickly mastered it and nodded. "Thank you for considering it, Miss Kelley."

When he was gone, Dione stared out at the Gulf for a long time, watching the eternal waves washing in with a froth of turquoise and sea-green, churning white as they rushed onto the sand. It was a good thing that her vacation was ending, that she'd already enjoyed almost two full weeks of utter contentment on the Florida panhandle, doing nothing more strenuous than walking in the tide. She'd already lazily begun considering her next job, but now it looked as if her plans had been changed.

After opening the envelope she held up the X rays one by one to the sun, and she winced when she saw the damage that had been done to a strong, vital human body. It was a miracle that he hadn't been killed outright. But the X rays taken after each successive operation revealed bones that had healed better than they should have, better than anyone could have hoped. Joints had been rebuilt; pins and plates had reconstructed his body and held it together. She went over the last set of X rays with excruciating detail. The surgeon had been a genius, or the results were a miracle, or perhaps a combination of both. She could see no physical reason why Blake couldn't walk again, provided the nerves hadn't been totally destroyed.

Beginning to read the surgeon's report, she concentrated fiercely on every detail until she understood exactly what damage had been done and what repairs had been made. This man *would* walk again; she'd make him! The end of the report mentioned that further improvement was prevented by the patient's lack of cooperation and depth of depression. She could almost feel the surgeon's sense of frustration as he'd written that; after all his painstaking work, after the unhoped-for success of his techniques, the patient had refused to help!

Gathering everything together, she started to replace the contents in the envelope and noticed that something else was inside, a stiff piece of paper that she'd neglected to remove. She pulled it out and turned it over. It wasn't just a piece of paper; it was a photograph.

Stunned, she stared into laughing blue eyes, eyes that sparkled and danced with the sheer joy of living. Richard Dylan was a sly one, too, knowing full well that few women would be able to resist the appeal of the dynamic man in the photograph. It was Blake Remington, she knew, as he had been before the accident. His brown hair was tousled, his darkly tanned face split by a rakish grin which revealed a captivating dimple in his left cheek. He was naked except for a brief pair of denim shorts, his body strong and well muscled, his legs the long, powerful limbs of an athlete. He was holding a good-sized marlin in the picture, and in the background she could make out the deep blue of the ocean; so he went deep-sea fishing, too. Wasn't there anything the man couldn't do? Yes, now there was, she reminded herself. Now he couldn't walk.

She wanted to refuse to take the case just to demonstrate to Richard Dylan that she couldn't be manipulated, but as she stared at the face in the photograph she knew that she would do just as he wanted, and she was disturbed by the knowledge. It had been such a long time since she'd been interested in any man at all that she was startled by her own reaction to a simple photograph.

Tracing the outline of his face with her fingertip, she wondered wistfully what her life would have been like if she'd been able to be a normal woman, to love a man and be loved in return, something that her brief and disastrous marriage had revealed to be impossible. She'd learned her lesson the hard way, but she'd never forgotten it. Men weren't for her. A loving husband and children weren't for her. The void left in her life by the total absence of love would have to be filled by her sense of satisfaction with her profession, with the joy she received from helping someone else. She might look at Blake Remington's photograph with admiration, but the daydreams that any other woman would indulge in when gazing at that masculine beauty were not for her. Daydreams were a waste of time, because she knew that she was incapable of attracting a man like him. Her ex-husband, Scott Hayes, had taught her with pain and humiliation the folly of enticing a man when she was unable to satisfy him.

Never again. She'd sworn it then, after leaving Scott, and she swore it again now. Never again would she give a man the chance to hurt her.

A sudden gust of salty wind fanned her cheeks, and she lifted her head, a little surprised to see that the sun was completely gone now and that she had been squinting at the photograph, not really seeing it as she dealt with her murky memories. She got to her feet and went inside, snapping on a tall floor lamp and illuminating the cool, summery interior of the beach house. Dropping into a plumply cushioned chair, Dione leaned her head back and began planning her therapy program, though of course she wouldn't be able to make any concrete plans until she actually met Mr. Remington and was better able to judge his condition. She smiled a little with anticipation. She loved a challenge more than she did anything else, and she had the feeling that Mr. Remington would fight her every inch of the way. She'd have to be on her toes, stay in control of the situation and use his helplessness as a lever against him, making him so angry that he'd go through hell to get better, just to get rid of her. Unfortunately, he really would have to go through hell; therapy wasn't a picnic.

She'd had difficult patients before, people who were so depressed and angry over their disabilities that they'd shut out the entire world, and she guessed that Blake Remington had reacted in the same way. He'd been so active, so vitally alive and in perfect shape, a real daredevil of a man; she guessed that it was killing his soul to be limited to a wheelchair. He wouldn't care if he lived or died; he wouldn't care about anything.

She slept deeply that night, no dreams disturbing her, and rose well before dawn for her usual run along the beach. She wasn't a serious runner, counting off the miles and constantly reaching for a higher number; she ran for the sheer pleasure of it, continuing until she tired, then strolling along and letting the silky froth of the tide wash over her bare feet. The sun was piercing the morning with its first blinding rays when she returned to the beach house, showered and began packing.

She'd made her decision, so she saw no need to waste time. She'd be ready when Mr. Dylan returned.

He wasn't even surprised when he saw her suitcases. "I knew you'd take the job," he said evenly.

Dione arched a slim black brow at him. "Are you always so sure of yourself, Mr. Dylan?"

"Please, call me Richard," he said. "I'm not always so certain, but Dr. Norwood has told me a great deal about you. He thought that you'd take the job because it was a challenge, and when I saw you, I knew that he was right."

"I'll have to talk with him about giving away my secrets," she joked.

"Not all of them," he said, and something in his voice made her wonder just how much he knew. "You have a lot of secrets left."

Deciding that Richard was far too astute, she turned briskly to her cases and helped him take them out to his car. Her own car was a rental, and after locking the beach house and returning the car to the rental office, she was ready to go.

Later, when they were in a private jet flying west to Phoenix, she began questioning Richard about her patient. What did he like? What did he hate? What were his hobbies? She wanted to know about his education, his politics, his favorite colors, the type of women he had dated, or about his wife if he were married. She'd found that wives were usually jealous of the close relationship that developed between therapist and patient, and she wanted to know as much as she could about a situation before she walked into it.

Richard knew an amazing amount about Mr. Remington's personal life, and finally Dione asked him what his relationship was to the man.

The firm mouth twisted. "I'm his vice-president, for one thing, so I know about his business operations. I'm also his brother-in-law. The only woman in his life who you'll have to deal with is my wife, Serena, who is also his younger sister."

Dione asked, "Why do you say that? Do you live in the same house with Mr. Remington?"

"No, but that doesn't mean anything. Since his accident, Serena has hovered over him, and I'm sure she won't be pleased when you arrive and take all of his attention. She's always adored Blake to the point of obsession. She nearly went insane when we thought he would die."

"I won't allow any interference in my therapy program," she warned him quietly. "I'll be overseeing his hours, his visitors, the food he eats, even the phone calls he receives. I hope your wife understands that."

"I'll try to convince her, but Serena is just like Blake. She's both stubborn and determined, and she has a key to the house."

"I'll have the locks changed," Dione planned aloud, perfectly serious in her intentions. Loving sister or not, Serena Dylan wasn't going to take over or intrude on Dione's therapy.

"Good," Richard approved, a frown settling on his austere brow. "I'd like to have a wife again."

It was beginning to appear that Richard had some other motive for wanting his brother-in-law walking again. Evidently, in the two years since Blake's accident, his sister had abandoned her husband in order to care for him, and the neglect was eroding her marriage. It was a situation that Dione didn't want to become involved in, but she had given her word that she would take the case, and she didn't betray the trust that people put in her.

Because of the time difference, it was only midafternoon when Richard drove them to the exclusive Phoenix suburb where Blake Remington lived. This time his car was a white Lincoln, plush and cool. As he drove up the circular drive to the hacienda-style house, she saw that it looked plush and cool, too. To call it a house was like calling a hurricane a wind; this place was a mansion. It was white and mysterious, keeping its secrets hidden behind its walls, presenting only a grateful facade to curious eyes. The landscaping was marvelous, a blend of the natural desert plants and lush greenery that was the product of careful and selective irrigation. The drive ran around to the back, where Richard told her the garage area was, but he stopped before the arched entry in front.

When she walked into the enormous foyer Dione thought she'd walked into the garden of paradise. There was a serenity to the place, a dignified simplicity wrought by the cool brown tiles on the floor, the plain white walls, the high ceiling. The hacienda was built in a U, around an open courtyard that was cool and fragrant, with a pink marble fountain in the center of it spouting clear water into the air. She could see all of that because the inner wall of the foyer, from ceiling to floor, was glass.

She was still speechless with admiration when the brisk clicking of heels on the tiles caught her attention, and she turned her head to watch the tall young woman approaching. This had to be Serena; the resemblance to the photo of Blake Remington was too strong for her to be anyone else. She had the same soft brown hair, the same dark blue eyes, the same clear-cut features.

But she wasn't laughing, as the man in the photo had been; her eyes were stormy, outraged.

"Richard!" she said in a low, wrathful tone. "Where have you been for the past two days? How dare you disappear without a word, then turn up with this...this gypsy in tow!"

Dione almost chuckled; most women wouldn't have attacked so bluntly, but she could see that this direct young woman had her share of the determination that Richard had attributed to Blake Remington. She opened her mouth to tell the truth of the matter, but Richard stepped in smoothly.

"Dione," he said, watching his wife with a cold eye, "I'd like to introduce my wife, Serena. Serena, this is Dione Kelley. I've hired Miss Kelley as Blake's new therapist, and I've been to Florida to pick her up and fly her back here. I didn't tell anyone where I was going because I had no intention of arguing over the matter. I've hired her, and that's that. I think that answers all of your questions." He finished with cutting sarcasm.

Serena Dylan wasn't a woman to be cowed, though a flush did color her cheeks. She turned to Dione and said frankly, "I apologize, though I refuse to take all of the blame. If my husband had seen fit to inform me of his intentions, I wouldn't have made such a terrible accusation."

"I understand." Dione smiled. "Under the same circumstances, I doubt that my conduct would have been as polite."

Serena smiled in return, then stepped forward and gave her husband a belated peck on the cheek. "Very well, you're forgiven," she sighed, "though I'm afraid you've wasted your time. You know that Blake won't put up with it. He can't stand having anyone hover over him, and he's been pushed at and pounded on enough.''

"Evidently not, or he'd be walking by now," Dione replied confidently.

Serena looked doubtful, then shrugged. "I still think you've wasted your time. Blake refused to have anything to do with the last therapist Richard hired, and he won't change his mind for you."

"I'd like to talk to him myself, if I may," Dione insisted, though in a pleasant tone.

Serena hadn't exactly stationed herself like a guard before the throne room, but it was evident that she was very protective of her brother. It wasn't all that unusual. When someone had been in a severe accident, it was only natural that the members of the family were over-protective for a while. Perhaps, when Serena found that Dione would be taking over the vast majority of Blake's time and attention, she would give her own husband the attention he deserved.

"At this time of day, Blake is usually in his room," Richard said, taking Dione's arm. "This way."

"Richard!" Again color rose in Serena's cheeks, but this time they were spots of anger. "He's lying down for a nap! At least leave him in peace until he comes downstairs. You know how badly he sleeps; let him rest while he can!"

"He naps every day?" Dione asked, thinking that if he slept during the day, no wonder he couldn't sleep at night.

"He tries to nap, but he usually looks worse afterward than he did before."

"Then it won't matter if we disturb him, will it?" Dione asked, deciding that now was the time to establish her authority. She caught a faint twitch of Richard's lips, signaling a smile, then he was directing her to the broad, sweeping stairs with his hand still warm and firm on her elbow. Behind them, Dione could feel the heat of the glare that Serena threw at them; then she heard the brisk tapping of heels as Serena followed.

From the design of the house, Dione suspected that all of the upstairs rooms opened onto the graceful gallery that ran along the entire U of the house, looking down on the inner courtyard. When Richard tapped lightly on a door that had been widened to allow a wheelchair to pass easily through it, then opened it at the low call that permitted entrance, she saw at once that, at least in this room, her supposition was correct. The enormous room was flooded with sunlight that streamed through the open curtains, though the sliding glass doors that opened onto the gallery remained closed.

The man at the window was silhouetted against the bright sunlight, a mysterious and melancholy figure slumped in the prison of a wheelchair. Then he reached out and pulled a chord, closing the curtains, and the room became dim. Dione blinked for a moment before her eyes adjusted to the sudden darkness; then the man became clear to her, and she felt her throat tighten with shock.

She'd thought that she was prepared; Richard had told her that Blake had lost weight and was rapidly deteriorating, but until she saw him, she hadn't realized exactly how serious the situation was. The contrast between the man in the wheelchair and the laughing man in the photo she'd seen was so great that she wouldn't have believed them to be the same man if it hadn't been for the dark blue eyes. His eyes no longer sparkled; they were dull and lifeless, but nothing could change their remarkable color.

He was thin, painfully so; he had to have lost almost fifty pounds from what he'd weighed when the photo had been taken, and he'd been all lean muscle then. His brown hair was dull from poor nutrition, and shaggy, as if it had been a long time since he'd had it trimmed. His skin was pale, his face all high cheekbones and gaunt cheeks.

Dione held herself upright, but inside she was shattering, crumbling into a thousand brittle pieces. She inevitably became involved with all her patients, but never before had she felt as if she were dying; never before had she wanted to rage at the injustice of it, at the horrible obscenity that had taken his perfect body and reduced it to helplessness. His suffering and despair were engraved on his drawn face, his bone structure revealed in stark clarity. Dark circles lay under the midnight blue of his eyes; his temples had become touched with gray. His once powerful body sat limp in the chair, his legs awkwardly motionless, and she knew that Richard had been right: Blake Remington didn't want to live.

He looked at her without a flicker of interest, then moved his gaze to Richard. It was as if she didn't exist. "Where've you been?" he asked flatly.

"I had business to attend to," Richard replied, his voice so cold that the room turned arctic. Dione could tell that he was insulted that anyone should question his actions; Richard might work for Blake, but he was in no way inferior. He was still angry with Serena, and the entire scene had earned his disapproval.

"He's so determined," Serena sighed, moving to her

brother's side. "He's hired another therapist for you, Miss...uh, Diane Kelley."

"Dione," Dione corrected without rancor.

Blake turned his disinterested gaze on her and surveyed her without a word. Dione stood quietly, studying him, noting his reaction, or rather, his lack of one. Richard had said that Blake had always preferred blondes, but even taking Dione's black hair into consideration, she had expected at least a basic recognition that she was female. She expected men to look at her; she'd grown used to it, though once an interested glance would have sent her into panic. She was a striking woman, and at last she had been able to accept that, considering it one of nature's ironies that she should have been given the looks to attract men when it was impossible for her to enjoy a man's touch.

She knew what he saw. She'd dressed carefully for effect, realizing that her appearance would either be intimidating or appealing; she didn't care which, as long as it gave her an edge in convincing him to cooperate. She'd parted her thick, vibrant black hair in the middle and drawn it back in a severe knot at the nape of her neck, where she'd secured it with a gold comb. Gold hoop earrings dangled from her ears. Serena had called her a gypsy, and her warm, honey-tanned skin made it seem possible. Her eyes were cat's eyes, slanted, golden, as mysterious as time and fringed with heavy black lashes. With her high cheekbones and strong, sculptured jawline, she looked Eastern and exotic, a prime candidate for a lusty sheik's harem, had she been born a century before.

She'd dressed in a white jumpsuit, chic and casual, and now she pushed her hands into the pockets, a posture that outlined her firm breasts. The line of her body was long and clean and sweeping, from her trim waist to her rounded bottom, then on down her long, graceful legs. Blake might not have noticed, but his sister had, and Serena had been stirred to instant jealousy. She didn't want Dione around either her husband or her brother.

After a long silence Blake moved his head slowly in a negative emotion. "No. Just take her away, Richard. I don't want to be bothered."

Dione glanced at Richard, then stepped forward, taking control and focusing Blake's attention on her. "I'm sorry you feel that way, Mr. Remington," she said mildly. "Because I'm staying anyway. You see, I have a contract, and I always honor my word."

"I'll release you from it," he muttered, turning his head away and looking out the window again.

"That's very nice of you, but *I* won't release *you* from it. I understand that you've given Richard your power of attorney, so the contract is legal, and it's also ironclad. It states, simply, that I'm employed as your therapist and will reside in this house until you're able to walk again. No time limit was set." She leaned down and put her hands on the arms of his wheelchair, bringing her face close to his and forcing him to give her his attention. "I'm going to be your shadow, Mr. Remington. The only way you'll be able to get rid of me is to walk to the door yourself and open it for me; no one else can do it for you."

"You're overstepping yourself, Miss Kelley!" Serena said sharply, her blue eyes narrowing with rage. She reached out and thrust Dione's hands away from the wheelchair. "My brother has said that he doesn't want you here!"

"This doesn't concern you," Dione replied, still in a mild tone.

"It certainly does! If you think I'll let you just move in here...why, you probably think you've found a meal ticket for life!"

"Not at all. I'll have Mr. Remington walking by Christmas. If you doubt my credentials, please feel free to investigate my record. But in the meantime, stop interfering." Dione straightened to her full height and stared steadily at Serena, the strength of her willpower blazing from her golden eyes.

"Don't talk to my sister like that," Blake said sharply.

At last! A response, even if it was an angry one! With secret delight Dione promptly attacked the crack in his indifference. "I'll talk to anyone like that who tries to come between me and my patient," she informed him. She put her hands on her hips and surveyed him with a contemptuous curl to her mouth. "Look at you! You're in such pitiful shape that you'd have to go into training to qualify for the ninety-eight-pound weakling category! You should be ashamed of yourself, letting your muscles turn into mush; no wonder you can't walk!"

The dark pupils of his eyes flared, a black pool in a sea of blue. "Damn you," he choked. "It's hard to do calisthenics when you're hooked up to more tubes than you have places for, and nothing except your face works when you want it to!"

"That was then," she said relentlessly. "What about now? It takes muscles to walk, and you don't have any! You'd lose a fight with a noodle, the shape you're in now."

"And I suppose you think you can wave your magic

wand and put me into working order again?'' he snarled.

She smiled. "A magic wand? It won't be as easy as that. You're going to work harder for me than you've ever worked before. You're going to sweat and hurt, and turn the air blue cussing me out, but you're going to work. I'll have you walking again if I have to half-kill you to do it.''

"No, you won't, lady,'' he said with cold deliberation. "I don't care what sort of contract you have; I don't want you in my house. I'll pay whatever it takes to get rid of you.''

"I'm not giving you that option, Mr. Remington. I won't accept a payoff.''

"You don't have to give me the option! I'm *taking* it!''

Looking into his enraged face, flushed with anger, Dione abruptly realized that the photograph of the laughing, relaxed man had been misleading, an exception rather than the rule. This was a man of indomitable will, used to forcing things to go his way by the sheer power of his will and personality. He had overcome every obstacle in his life by his own determination, until the fall down the cliff had changed all that and presented him with the one obstacle that he couldn't handle on his own. He'd never had to have help before, and he hadn't been able to accept that now he did. Because he couldn't make himself walk, he was convinced that it wasn't possible.

But she was determined, too. Unlike him, she'd learned early that she could be struck down, forced to do things she didn't want to do. She'd pulled herself out of the murky depths of despair by her own silent, stubborn belief that life *had* to be better. Dione had forged her strength in the fires of pain; the woman she had become, the independence and skill and reputation she'd built, were too precious to her to allow her to back down now. This was the challenge of her career, and it would take every ounce of her willpower to handle it.

So, insolently, she asked him, "Do you *like* having everyone feel sorry for you?"

Serena gasped; even Richard made an involuntary sound before bringing himself back under control. Dione didn't waste a glance on them. She kept her eyes locked with Blake's, watching the shock in them, watching the angry color wash out of his face and leave it utterly white.

"You bitch," he said in a hollow, shaking voice.

She shrugged. "Look, we're getting nowhere like this. Let's make a deal. You're so weak, I'll bet you can't beat me at arm wrestling. If I win, I stay and you agree to therapy. If you win, I walk out that door and never come back. What do you say?"

Chapter Two

His head jerked up, his eyes narrowing as they swept over her slender form and graceful, feminine arms. Dione could almost read his thoughts. As thin as he was, he still outweighed her by at least forty, possibly even fifty, pounds. He knew that even if a man and a woman were the same weight, the man would be stronger than the woman, under normal circumstances. Dione refused to let a smile touch her lips, but she knew that these weren't normal circumstances. Blake had been inactive for two years, while she was in extremely good shape. She was a therapist; she had to be strong in order to do her job. She was slim, yes, but every inch of her was sleek, strong muscle. She ran, she swam, she did stretching exercises regularly, but most importantly, she lifted weights. She had to have considerable arm strength to be able to handle patients who couldn't handle themselves. She looked at Blake's thin, pale hands, and she knew that she would win.

"Don't do it!" Serena said sharply, twisting her fingers into knots.

Blake turned and looked at his sister in disbelief. "You think she can beat me, don't you?" he murmured, but the words were more a statement than a question.

Serena was tense, staring at Dione with an odd, pleading look in her eyes. Dione understood: Serena didn't want her brother humiliated. And neither did she.

But she did want him to agree to therapy, and she was willing to do whatever was necessary to make him see what he was doing to himself. She tried to say that with her eyes, because she couldn't say the words aloud.

"Answer me!" Blake roared suddenly. Every line of him was tense.

Serena bit her lower lip. "Yes," she finally said. "I think she can beat you."

Silence fell, and Blake sat as though made of stone. Watching him carefully, Dione saw the moment he made the decision. "There's only one way to find out, isn't there?" he challenged, turning the wheelchair with a quick pressure of his finger on a button. Dione followed him as he led the way to his desk and positioned the wheelchair beside it.

"You shouldn't have a motorized wheelchair," she observed absently. "A manual chair would have kept your upper body strength at a reasonable level. This is a fancy chair, but it isn't doing you any good at all."

He shot her a brooding glance, but didn't respond to her comment. "Sit down," he said, indicating his desk.

Dione took her time obeying him. She felt no joy, no elation, in knowing that she would win; it was something she had to do, a point that she had to make to Blake.

Richard and Serena flanked them as they positioned themselves, Blake maneuvering himself until he was satisfied with his location, Dione doing the same. She propped her right arm on the desk and gripped her bicep with her left hand. "Ready when you are," she said.

Blake had the advantage of a longer arm, and she realized that it would take all of the strength in her hand and wrist to overcome the leverage he would have. He positioned his arm against hers and wrapped his fingers firmly around her much smaller hand. For a moment he studied the slim grace of her fingers, the delicate pink of her manicured nails, and a slight smile moved his lips. He probably thought it would be a cake walk. But she felt the coldness of his hands, indicating poor circulation, and knew the inevitable outcome of their little battle.

"Richard, you start it," Blake instructed, lifting his eyes and locking them with hers. She could feel his intensity, his aggressive drive to win, and she began to brace herself, concentrating all her energy and strength into her right arm and hand.

"Go," said Richard, and though there was no great flurry of movement between the two antagonists, their bodies were suddenly tense, their arms locked together.

Dione kept her face calm, revealing nothing of the fierce effort it took to keep her wrist straight. After the first moments, when he was unable to shove her arm down, Blake's face reflected first astonishment, then anger, then a sort of desperation. She could feel his first burst of strength ebbing and slowly, inexorably, she began forcing his arm down. Sweat broke out on his forehead and slipped down one side of his face as he struggled to reverse the motion, but he had already used his meager strength and had nothing in reserve. Knowing that she had him, and regretting her victory even though she knew it was necessary, Dione quickly settled the matter by forcing his arm down flat on the desk.

He sat in his wheelchair, a shattered expression in his eyes for a flashing moment before he closed himself off and made his face a blank wall.

The silence was broken only by his rapid breathing. Richard's face was grim; Serena looked torn between the desire to comfort her brother and a strong inclination to throw Dione out herself.

Dione moved briskly, rising to her feet. "That settles that," she said casually. "In another two months I won't be able to do that. I'll put my things in the room next to this one—"

"No," said Blake curtly, not looking at her. "Serena, give Miss Kelley the guest suite."

"That won't do at all," Dione replied. "I want to be close enough to you that I'll be able to hear you if you call. The room next door will do nicely. Richard, how soon can you have those changes made that I stipulated?"

"What changes?" Blake asked, jerking his head up.

"I need some special equipment," she explained, noting that the diversion had worked, as she'd intended it to. He'd already lost that empty look. She'd evidently made the right decision in being so casual about beating him at arm wrestling, treating the incident as nothing unusual. Now was not the time to rub it in, or to let him know that there were a lot of men walking the earth who couldn't match her in arm wrestling. He'd find out soon enough when they got into the weight-lifting program.

"What sort of special equipment?" he demanded.

She controlled a smile. His attention had certainly been caught by the possibility of any changes in his beloved home. She outlined her needs to him. "A whirlpool is a necessity. I'll also need a treadmill, weight bench, sauna, things like that. Any objections?"

"There might be. Just where do you plan to put all this?"

"Richard said he could outfit a gym for me on the ground floor, next to the pool, which will be very convenient, because you'll be doing a lot of work in the pool. Water is a great place for calisthenics,'' she said enthusiastically. ''Your muscles still get the workout, but the water supports your weight.''

''You're not putting in a gym,'' he said grimly.

''Read my contract.'' She smiled. ''The gym is going in. Don't make such a fuss; the house won't be disfigured, and the equipment is necessary. An Olympic trainee won't be getting the workout you're facing,'' she said with quiet truth. ''It's going to be hard work, and it's going to be painful, but you'll do it if I have to drive you like a slave. You can put money on it: You'll be walking by Christmas.''

A terrible longing crossed his face before he brought his thin hand up to rub his forehead, and Dione sensed his indecision. But it wasn't in him to give in to anyone else easily, and he scowled. ''You won the right to stay here,'' he said grudgingly. ''But I don't like it, and I don't like you, Miss Kelley. Richard, I want to see that contract she keeps harping about.''

''I don't have it with me,'' Richard lied smoothly, taking Serena's arm and edging her toward the door. ''I'll bring it with me the next time I'm over.''

Serena had time for only an incoherent protest before Richard had her out the door. Trusting Richard to keep his wife away, at least for the time being, Dione smiled at Blake and waited.

He eyed her warily. ''Don't you have something else to do besides staring at me?''

''I certainly do. I was just waiting to see if you have any questions. If you don't, I need to be unpacking.''

''No questions,'' he muttered.

That wouldn't last long, she thought, leaving him

without another word. When he found out the extent of her therapy, he'd have plenty to say about it.

It was evidently up to her to find her way around the house, but because the design was so simple, she had no difficulty exploring. Her suitcases were sitting in the foyer, and she took them upstairs herself, finally examining the room she'd chosen for her own. It was a room for a man, done in masculine browns and creams, but it was comfortable and suited her; she wasn't picky. She unpacked, a chore that didn't take long because she didn't burden herself with a lot of clothing. What she had was good and adaptable, so she could use one outfit for several different things just by changing a few accessories. The way she traveled around, from one case to another, a lot of clothing would have been a hindrance.

Then she went in search of the cook and housekeeper; a house that size had to have some sort of staff, and she needed everyone's cooperation. It might have been easier if Richard had remained to introduce her, but she was glad that he'd taken Serena out of the way.

She found the kitchen without difficulty, though the cook who occupied it was something of a surprise. She was tall and lean, obviously part Indian, despite the pale green of her eyes. Though her age was impossible to determine, Dione guessed her to be at least in her fifties, possibly sixties. Her raven black hair didn't hint at it, but there was something in the knowledge in her eyes, the dignity of her features, that suggested age. She was as imperial as a queen, though the look she turned on the intruder into her kitchen wasn't haughty, merely questioning.

Quickly Dione introduced herself and explained why she was there. The woman washed her hands and dried them with unhurried motions, then held her hand out. Dione took it. "My name is Alberta Quincy," the cook said in a deep, rich voice that could have been a man's. "I'm glad that Mr. Remington has agreed to therapy."

"He didn't exactly agree," Dione replied honestly, smiling. "But I'm here anyway, and I'm staying. I'll need everyone's cooperation to handle him, though."

"You just tell me what you want," Alberta said with pure confidence. "Miguel, who takes care of the grounds and drives Mr. Remington's car, will do as I tell him. My stepdaughter, Angela, cleans the house, and she'll also do as I say."

Most people would, Dione thought privately. Alberta Quincy was the most regal person she'd ever met. There wasn't much expression in her face and her voice was even and deliberate, but there was a force to the woman that most people wouldn't be able to resist. She would be an indispensable ally.

Dione outlined the diet she wanted Blake to follow, and explained why she wanted changes made. The last thing she wanted to do was offend Alberta. But Alberta merely nodded. "Yes, I understand."

"If he gets angry, put all the blame on me," Dione said. "At this point, I *want* him to be angry. I can use anger, but I can't work with indifference."

Again Alberta nodded her regal head. "I understand," she said again. She wasn't a talkative woman, to understate the matter, but she did understand, and to Dione's relief she didn't express any doubts.

There was one other problem, and Dione broached it cautiously. "About Mr. Remington's sister..."

Alberta blinked once, slowly, and nodded. "Yes," she said simply.

"Does she have a key to the house?" Gold eyes met

green ones, and the communication between the two women was so strong that Dione had the sudden feeling that words were unnecessary.

"I'll have the locks changed," Alberta said. "But there'll be trouble."

"It'll be worth the benefits. I can't have his routine interrupted once I get him started on it, at least until he can see some improvement for himself and will want to continue with it. I think Mr. Dylan can handle his wife."

"If he even wants to any longer," Alberta said calmly.

"I think he does. He doesn't seem like a man to give up very easily."

"No, but he's also very proud."

"I don't want to cause trouble between them, but Mr. Remington is my concern, and if that causes friction, then they have to handle it as best they can."

"Mrs. Dylan worships her brother. He raised her; their mother died when Mrs. Dylan was thirteen."

That explained a lot, and Dione spared a moment of sympathy for both Serena and Richard; then she pushed thoughts of them away. She couldn't consider them; Blake would take all her concentration and energy.

Suddenly she was very tired. It had been a full day, and though it was only late afternoon, she needed to rest. The battle would begin in earnest in the morning, and she'd need a good night's sleep in order to face it. Starting tomorrow, her hands would be full.

Alberta saw the sudden fatigue that tightened Dione's features and within minutes had a sandwich and a glass of milk sitting on the table. "Eat," she said, and Dione knew better than to argue. She sat down and ate.

*   *   *

Dione's alarm clock went off at five-thirty the next morning. She rose and took a shower, her movements brisk and certain from the moment she got out of bed. She always woke instantly, her mind clear, her coordination in perfect sync. It was one reason why she was such a good therapist; if a patient needed her during the night, she didn't stumble around rubbing her eyes. She was instantly capable of doing whatever was required of her.

Something told her that Blake wouldn't be such a cheerful riser, and she could feel her heartbeat speeding up as she brushed her long hair and braided it in one thick braid. Anticipation of the coming battle ran through her veins like liquid joy, making her eyes sparkle and giving a rosy flush to her skin.

The morning was still cool, but she knew from experience that exertion would make her warm, so she dressed in brief blue shorts, a sleeveless cotton shirt with cheerful polka dots in red, blue and yellow, and an old pair of tennis shoes. She touched her toes twenty times, stretching her back and legs, then did twenty sit-ups. She was capable of many more than that, but this was only a quick routine to warm up.

She was smiling when she entered Blake's room after a quick tap on the door. "Good morning," she said cheerfully as she crossed the floor to the balcony and opened the curtains, flooding the room with light.

He was lying on his back, his legs positioned a little awkwardly, as if he'd tried to move them during the night. He opened his eyes, and Dione saw the flare of panic in them. He twitched and tried to sit up, groping at his legs; then he remembered and fell back, his face bleak.

How often did that happen? How often did he wake, not remembering the accident, and panic because he couldn't move his legs? He wouldn't do that for very much longer, she determined grimly, going over to sit on the bed beside him.

"Good morning," she said again.

He didn't return the greeting. "What time is it?" he snapped.

"About six o'clock, maybe a little earlier."

"What're you doing here?"

"Beginning your therapy," she replied serenely. He was wearing pajamas, she saw, and wondered if he were able to completely dress himself or if someone had to help him.

"No one's up at this hour," he grumbled, closing his eyes again.

"I am, and now you are. Come on; we've got a lot to do today." She rolled the wheelchair to the side of the bed and threw the covers back, revealing his pitifully thin legs clad in the pale blue pajamas. His feet were covered with white socks.

He opened his eyes and the anger was there again. "What're you doing?" he snarled, reaching out an arm to whip the covers back over himself again.

He didn't want her to see him, but she couldn't permit any modesty to interfere. Before long she'd be as familiar with his body as she was with her own, and he had to realize that. If he were ashamed of his physical condition, then he'd simply have to work to improve it.

She snatched the covers away again, and with a deft movement scooped his legs around until they were hanging off the side of the bed. "Get up," she said relentlessly. "Go to the bathroom before we get started. Do you need any help?"

Pure fire sparked from his blue, blue eyes. "No," he growled, so angry that he could barely speak. "I can go to the bathroom by myself, Mama!"

"I'm not your mother," she returned. "I'm your therapist, though the two do have a lot in common."

She held the chair while he levered himself into it; then he shot across the room and was in the adjoining bathroom before she could react. She laughed silently to herself. When she heard the lock click she called out, "Don't think you can lock yourself in there all morning! I'll take the door off the hinges if I have to."

A muffled curse answered her, and she laughed again. This was going to be interesting!

By the time he finally came out she had begun to think she really would have to take the door down. He'd combed his hair and washed his face, but he didn't look any more pleased with being awake than he had before.

"Do you have any underwear on?" she asked, not making any comment on the length of time he'd spent in the bathroom. He'd timed that very nicely, stalling as long as he could, but coming out just before she did something about it.

Shock froze his features. "What?" he asked.

"Do you have any underwear on?" she repeated.

"What business is it of yours?"

"Because I want your pajamas off. If you don't have any underwear on, you may want to put on a pair, but it really doesn't matter to me. I've seen naked men before."

"I'm sure you have," he muttered snidely. "I have underwear on, but I'm not taking my pajamas off for you."

"Then don't. I'll take them off for you. I think you learned yesterday that I'm strong enough to do it. But those pajamas are coming off, the easy way or the hard way. Which is it?''

"Why do you want them off?'' he stalled. "It can't be so you can admire my build," he said bitterly.

"You're right about that," she said. "You look like a bird. That's why I'm here; if you didn't look like a bird, you wouldn't need me."

He flushed.

"The pajamas," she prodded.

Furiously he unbuttoned the shirt and threw it across the room. She could sense that he would have liked to do the same to the bottoms, but they were a bit more difficult to remove. Without a word Dione helped him back onto the bed, then pulled the garment down his thin legs and draped it over the arm of the wheelchair. "On your stomach," she said, and deftly rolled him over.

"Hey!" he protested, his face smothered in the pillow. He swept the pillow aside. He was shaking with fury.

She popped the elastic waistband of his shorts. "Calm down," she advised. "This will be painless this morning."

Her impertinent little gesture made his temper flare so hotly that his entire torso flushed. Smiling at his response, she began to firmly knead his shoulders and back.

He grunted. "Take it easy! I'm not a side of beef!"

She laughed. "How delicate you are!" she mocked. "There's a reason for this."

"Like what? Punishment?"

"In a word, circulation. Your circulation is terrible. That's why your hands are cold, and why you have to wear socks to keep your feet warm, even in bed. I'll bet they're icy cold right now, aren't they?''

Silence was her answer.

''Muscles can't work without a good blood supply,'' she commented.

''I see,'' he said sarcastically. ''Your magical massage is going to zip me right onto my feet.''

''No way. My magical massage is mere groundwork, and you should learn to like it, because you're going to be getting a lot of it.''

''God, you're just loaded down with charm, aren't you?''

She laughed again. ''I'm loaded down with knowledge, and I also come equipped with a thick hide, so you're wasting your time.'' She moved down to his legs; there was no flesh there to massage. She felt as if she were merely moving his skin over his bones, but she kept at it, knowing that the hours and hours of massage that she would give him would eventually pay off. She pulled his socks off and rubbed his limp feet briskly, feeling some of the chill leave his skin.

The minutes passed as she worked in silence. He grunted occasionally in protest when her vigorous fingers were a little too rough. A fine sheen of perspiration began to glow on her face and body.

She shifted him onto his back and gave her attention to his arms and chest and his hollow belly. His ribs stood out white under his skin. He lay with his eyes fixed on the ceiling, his mouth grim.

Dione moved down to his legs again.

''How much longer are you going to keep this up?'' he finally asked.

She looked up and checked the time. It had been a

little over an hour. "I suppose that's enough for right now," she said. "Now we do the exercises."

She took first one leg, then the other, bending them, forcing his knees up to his chest, repeating the motion over and over. He bore it in silence for about fifteen minutes, then suddenly rolled to a sitting position and shoved her away.

"Stop it!" he shouted, his face drawn. "My God, woman, do you have to keep on and on? It's a waste of time! Just leave me alone!"

She regarded him in amazement. "What do you mean, 'a waste of time'? I've just started. Did you really expect to see a difference in an hour?"

"I don't like being handled like so much putty!"

She shrugged, hiding a smile. "It's almost seven-thirty anyway. Your breakfast will be ready. I don't know about you, but I'm hungry."

"I'm not hungry," he said, and then a startled look crossed his face and she knew that he'd just realized that he *was* hungry, probably for the first time in months. She helped him to dress, though her aid managed to send him off into a black temper again. He was as sullen as a child when they entered the elevator that had been installed especially for him.

But the sullenness fled when he saw what was on his plate. Watching him, Dione had to bite her lip to keep from laughing aloud. First horror, then outrage contorted his features. "What's that mess?" he roared.

"Oh, don't worry," she said casually. "That's not all you're getting, but that's what you'll start off with. Those are vitamins," she added in a helpful tone.

They could have been snakes from the way he was staring at them. She had to admit that the collection was a little impressive. Alberta had counted them out exactly as Dione had instructed, and she knew that there were nineteen pills.

"I'm not taking them!"

"You're taking them. You need them. You'll need them even more after a few days of therapy. Besides, you don't get anything to eat until after you've taken them."

He wasn't a good loser. He snatched them up and swallowed them several at a time, washing them down with gulps of water. "There," he snarled. "I've taken the damned things."

"Thank you," she said gravely.

Alberta had evidently been listening, because she promptly entered with their breakfast trays. He looked at his grapefruit half, whole wheat toast, eggs, bacon and milk as if it were slop. "I want a blueberry waffle," he said.

"Sorry," Dione said. "That's not on your diet. Too sweet. Eat your grapefruit."

"I hate grapefruit."

"You need the vitamin C."

"I just took a year's supply of vitamin C!"

"Look," she said sweetly, "this is your breakfast. Eat it or do without. You're not getting a blueberry waffle."

He threw it at her.

She'd been expecting something like that, and ducked gracefully. The plate crashed against the wall. She collapsed against the table, the laughter that she'd been holding in all morning finally bursting out of her in great whoops. His hair was practically standing on end, he was so angry. He was beautiful! His cobalt blue eyes were as vivid as sapphires; his face was alive with color.

As dignified as a queen, Alberta marched out of the

kitchen with an identical tray and set it before him. "She said you'd probably throw the first one," she said without inflection.

Knowing that he'd acted exactly as Dione had predicted made him even angrier, but now he was stymied. He didn't know what to do, afraid that whatever he did, she would have anticipated it. Finally he did nothing. He ate silently, pushing the food into his mouth with determined movements, then balked again at the milk.

"I can't stand milk. Surely coffee can't hurt!"

"It won't hurt, but it won't help, either. Let's make a deal," she offered. "Drink the milk, which you need for the calcium, and then you can have coffee."

He took a deep breath and drained the milk glass.

Alberta brought in coffee. The remainder of the meal passed in relative peace. Angela Quincy, Alberta's stepdaughter, came in to clear the mess that Blake had made with his first breakfast, and he looked a little embarrassed.

Angela, in her way, was as much of an enigma as Alberta was. She showed her age, unlike Alberta; she was about fifty, as soft and cuddly as Alberta was lean and angular. She was very pretty, could even have been called beautiful, despite the wrinkling of her skin. She was the most serene person Dione had ever seen. Her hair was brown, liberally streaked with gray, and her eyes were a soft, tranquil brown. She had once been engaged, Dione would learn later, but the man had died, and Angela still wore the engagement ring he'd given her so many years before.

She wasn't disturbed at all by having to clean egg off the wall, though Blake became increasingly restless as she worked. Dione leisurely finished her meal, then laid her napkin aside.

"Time for more exercises," she announced.

"No!" he roared. "I've had enough for today! A little of you goes a long way, lady!"

"Please, call me Dione," she murmured.

"I don't want to call you anything! My God, would you just leave me alone!"

"Of course I will, when my job is finished. I can't let you ruin my record of successful cases, can I?"

"Do you know what you can do with your successful record?" he snarled, sending the chair jerking backward. He jabbed the forward button. "I don't want to see your face again!" he shouted as the chair rolled out of the room.

She sighed and lifted her shoulders helplessly when her eyes met Angela's philosophic gaze. Angela smiled, but didn't say anything. Alberta wasn't talkative, and Angela was even less so. Dione imagined that when the two of them were together, the silence was deafening.

When she thought that Blake had had enough time to get over his tantrum, she went upstairs to begin again. It would probably be a waste of time to try his door, so she entered her room and went straight through to the gallery. She tapped on the sliding glass doors in his room, then opened them and stepped in.

He regarded her broodingly from his chair. Dione went to him and placed her hand on his shoulder. "I know it's difficult," she said softly. "I can't promise you that any of this will be easy. Try to trust me; I really am good at my job, and at the very worst you'll still be in much better health than you are now."

"If I can't walk, why should I care about my health?" he asked tightly. "Do you think I want to live like this? I would rather have died outright on that cliff than have gone through these past two years."

"Have you always given up so easily?"

"Easily!" His head jerked. "You don't know anything about it! You don't know what it was like—"

"I can tell you what it wasn't like," she interrupted. "I can tell you that you've never looked down at where your legs used to be and seen only flat sheet. You've never had to type by punching the keys with a pencil held in your teeth because you're paralyzed from the neck down. I've seen a lot of people who are a lot worse off than you. You're going to walk again, because I'm going to make you."

"I don't want to hear about how bad other people have it! They're not *me!* My life is my own, and I know what I want out of it, and what I can't...what I *won't* accept."

"Work? Effort? Pain?" she prodded. "Mr. Remington, Richard has told me a great deal about you. You lived life to the fullest. If there were even the slimmest chance that you could do all of that again, would you go for it?"

He sighed, his face unutterably weary. "I don't know. If I really thought there was a chance...but I don't. I can't walk, Miss Kelley. I can't move my legs at all."

"I know. You can't expect to move them right now. I'll have to retrain your nerve impulses before you'll be able to move them. It'll take several months, and I can't promise that you won't limp, but you *will* walk again...if you cooperate with me. So, Mr. Remington, shall we get started again on those exercises?"

Chapter Three

He submitted to the exercises with ill grace, but that didn't bother her as long as he cooperated at all. His muscles didn't know that he lay there scowling the entire time; the movement, the stimulation, were what counted. Dione worked tirelessly, alternating between exercising his legs and massaging his entire body. It was almost ten-thirty when she heard the noise that she'd been unconsciously listening for all morning: the tapping of Serena's heels. She lifted her head, and then Blake heard it, too. "No!" he said hoarsely. "Don't let her see me like this!"

"All right," she said calmly, flipping the sheet up to cover him. Then she walked to the door and stepped into the hallway, blocking Serena's way as she started to enter Blake's room.

Serena gave her a startled look. "Is Blake awake? I was just going to peek in; he usually doesn't get up until about noon."

No wonder he'd been so upset when I got him up at six! Dione thought, amused. To Serena she said blandly, "I'm giving him his exercises now."

"So early?" Serena's brows arched in amazement. "Well, I'm certain you've done enough for the day. Since he's awake early he'll be ready for his breakfast. He eats so badly. I don't want him to miss any meals. I'll go in and see what he'd like—"

As Serena moved around Dione to enter Blake's bed-room, Dione deftly sidestepped until she once more blocked the door. "I'm sorry," she said as gently as possible when Serena stared at her in disbelief. "He's already had his breakfast. I've put him on a schedule, and it's important that he stay on it. After another hour of exercise we'll come downstairs for lunch, if you'd like to wait until then."

Serena was still staring at her as if she couldn't be-lieve what she was hearing. "Are you saying..." she whispered, then stopped and began again, her voice stronger this time. "Are you saying that I can't see my brother?"

"At this time, no. We need to complete these exer-cises."

"Does Blake know I'm here?" Serena demanded, her cheeks suddenly flushing.

"Yes, he does. He doesn't want you to see him right now. Please, try to understand how he feels."

Serena's marvelous eyes widened. "Oh! Oh, I see!" Perhaps she did, but Dione rather doubted it. Hurt shim-mered in Serena's eyes for a moment; then she shrugged lightly. "I'll...see him in an hour, then." She turned away, and Dione watched her for a moment, reading wounded emotions in every line of her straight back. It wasn't unusual for the one closest to the patient to be-come jealous of the intimacy that was necessary be-tween patient and therapist, but Dione never failed to feel uncomfortable when it happened. She knew that the intimacy was only fleeting, that as soon as her patient was recovered and no longer needed her services, she would go on to some other case and the patient would forget all about her. In Blake's case, there was nothing to be jealous of anyway. The only emotion he felt for her was hostility.

When she reentered the bedroom he twisted his head around to stare at her. "Is she gone?" he questioned anxiously.

"She's going to wait downstairs to eat lunch with you," Dione answered, and saw the relief that crossed his face.

"Good. She...nearly went to pieces when this happened to me. She'd be hysterical if she saw what I really look like." Pain darkened his eyes. "She's special to me; I practically raised her. I'm all the family she has."

"No, you're not," Dione pointed out. "She has Richard."

"He's so wrapped up in his work, he seldom remembers that she's alive," he snorted. "Richard's a great vice-president, but he's not a great husband."

That wasn't the impression Dione had gotten from Richard; he'd seemed to her to be a man very much in love with his wife. On the surface Richard and Serena were opposites; he was reserved, sophisticated, while she was as forceful as her brother, but perhaps they were each what the other needed. Perhaps her fire made him more spontaneous; perhaps his reserve tempered her rashness. But Dione didn't say anything to Blake. She began the repetitive exercises again, forcing his legs through the same motions.

It was tiring, boring work; tiring for her, boring for him. It made him irritable all over again, but this time when he snapped at her to stop, she obeyed him. She didn't want to browbeat him, to force her wishes on him in everything. He'd put in the most active morning he'd had since the accident, and she wasn't going to push him any further. "Whew!" she sighed, wiping her forehead with the back of her hand and feeling the moisture there. "I need a shower before lunch! Breaking off a little early is a good idea."

He looked at her, and his eyes widened in surprise. She knew that he didn't really see her all morning; he'd been preoccupied with his own condition, his own despair. She'd told him that he'd have to work hard, but now for the first time he realized that she'd be working hard, too. It wasn't going to be a picnic for her. She knew that she looked a mess, all sweaty and flushed.

"A bath wouldn't hurt you," he agreed dryly, and she laughed.

"Don't be such a gentleman about it," she teased. "You just wait. I won't be the only one working up a sweat before long, and I won't show you any mercy!"

"I haven't noticed you showing any, anyway," he grumbled.

"Now, I've been very good to you. I've kept you entertained all morning; I made certain you had a good breakfast—"

"Don't push your luck," he advised, giving her a black look, which she rewarded with a smile. It was important that he learn to joke and laugh with her, to ease the stress of the coming months. She had to become the best friend he had in the world, knowing as she did so that it was a friendship that was doomed from the outset, because it was based on dependence and need. When he no longer needed her, when his life had regained its normal pace, she would leave and be promptly forgotten. She knew that, and she had to keep a part of herself aloof, though the remainder of her emotions and mental effort would be concentrated entirely on him.

While she was helping him to dress, a process that

didn't anger him as it had that morning, he said thoughtfully, ''You'll be spending most of your time dressing and undressing me, it seems. If this is the routine you're going to be following it'll save a lot of time if I just wear a pair of gym shorts; I can put on a robe before we eat, and Alberta can bring trays up here.''

Dione successfully hid her delight, merely saying, ''That's your second good idea of the day.'' Secretly she was elated. From a practical standpoint he was right: It would save a lot of time and effort; however, it would also exclude Serena from most of their meals. That would be a big help.

If wasn't that she disliked Serena; if she had met her under different circumstances, Dione felt that she would have liked Serena very much. But Blake was her concern now, and she didn't want anyone or anything interfering with her work. While she was working on a case she concentrated on her patient to the extent that everyone else faded into the background, became gray cardboard figures rather than three-dimensional human beings. It was one of the things that made her so successful in her field. Already, after only one morning, Blake so filled her thoughts, and she was so much in tune with him, that she felt she knew him inside and out. She could practically read his mind, know what he was going to say before he said it. She ached for him, sympathized with him, but most of all she was happy for him, because she could look at his helplessness now and know that in a few months he would be strong and fit again. Already he was looking better, she thought proudly. It was probably due more to his anger than her efforts, but his color was much improved. He could stay angry with her for the entire time if it would keep him active and involved.

She was feeling satisfied with the morning's work as she walked beside him into the dining room, but that feeling was shattered when Serena plunged toward Blake, her lovely face bathed in tears. "Blake," she said brokenly.

Instantly he was alert, concerned, as he reached for her hand. "What is it?" he asked, a note of tenderness creeping into his voice, a particular tone that was absent when he talked to everyone else. Only Serena inspired that voice of love.

"The patio!" she wailed. "Mother's bench...it's ruined! They've turned the pool into a madhouse! It looks awful!"

"What?" he asked, his brows snapping together. "What're you talking about?"

Serena pointed a shaking finger at Dione. "*Her* gym! They've torn up the entire patio!"

"I don't think it's that bad," Dione said reasonably. "It may be disorganized now, but nothing should be torn up. Richard's overseeing the installation of the equipment, and I'm sure he wouldn't let anything be damaged."

"Come see for yourself!"

Dione checked her watch. "I think we should have lunch first. The patio isn't going anywhere, but the food will be cold."

"Stalling?" Blake inquired coldly. "I told you, Miss Kelley, that I don't want this house changed."

"I can neither deny nor confirm what changes have been made, because I haven't been outside. I've been with you all morning. However, I trust Richard's good sense, even if you don't," she said pointedly, and Serena flushed furiously.

"It isn't that I don't trust my husband," she began heatedly, but Blake cut her off with a lifted hand.

"Not now," he said shortly. "I want to see the patio."

Serena fell into immediate silence, though she looked sulky. Evidently Blake was still very much the big brother, despite his obvious ill health. His voice carried the unmistakable ring of command. Blake Remington was accustomed to giving orders and having them carried out immediately; his morning with Dione must have gone completely against the grain.

It was the first time Dione had been on the patio, and she found it beautifully landscaped, cool and fragrant, despite the brutal Arizona sun. Yucca plants and different varieties of cactus grew in perfect harmony with plants normally found in a much more congenial climate. Careful watering explained the unusual variety of plants, that and the well-planned use of shade. White flagstones had been laid out to form a path, while a central fountain spewed its musical water upward in a perfect spray. At the back of the patio, where a tall gate opened onto the pool area, was a beautifully carved bench in a delicate pearl-gray color. Dione had no idea what type of wood it was, though it was gorgeous.

The patio *was* disorganized; evidently the workers Richard had hired had used the patio to store the pool furniture that was in the way, and also the materials that they didn't need at the moment. However, she saw that they had been careful not to disturb any of the plants; everything was placed carefully on the flagstones. But Serena ran to the lovely bench and pointed out a long gouge on its side. "See!" she cried.

Blake's eyes flashed. "Yes, I see. Well, Miss Kelley, it looks as if your workers have damaged a bench that

I consider priceless. My father gave it to my mother when they moved into this house; she sat here every evening, and it's here that I see her in my mind. I want this whole thing called off before something else is ruined, and I want you out of my house.''

Dione was distressed that the bench had been damaged, and she opened her mouth to apologize; then she saw the flash of triumph in Serena's eyes and she paused. To give herself time to think, she walked to the bench and bent down to examine the scarred wood. Thoughtfully she ran a finger over the gouge; a quick glance at Serena caught a hint of apprehension in those amazingly expressive eyes. What was Serena worried about? Looking back at the bench, the answer became readily apparent: The bench was undoubtedly damaged, but the gouge was old enough to have weathered. It certainly hadn't been done that morning.

She could have accused Serena of deliberately trying to cause trouble, but she didn't. Serena was fighting for the brother she loved, and though her battle was useless, Dione couldn't condemn her for it. She would just have to separate Serena from Blake so her work could continue without a constant stream of interruptions. Richard would have to bring that laser brain of his into use and keep his wife occupied.

"I can understand why you're both upset," she said mildly, "but this gouge wasn't done tonight. See?" she asked, pointing at the wood. "It isn't a fresh scar. I'd guess that this has been here for several weeks.''

Blake moved his wheelchair closer and leaned down to inspect the bench for himself. He straightened slowly. "You're right," he sighed. "In fact, I'm afraid I'm the culprit.''

Serena gasped. "What do you mean?''

"A few weeks ago I was out here and I bumped the wheelchair into the bench. You'll notice that the gouge is the same height as the hub of my wheel." He rubbed his eyes with a thin hand that trembled with strain. "God, I'm sorry, Serena."

"Don't blame yourself!" she cried, rushing to his side and clutching his hand. "It doesn't matter; please don't be upset. Come inside and let's have lunch. I know you must be tired. It can't do any good for you to tire yourself out like this. You need to rest."

Dione watched as Serena walked beside the wheelchair, all concern and love. Shaking her head a little in amused exasperation, she followed them.

Serena remained close by Blake's side for the rest of the day, fussing over him like a hen with one chick. Blake *was* tired after his first day of therapy, and he let her coddle him. Though Dione had planned to have another session of exercise and massage, she let it go rather than fight a battle to do it. Tomorrow...well, tomorrow would be another story.

Richard arrived for dinner, a practice that Alberta had told Dione was the usual whenever Serena came over, which was every day. He watched silently as Serena hovered anxiously over Blake, and though Richard had the original poker face, Dione sensed that he wasn't happy with the situation. After dinner, while Serena got Blake settled in his study, Dione took the opportunity to speak privately to Richard.

They went out to the patio and sat on one of the benches that were scattered around. Dione looked up at the countless stars that were visible in the clear desert night. "I'm having a problem with Serena," she said without preamble.

He sighed. "I know. I've had a problem with her

since Blake had his accident. I understand how she feels, but it's still driving me crazy.''

"He said something today about raising her."

"Practically. Serena was thirteen when their mother died, and it was quite a shock to her. It was weeks before she could bear for Blake to be out of her sight; it must've seemed to her as if everyone she loved was dying. First her father, then her mother. She was especially close to her mother. I know that she's terrified something will happen to Blake, but at the same time I can't help resenting it.''

" 'Forsaking all others,' '' Dione quoted, a little sadly.

"Exactly. I want my wife back.''

"Blake said that you don't pay any attention to her, that you're wrapped up in your work.''

He rubbed the back of his neck with restless fingers. "I have a lot of work to do, with Blake like he is. My God, what I wouldn't give to go home to just a little of the tender loving care that she smothers Blake with every day!''

"I spoke to Alberta about having the locks on the doors changed, but the more I think about it, the more I think it isn't such a good idea," she confessed. "Blake would be furious if anyone locked his sister out of his house. The problem is, I can't keep him on a schedule if she keeps interrupting.''

"I'll see what I can do," he said doubtfully. "But any suggestion that will keep her away from Blake will go over like an outbreak of plague." He looked at her, and his teeth suddenly flashed white as he grinned. "You must have the steadiest nerves I've ever seen. Was it interesting today?''

"It had its moments," she replied, laughing a little. "He threw his breakfast at me.''

Richard laughed aloud. "I wish I could've seen that! Blake's always had a hot temper, but for the past year he's been so depressed that you couldn't make him angry if you tried all day. It would've been like old times if I had been here to see him."

"I hope I can get him to the point where he doesn't need to be angry," she said. "I'm certain that he'll progress more rapidly if we aren't interrupted. I'm relying on you to think of something that'll keep Serena occupied."

"If I could, I'd have used it before now," he said in disgust. "Short of kidnapping her, I can't think of anything that will work."

"Then why don't you?"

"What?"

"Kidnap her. Take her on a second honeymoon. Whatever it takes."

"The second honeymoon sounds good," he admitted. "But there's no way I can get free until Blake returns to work and takes over again. Any more ideas?"

"I'm afraid you'll have to think of something on your own. I don't know her that well. But I need privacy to work with Blake."

"Then you'll have it," he promised after a moment's thought. "I don't know what I'll do, but I'll keep her away as much as I can. Unless Blake's completely dead, it shouldn't take him long to realize that he'd rather have you fussing over him than his sister, anyway."

At the obvious admiration in his voice, Dione shifted uncomfortably. She was aware of her looks, but at the same time she didn't want anyone to comment on them. Blake was her patient; it was out of the question for her to become involved with him in any sort of sexual relationship. Not only was it against her professional ethics, it was impossible for her. She no longer woke up in the middle of the night trying desperately to scream, her throat constricted by sheer terror, and she wasn't going to do anything to reawaken those nightmares. She'd put the horror behind her, where it had to stay.

Sensing her unease, Richard said, "Dione?" His voice was low, puzzled. "Is something wrong?" He put his hand on her arm, and she jumped as if she'd been stung, unable to bear the touch. He got to his feet, alarmed by her action. "Dione?" he asked again.

"I...I'm sorry," she murmured, wrapping her arms tightly around herself in an effort to control the trembling that had seized her. "I can't explain.... I'm sorry—"

"But what's wrong?" he demanded, reaching out his hand to her again, and she drew back sharply, jumping to her feet.

She knew that she couldn't explain, but neither could she stand there any longer. "Good night," she said rapidly, and walked away from him. She entered the house and almost bumped into Serena, who was stepping out onto the patio.

"There you are," she said. "Blake's gone to bed; he was so tired."

"Yes, I thought he would be," Dione said, gathering her composure enough to answer Serena evenly. Suddenly she felt very tired, too, and she was unable to stifle a yawn. "I'm sorry," she said. "It's been a long day."

Serena gave her an odd, considering look. "Then Richard and I will be leaving; I don't want to keep you up. I'll see Blake tomorrow."

"I'll be increasing his exercises tomorrow," Dione

informed her, taking the opportunity to let Serena know that her presence would hinder rather than help. "It would be better if you waited until late afternoon, say after four."

"But that's too much!" Serena gasped. "He isn't strong enough!"

"At this point, I'm doing most of the work," Dione reassured her dryly. "But I'll be careful not to let him do too much."

If Serena heard the sarcasm that Dione couldn't quite suppress, she didn't let on. Instead she nodded. "I see," she said coldly. "Very well. I'll see Blake tomorrow afternoon."

Well, will wonders never cease, Dione thought wryly to herself as she made her way upstairs. All she'd had to do was mention that Blake would be busy, and though Serena hadn't been happy with the situation, she'd agreed to it.

After she'd gotten ready for bed, she tapped lightly on Blake's door; when she didn't hear an answer she opened the door just enough to peek inside. He was sound asleep, lying on his back, his head rolled against his shoulder. With only the light from the hallway on him, he looked younger, the lines of suffering not visible now.

Quietly she closed the door and returned to her room. She was tired, so tired that her limbs ached, but after she was in bed she found that sleep eluded her. She knew why, and lay awake staring at the ceiling, knowing that she might not sleep at all that night. Such a silly, trivial thing…just because Richard had touched her.

Yet it wasn't trivial, and she knew it. She might have pushed the nightmare away, she might have restructured her life completely, but her past was hers, a part of her, and it hadn't been trivial. Rape wasn't trivial. Since that night she hadn't been able to bear for anyone to touch her. She'd worked out a compromise with herself, satisfying her human need for warmth and touching by working with her patients, touching them, but she could bear the contact only as long as she was the one in control.

On the surface she had recovered completely; she had built a wall between who she was now and who she had been then, never dwelling on what had happened, literally forcing herself to gather together the shattered pieces of her life and, with fierce concentration and willpower, actually mending the pieces into a stronger fabric. She could laugh and enjoy life. More importantly, she had learned how to respect herself, which had been the hardest task of all.

But she couldn't tolerate a man's touch.

That night had effectively prevented her from marrying and having a family. Since that part of life was denied her, she ignored it, and never cried for what might have been. Instead she became a vagabond of sorts, traveling around the country and helping other people. While she was on a case she had an intense relationship full of love and caring, but without any sexual overtones. She loved her patients, and, inevitably, they loved her…while it lasted. They became her family, until the day when it was over and she left them with a smile on her face, ready to continue on to her next case and her next "family."

She had wondered, when she began her training, if she would ever be able to work with a man at all. The problem worried her until she decided that, if she couldn't, she would be handicapping her career terribly and made up her mind to do what was necessary. The first time she worked with a man she'd had to grit her teeth and use all her considerable determination to make herself touch him, but after a few minutes she had realized that a man who needed therapy obviously wasn't in any shape to be attacking her. Men were human beings who needed help, just like everyone else.

She preferred working with children, though. They loved so freely, so wholeheartedly. A child's touch was the one touch she could tolerate; she had learned to enjoy the feel of little arms going about her neck in a joyous hug. If there was one regret that sometimes refused to go away, it was the regret that she would never have children of her own. She controlled it by channeling extra devotion into her efforts for the children she worked with, but deep inside her was the need to have someone of her own, someone who belonged to her and who she belonged to, a part of herself.

Suddenly a muffled sound caught her attention, and she lifted her head from the pillow, waiting to see if it was repeated. Blake? Had he called out?

There was nothing but silence now, but she couldn't rest until she had made certain that he was all right. Getting out of bed, she slipped on her robe and walked silently to the room next door. Opening the door enough to look inside, she saw him lying in the same position he'd been in before. She was about to leave when he tried to roll onto his side, and when his legs didn't cooperate, he made the same sound she'd heard before, a half sigh, half grunt.

Did no one ever think to help him change his position? she wondered, gliding silently into the room on her bare feet. If he'd been lying on his back for two years, no wonder he had the temperament of a water buffalo.

She didn't know if he were awake or not; she didn't think so. Probably he was just trying to change positions as people do naturally during sleep. The light in the hallway wasn't on now, since everyone was in bed, and in the dim starlight coming through the glass doors she couldn't see well enough to decide. Perhaps, if he were still asleep, she could gently adjust his position without his ever waking up. It was something she did for most of her patients, a gesture of concern that they usually never realized.

First she touched his shoulder lightly, just placing her hand on him and letting his subconscious become accustomed to the touch. After a moment she applied a little pressure and he obeyed it, trying to roll to his right side, facing her. Gently, slowly, she helped him, moving his legs so they didn't hold him back. With a soft sigh he burrowed his face into the pillow, his breathing becoming deeper as he relaxed.

Smiling, she pulled the sheet up over his shoulder and returned to her room.

Blake wasn't like her other patients. Still lying awake over an hour later, she tried to decide why she was so determined to make him walk again. It wasn't just her normal devotion to a patient; in some way she didn't yet understand, it was important to her personally that he once again become the man he had been. He had been such a strong man, a man so vibrantly alive that he was the center of attention wherever he went. She *knew* that. She had to restore him to that.

He was so near to death. Richard had been correct in saying that he wouldn't live another year the way he was. Blake had been willing himself to die. She had gotten his attention that morning with her shock tactics, but she had to keep it until he could actually see himself progressing, until he realized that he could recover. She would never be able to forgive herself if she failed him.

She finally slept for about two hours, rising before dawn with a restless anticipation driving her. She would have loved to run on the beach, but Phoenix didn't have a beach, and she didn't know the grounds well enough to go trotting around them in the dark. For all she knew Blake had attack dogs patrolling at night. But despite her lack of sleep she was brimming with energy. She tried to burn off some of it by doing a brisk routine of exercises, but the shower she took afterward so refreshed her that she felt she was ready to tackle the world. Well, at least Blake Remington!

It was even earlier than it had been the morning before when she gave in to her enthusiasm and bounded into his room, snapping on the light as she did, because it was still dark.

"Good morning," she chirped.

He was still on his side; he opened one blue eye, surveyed her with an expression of horror, then uttered an explicit word that would have gotten his mouth washed out with soap if he'd been younger. Dione grinned at him.

"Are you ready to start?" she asked innocently.

"Hell, no!" he barked. "Lady, it's the middle of the night!"

"Not quite. It's almost dawn."

"*Almost?* How close to almost?"

"In just a few minutes," she soothed, then ruined it by laughing as she threw the covers off him. "Don't you want to see the sunrise?"

"No!"

"Don't be such a spoilsport," she coaxed, swinging his legs off the bed. "Watch the sunrise with me."

"I don't want to watch the sunrise, with you or anyone else," he snarled. "I want to sleep!"

"You've been asleep for hours, and you don't want to pass this sunrise up; it's going to be a special one."

"What makes this sunrise so special? Does it mark the beginning of the day you're going to torture me to death?"

"Only if you *don't* watch it with me," she promised him cheerfully, catching his hand and urging him upright. She helped him into the wheelchair and covered him with a blanket, knowing that the air would feel cool to him. "Where's the best place to watch it from?" she asked.

"By the pool," he grunted, rubbing his face with both hands and mumbling the words through his fingers. "You're crazy, lady; a certified lunatic if I've ever seen one."

She smoothed his tousled hair with her fingers, smiling down at him tenderly. "Oh, I don't know about that," she murmured. "Didn't you sleep well last night?"

"Of course I did!" he snapped. "You had me so tired I couldn't hold my head up!" As soon as the words left his mouth a sheepish expression crossed his face. "All right, so it was the best night I've had in two years," he admitted, grudgingly, it was true, but at least he said it.

"See what a little therapy can do for you?" she teased, then changed the subject before he could flare up at her again. "You'll have to lead the way to the pool; I don't want to go through the courtyard, since the workers have put so much of their equipment there. It could be tricky in the dark.''

He wasn't enthusiastic, but he put the chair in motion and led her through the silent house to the rear entrance. As they circled around the back to the pool, a bird chirped a single, liquid note in greeting of the new day, and his head lifted at the sound.

Had it been two years since he'd heard a bird sing?

Sitting beside the pool, with the quiet ripple of the water making its own music, they silently watched the first graying of dawn; then at last the first piercing ray of the sun shot over the rim of the mountains. There were no clouds to paint the sky in numberless hues of pink and gold, only the clear, clear blue sky and the white-gold sun, but the utter serenity of the new day made the scene as precious as the most glamorous sunrise she'd ever seen. As fast as that, the day began to warm, and he pushed the blanket down from his shoulders.

''I'm hungry,'' he announced, a prosaic concern after the long silence they had shared.

She looked at him and chuckled, then rose from her cross-legged position on the concrete. ''I can see how much you appreciate the finer things in life,'' she said lightly.

''If you insist on getting me up at midnight, naturally I'm hungry by the time dawn rolls around! Am I getting the same slop today that I had yesterday morning?''

''You are,'' she said serenely. ''A nutritious, high-protein breakfast, just what you need to put weight on you.''

''Which you then try your damnedest to beat off of me,'' he retorted.

She laughed at him, enjoying their running argument. "You just wait," she promised. "By this time next week you're going to think that yesterday was nothing!"

Chapter Four

Dione lay awake, watching the patterns of light that the new moon was casting on the white ceiling. Richard had worked miracles and informed her at dinner that night that the gym was now ready for use, but her problem was with Blake. Unaccountably he'd become withdrawn and depressed again. He ate what Alberta put before him, and he lay silent and uncomplaining while Dione exercised his legs, and that was all wrong. Therapy wasn't something for a patient to passively accept, as Blake was doing. He could lie there and let her move his legs, but when they started working in the gym and in the pool, he'd have to actively participate.

He wouldn't talk to her about what was bothering him. She knew exactly when it had happened, but she couldn't begin to guess what had triggered it. They had been sniping at each other while she gave him a massage before beginning the exercises, and all of a sudden his eyes had gotten that blank, empty look, and he'd been unresponsive to any of her gibes since then. She didn't think it was anything she'd said; her teasing that day had been lighthearted, because of his greatly improved spirits.

Turning her head to read the luminous dial of the clock, she saw that it was after midnight. As she had done every night, she got up to check on Blake. She hadn't heard the sounds that he usually made when he tried to turn over, but she'd been preoccupied with her thoughts.

As soon as she entered his room she saw that his legs had that awkward, slightly twisted look that meant he'd already tried to shift his position. Gently she put her left hand on his shoulder and her right on his legs, ready to move him.

"Dione?"

His quiet, uncertain voice startled her, and she leaped back. She'd been so intent on his legs that she hadn't noticed his open eyes, though the moonlight that played across the bed was bright enough for her to see him.

"I thought you were asleep," she murmured.

"What were you doing?"

"Helping you to roll over on your side. I do this every night; this is the first time you've been disturbed by it."

"No, I was already awake." Curiosity entered his tone as he shifted his shoulders restlessly. "Do you mean you come in here in the middle of every night and roll me around?"

"You seem to sleep better on your side," she said by way of explanation.

He gave a short, bitter laugh. "I sleep better on my stomach, or at least I did before. I haven't slept on my stomach in two years now."

The quiet intimacy of the night, the moonlit room, made it seem as if they were the only two people on earth, and she was aware of a deep despair in him. Perhaps he felt a special closeness with her, too; perhaps now, with the darkness as a partial shield, he would talk to her and tell her what was bothering him. Without hesitation she sat down on the edge of the bed and pulled her nightgown snugly around her legs.

"Blake, what's wrong? Something's bothering you," she said softly.

"Bingo," he muttered. "Did you take psychology, too, when you were in training to be Superwoman?"

She ignored the cut and put her hand on his arm. "Please tell me. Whatever it is, it's interfering with your therapy. The gym is ready for you, but you aren't ready for it."

"I could've told you that. Look, this whole thing is a waste of time," he said, and she could almost feel the weariness in him, like a great stone weighing him down. "You may feed me vitamins and rev up my circulation, but can you promise that I'll ever be exactly like I was before? Don't you understand? I don't want just 'improvement,' or any other compromise. If I can't be back, one hundred percent, the way I was before, then I'm not interested."

She was silent. No, she couldn't honestly promise him that there wouldn't always be some impairment, a limp, difficulties that would be with him for the rest of his life. In her experience, the human body could do wonders in repairing itself, but the injuries it suffered always left traces of pain and healing in the tissue.

"Would it matter so much to you if you walked with a limp?" she finally asked. "I'm not the way I would like to be, either. Everyone has a weakness, but not everyone just gives up and lets himself rot because of it, either. What if your position were reversed with say, Serena? Would you want her to just lie there and slowly deteriorate into a vegetable? Wouldn't you want her to fight, to try as hard as she could to overcome the problem?"

He flung his forearm up to cover his eyes. "You fight dirty, lady. Yes, I'd want Serena to fight. But I'm not

Serena, and my life isn't hers. I'd never really realized, before the accident, how important the quality of my life was. The things I did were wild and dangerous, but, my God, I was alive! I've never been a nine-to-five man; I'd rather be dead, even though I know that millions of people are perfectly happy and content with that kind of routine. That's fine for them, but it's not *me*."

"Would a limp prevent you from doing all those things again?" she probed. "You can still jump out of airplanes, or climb mountains. You can still fly your own jets. Is the rhythm of your walk so important to you that you're willing to die because of it?"

"Why do you keep saying that?" he asked sharply, jerking his arm down and glaring at her. "I don't remember heading my wheelchair down the stairs, if that's what you're thinking."

"No, but you're killing yourself just as surely in a different way. You're letting your body die of neglect. Richard was desperate when he tracked me down in Florida; he told me that you wouldn't live another year the way you were going, and after seeing you, I agree with him."

He lay in silence, staring up at the ceiling that he had already looked at for more hours than she could imagine. She wanted to gather him into her arms and soothe him as she did the children she worked with; he was a man, but in a way he was as lost and frightened as any child. Confused suddenly by the unfamiliar need to touch him, she folded her hands tightly in her lap.

"What's your weakness?" he asked. "You said that everyone has one. Tell me what torments you, lady."

The question was so unexpected that she couldn't stop the welling of pain, and a shudder shook her entire body. His weakness was obvious, there for everyone to see in his limp, wasted legs. Hers was also a wound that had almost been fatal, for all that it couldn't be seen. There had been a dark time when death had seemed like the easiest way out, a soft cushion for a battered mind and body that had taken too much abuse. But there had been, deep inside her, a bright and determined spark of life that had kept her from even the attempt, as if she knew that to take the first step would be one step too many. She had fought, and lived, and healed her wounds as best she could.

"What's wrong?" he jeered softly. "You can pry into everyone else's secrets, so why can't you share a few of your own? What are your weaknesses? Do you shoplift for kicks? Sleep with strangers? Cheat on your taxes?"

Dione shuddered again, her hands clenched so tightly that her knuckles were white. She couldn't tell him, not all of it, yet in a way he had a right to know some of her pain. She had already witnessed a lot of his, knew what he thought, knew his longing and despair. None of her other patients had demanded so much from her, but Blake wasn't like the others. He was asking for more than he knew, just as she was asking him for superhuman effort. If she put him off now, she knew in her bones that he wouldn't respond to her anymore. His recovery depended on her, on the trust she could foster between them.

She was shaking visibly, her entire body caught up in the tremors that shook her from head to foot. She knew that the bed was vibrating, knew that he could feel it. His brows snapped together and he said uncertainly, "Dione? Listen, I—"

"I'm illegitimate," she grounded out, her teeth chattering. She was panting with the effort it took her to speak at all, and she felt a film of perspiration break out on her body. She sucked in her breath on a sob that shuddered through her; then with a grinding force of will she held her body still. "I don't know who my father was; my mother didn't even know his name. She was drunk, he was there, and presto! She had a baby. Me. She didn't want me. Oh, she fed me, I suppose, since I'm alive to tell about it. But she never hugged me, never kissed me, never told me that she loved me. In fact, she went out of her way to tell me that she hated me, hated having to take care of me, hated even seeing me. Except for the welfare check she got for me, she would probably have dumped me in a trash can and left me."

"You don't know that!" he snapped, heaving himself up on one elbow. She could tell that he was taken aback by the harsh bitterness in her voice, but now that she had started, she couldn't stop. If it killed her, the poison had to spew out now.

"She told me," she insisted flatly. "You know how kids are. I tried every way I knew how to make her love me. I couldn't have been more than three years old, but I can remember climbing up on chairs, then onto the cabinets so I could reach the whiskey bottle for her. Nothing worked, of course. I learned not to cry, because she slapped me if I cried. If she wasn't there, or if she was passed out drunk, I learned to eat whatever I could. Dry bread, a piece of cheese, it didn't matter. Sometimes there wasn't anything to eat, because she'd spent all the check on whiskey. If I waited long enough she'd go off with some man and come back with a little money, enough to get by until the next check, or the next man."

"Dee, stop it!" he ordered harshly, putting his hand

on her arm and shaking her. Wildly she jerked away
from him.

"You wanted to know!" she breathed, her lungs aching with the effort they were making to draw air into
her constricted chest. "So you can hear it!... Whenever
I made the mistake of bothering her, which didn't take
much, she slapped me. Once she threw a whiskey bottle
at me. I was lucky that time, because all I got was a
little cut on my temple, though she was so angry at the
wasted whiskey that she beat me with her shoe. Do you
know what she told me, over and over? 'You're just a
bastard, and nobody loves a bastard!' Over and over,
until finally I had to believe it. I know the exact day
when I learned to believe it. My seventh birthday. I'd
started to go to school, you see, and I knew then that
birthdays were supposed to be something special. Birthdays were when your parents gave you presents to show
you how much they loved you. I woke up and went
running into her room, sure that today was the day that
she would finally love me. She slapped me for waking
her up and shoved me into the closet. She kept me
locked in the closet all day long. That's what she
thought of my birthday, you see. She hated the sight of
me."

She was bent over, her body tight with pain, but her
eyes were dry and burning. "I was living in the streets
by the time I was ten," she whispered, her strength
beginning to leave her. "It was safer than home. I don't
know what happened to her. I went back one day, and
the place was empty."

Her rasping breath was the only sound in the room.
He lay as if he had been turned to stone, his eyes burning on her. Dione could have collapsed, she was sud-

denly so tired. With an effort she drew herself upright.
"Any more questions?" she asked dully.

"Just one," he said, and her body clenched painfully,
but she didn't protest. She waited, wondering in exhaustion what he would ask of her next.

"Were you eventually adopted?"

"No," she breathed, closing her eyes, swaying a little. "I eventually wound up in an orphanage, and it was
as good a place as any. I had food, and a place to sleep,
and I was able to go to school regularly. I was too old
for adoption, and no one wanted me as a foster child.
My looks were too odd, I suppose." Moving like an
old woman, she got to her feet and slowly left the room,
knowing that the air was still heavy with questions that
he wanted to ask, but she'd remembered enough for one
night. No matter what she had accomplished, no matter
how many years had passed since she was a lonely,
bewildered child, the lack of her mother's love was still
an emptiness that hadn't been filled. A mother's love
was the basis of every child's life, and the absence of
it had left her crippled inside just as surely as the accident had crippled Blake's legs.

Not surprisingly, she fell facedown on her bed and
slept heavily, without dreaming, to awaken promptly
when the alarm went off. She had learned, over the
years, how to function even when she felt as if a part
of her had been murdered, and she did so now. At first
she had to force herself to go through the regular routine, but in only a moment the hard self-discipline had
taken over, and she shoved the crisis of the night away.
She would *not* let it drag her down! She had a job to
do, and she'd do it.

Perhaps something of her determination was written
on her face when she entered Blake's bedroom, because

he promptly raised his hands and said mildly, "I surrender."

She stopped in her tracks and regarded him quizzically. He was smiling a little, his pale, thin face weary, but no longer locked in a mask of detachment. "But I haven't even attacked yet," she protested. "You're taking all the fun out of it."

"I know when I'm outgunned." He grimaced and admitted, "I don't see how I can give up without at least trying again. You didn't give up, and I've never been a man to back down from a challenge."

The hard knot of apprehension that had been tied in her stomach since he'd lapsed into depression slowly eased, then relaxed completely. Her spirits soared, and she gave him a blinding smile. With his cooperation, she felt that she could do anything.

At first he was capable of very little with the weights. Even the smaller ones were too much for him, though he kept gritting his teeth and trying to continue even when she wanted him to stop. *Stubborn* was too mild a word to describe him. He was hell-bent and determined to push himself to the limits of his endurance, which unfortunately wasn't far. It always took a long session in the whirlpool afterward to ease the pain from his tortured muscles, but he kept at it, even knowing that he was going to have to pay with pain.

To her relief he asked no more questions and in no way referred to what she'd told him of her childhood. Because of the extra demand he was making on his body, he was always sound asleep when she checked on him at night, so there were no repeats.

Over Serena's protests Dione also began giving him therapy in the pool. Serena was terrified that he'd drown, since his legs were useless and he obviously couldn't kick, but Blake himself overruled her objections. He'd said that he liked challenges, and he wasn't backing off from this one. With his engineering expertise, he designed and directed the construction of a system of braces and pulleys that enabled Dione to lower him into the pool and hoist him out when the session was ended, something that he would soon be able to do for himself.

One morning, after she'd been here a little over two weeks, Dione watched him as he devoured the breakfast that Alberta had prepared. Already it seemed that he was gaining weight. His face had fleshed out and wasn't as gray as it had been. He'd burned a little during the first few days he'd been in the sun, but he hadn't peeled, and now the light tan he'd acquired made his blue eyes seem even bluer.

"What're you staring at?" he demanded as Alberta removed the plate before him and replaced it with a bowl of fresh strawberries in cream.

"You're gaining weight," Dione told him with immense satisfaction.

"Shouldn't wonder," Alberta snorted as she left the room. "He's eating like a horse."

Blake scowled at her, but dipped his spoon into the bowl and lifted a plump strawberry. His white teeth sank into the red fruit; then his tongue captured the juice that stained his lips. "That's what you wanted, isn't it?" he demanded grumpily. "To fatten me up?"

She smiled and didn't reply, watching as he demolished the fruit. Just as he was finishing Angela glided in with a telephone, which she placed on the table before him. After plugging it in, she gave him a shy smile and left.

Blake sat there, staring at the phone. Dione hid a grin. "I think that means you have a call," she prompted.

He looked relieved. "Good. I was afraid you wanted me to eat it."

She chuckled and got to her feet. As he lifted the receiver and put it to his ear, she touched his shoulder lightly and murmured, "I'll be in the gym; come down when you're finished."

He met her eyes and nodded, already embroiled in conversation. She heard enough to know that he was talking to Richard, and just the thought of Richard was enough to pucker her brow in a line of worry.

Serena had been very good after that first day; she'd come to see Blake only in the late afternoon, when Dione had completed her schedule for the day. She'd also learned not to wait until too late to arrive, or Blake would already be asleep. Most nights, Richard also arrived for dinner.

Richard was a witty, entertaining man, with a dry sense of humor and a repertoire of jokes that often had her chuckling in her seat, but which couldn't be repeated when Blake or Serena asked what was so funny.

Dione couldn't say that Richard had been less than a gentleman. In no way had he said or done anything that could be termed suggestive. It was just that she could read the deepening admiration in his eyes, sense the growing gentleness in the way he treated her. She wasn't the only one who felt that perhaps Richard was becoming too fond of her; Serena was subtle, but she watched her husband sharply when he was talking with Dione. In a way, Dione was relieved; it meant that Serena was at least paying attention to her husband. But she didn't want complications of that sort, especially when there was nothing to it.

She didn't feel that she could say anything to Richard about it either. How could she scold him when he'd been nothing but polite? He loved his wife, she was sure. He liked and admired his brother-in-law. But still, he responded to Dione in a way that she knew she hadn't mistaken.

She'd been the object of unwanted attention before, but this was the first time that attention hadn't been obvious. She had no idea how to handle it. She knew that Richard would never try to force himself on her, but Serena was jealous. Part of Dione, the deeply feminine part of her, was even flattered by his regard. If Serena had been giving her husband the attention he deserved, none of this would be happening.

But they weren't important, she told herself. She couldn't let them be important to her. Only Blake mattered. He was coming out of the prison of his disability, more and more revealing himself as the man he'd been before the accident. In another month she hoped to have him standing. Not walking, but standing. Letting his legs get used to supporting the weight of his body again. What she was doing now was dealing with the basics, restoring him to health and building his strength up enough that he would be able to stand when she demanded it of him.

She ran hot water in a plastic container and set the flask of oil that she used down in it to warm it for the massage that she always gave him before he went in the pool, in an effort to protect him from any chill. Not that a chill was likely in the hundred-plus-degree heat of a summer day in Phoenix, she thought wryly, but he was so thin, still so weakened, that she didn't take any chances with him. Besides, he seemed to enjoy the feel

of the warm oil being massaged into him, and he had
little enough joy in his life.

She was restless, and she prowled aimlessly about the
converted game room, pausing to stretch her body. She
needed a good workout to release some of her energy,
she decided, and positioned herself on the weight bench.

She liked lifting weights. Her aim was strength, not
bulk, and the program that she followed was designed
with that in mind. For Blake, she was altering the program enough to build up the bulk of his muscles without
pumping him up like a Mr. Universe. Carefully regu-
lating her breathing, concentrating on what she was doing, she began her sets. Up, down. Up, down.

She finished her leg sets and adjusted the system of
pulleys and weights to what she wanted for her arms.
Puffing, she began again. The demand she was making
on her muscles reached a plateau that was almost pleasure. Again. Again.

"You damned cheat!" The roar startled her, and she
jerked upright, alarm skittering across her features. Confused, she stared at Blake. He sat in his wheelchair, just
inside the door, his face dark red and contorted with
fury.

"What?" she spluttered.

He pointed at the weights. "You're a weight lifter!"
he bellowed, so furious that he was shaking. "You little
cheat. You knew the day you beat me at arm wrestling
that you'd win! Hell, how many men *could* beat you?"

She blushed. "Not everyone," she said with modesty, which seemed to make him even angrier.

"I can't believe it!" He was yelling, getting louder
and louder. "Knowing how it would make me feel that
a woman could beat me at arm wrestling, you made a
bet on it anyway, and you *rigged* it!"

"I never said that I wasn't good at it," she pointed out, trying to keep the laughter out of her voice. He looked wonderful! If sheer rage could have put him back on his feet, he'd have been walking right then. A giggle escaped her control, and at the sound of it he began pounding his fist on the arm of the wheelchair; unfortunately he was pounding on the controls, and the chair began jumping back and forth like a bronc trying to rid itself of an unwanted rider.

Dione couldn't help it; she gave up even trying to keep a straight face and laughed until tears ran down her face. She howled. She beat the weight bench with her fist in mute mockery of the way he'd pounded the wheelchair controls; she clutched her arms across her stomach, gasping for breath, and every new eruption of rage from him sent her off into renewed paroxysms.

"Stop laughing!" he thundered, his voice booming off the walls. "Sit down! We'll see who wins this time!"

She was so weak that she had to haul herself to the massage table where he'd propped his elbow and was waiting for her with a face like doom. Still giggling, she collapsed against the table.

"This isn't fair!" she protested, putting her hand in his grip. "I'm not ready. Wait until I stop laughing."

"Was it fair when you let me think I was wrestling a frail, *normal* woman?" he seethed.

"I'm perfectly normal!" she hooted. "You got beat fair and square, and you know it!"

"I don't know any such thing! You cheated, and I want a rematch."

"All right, all right. Just give me a minute." Quickly she squelched the remaining laughter that wanted to bubble out and flexed her hand in his. She began tightening her muscles. "Okay. I'm ready."

"On the count of three," he said. "One...twothree!"

It was fortunate that she was ready for the quick count he gave. She threw her entire body into the effort, realizing that the extra weight he'd gained and the few days of workouts that he'd had with the weights had increased his strength. Not by much, perhaps, but with the added impetus of his anger and the laughter that had weakened her, perhaps it would be enough to win the match for him.

"You cheated!" she accused in turn, gritting her teeth as she bore down with all her strength against the force of his arm.

"You deserved it!"

They panted and huffed and grunted for several minutes, and sweat began to run down their faces. They were close together, almost face to face, as their locked arms strained harder and harder. Dione groaned aloud. His initial burst of strength had been greater than hers, but not enough to make a quick end to it. Now it was a matter of stamina, and she thought that she could outlast him. She could have let him win, to soothe his ego, but it wasn't in her to trick him that way. If he won, it would be despite everything she could do.

Something of her determination must have shown in her face, because he growled, "Damn it, this is the part where you're supposed to let me win!"

She puffed, sucking in much-needed oxygen. "If you want to beat me, you're going to have to work for it," she panted. "I don't *let* anybody win!"

"But I'm a patient!"

"You're an opportunist!"

He ground his teeth and pushed harder. Dione ducked

her head, a movement that placed her head in the hollow of his shoulder, and counteracted his move with everything she had. Slowly, slowly, she felt his arm begin to move back. The rush of strength that winning always gave her zoomed through her veins, and with a cry she slammed his arm down flat on the table.

Their panting breaths filled the room, and her heartbeat thundered in her ears like the hoofbeats of a galloping horse. She was still slumped against him, her head on his shoulder, and she could feel the pounding of his heart throughout his entire body. Slowly she pushed herself off him, letting her weight fall against the table. Like a rag doll, he slumped forward onto the table, too, his color fading almost to normal as he sucked in deep breaths of air.

After a moment he propped his chin on his folded arm and regarded her out of dark blue eyes that still held storm clouds.

Dione drew a deep breath, staring at him. "You're beautiful when you're angry," she told him.

He blinked in astonishment. Stunned, he stared at her for a long, long minute that hung suspended in time; then an odd little gurgle sounded in his throat. He gulped. The next sound was a full-throated roar of laughter. He threw his head back and clutched helplessly at his stomach. Dione began to giggle again.

He was rolling, howling with mirth, rocking back and forth. The abused controls of the wheelchair caught the impact of his fist again, and this time the jerky movements combined with his back and forth motion to pitch him out on his face. It was lucky that he wasn't hurt, because Dione couldn't have stopped laughing if her life had depended on it. She fell off her stool to lie beside him, drawing her legs up to her stomach. "Stop it! Stop it!" she shrieked as tears rolled down her face.

"Stop it! Stop it!" he mimicked, catching her and digging his fingers into her ribs.

In all her life, Dione had never been tickled. She'd never known what it was to play. She was so startled by the unbearably ticklish sensation of his fingers on her ribs that she couldn't even be alarmed at his touch. She was screaming her head off, rolling helplessly in an effort to get away from those tormenting fingers, when another voice intruded on them.

"Blake!" Serena didn't stop to interpret the scene before her. She saw her brother on the floor, she heard Dione screaming and she immediately assumed that a terrible accident had happened. She added her despairing cry to the din and dove for him, her desperate hands catching him and rolling him to her.

Though Serena wasn't supposed to be there during the day, Dione was grateful to her for the interruption. Shakily she rolled away from Blake and sat up, only then realizing that Serena was almost hysterical.

"Serena! There's nothing wrong," Blake was saying strongly, deliberately, having sensed his sister's state of mind before Dione had. "We were just playing around. I'm not hurt. I'm not hurt," he repeated.

Serena calmed down, her white face regaining some of its color. Blake pushed himself to a sitting position and reached for the blanket that usually covered his legs. As he covered himself, he demanded harshly, "What're you doing here? You know you're not supposed to come during the day."

She looked as if he'd slapped her, drawing back sharply and staring at him with a stunned look in her eyes. Dione bit her lip. She knew why he'd spoken so sharply. He'd become used to her seeing him, and in her presence he could sit around wearing nothing but a pair of briefs or gym shorts, but he was still sensitive about his body with everyone else, Serena most of all.

Serena recovered, lifting her chin proudly. "I thought this was supposed to be therapy, not play period." She lashed out as sharply as he had, and rose to her feet. "Excuse me for interrupting; I had a reason for seeing you, but it can wait."

Her outraged temper was evident in every line of her straight back as she marched out the door, ignoring Blake's rueful call.

"Damn!" he said softly. "Now I'll have to apologize. It's just so awkward explaining...."

Dione chuckled. "She's definitely your sister, isn't she?"

He eyed her warningly. "Don't be acting so cocky, young lady. I've found the weakness in your fortress, now. You're as ticklish as a baby!"

She prudently scooted out of his reach. "If you tickle me again I'll sneak up on you when you're asleep and pour ice water on you."

"You would, too, you wretch," he snorted, and glared at her. "I want a rematch in two weeks."

"You're a glutton for punishment, aren't you?" she asked gleefully, getting to her feet and contemplating the problem of getting him from the floor to the table.

"Don't even try it," he ordered, seeing the speculative look on her face as she looked at him. She smiled sheepishly, because she'd been about to try lifting him herself. "Call Miguel to help you."

Miguel was Blake's chauffeur, handyman and, Dione suspected, bodyguard. He was short and lean, as hard as rock, and his dark face was marred by a scar that puckered his left cheek. No one had said how Blake had acquired his services, and Dione wasn't sure she wanted to know. She didn't even know where Miguel was from; it could have been any Latin nation. She did know that he spoke Portuguese as well as Spanish and English, so she suspected that he was from South America, but again, no one volunteered the information and she didn't ask. It was enough that he was dedicated to Blake.

Miguel wasn't one for asking questions, either. If he was surprised to find his employer on the floor, none of that surprise was reflected on his face. Together he and Dione lifted Blake and put him on the table.

"Miguel, I need another contraption rigged for me in here like the one by the pool," Blake instructed. "We can bolt a bar across the ceiling, this way," he said, indicating the length of the room. "With the pulley arm swinging in any direction we want, and running the length of the bar, I can get myself up and down as I please."

Miguel studied the ceiling, getting in his mind exactly what Blake wanted. "No problem," he finally allowed. "Will tomorrow be soon enough?"

"If you can't do it any faster than that, I suppose it will."

"You're a brutal slave driver," Dione told him as she was massaging his back with the warm oil.

"I've been taking lessons from you," he murmured sleepily, burrowing his head deeper into the cradle of his arm. The comment earned him a pinch on his side, and he laughed. "One thing about it," he continued. "I haven't been bored since you bulldozed into my life."

He was already awake the next morning when she went into his room; he was bending from the waist and rubbing his thighs and calves. She regarded him with satisfaction, glad that he was taking an active part in his recovery.

"I had a long talk with Serena last night," he grunted, not looking up from what he was doing.

"Good. I expect the apology was good for your soul," she said, slipping behind him and kneading his back and shoulders.

"She was upset. It seems Richard has been leaving again as soon as he takes her home at night, and she thinks he's seeing another woman."

Dione's fingers stilled. Was it possible? She hadn't thought him the type to sneak around. It seemed so tawdry, and Richard wasn't a tawdry man.

Blake swiveled his head around to look at her. "Serena thinks he's seeing you," he said bluntly.

She resumed the motion of her fingers. "What did you tell her?" she asked, trying to stay calm. She concentrated on the feel of his flesh under her hands, noting that he didn't feel as bony as he had at first.

"I told her that I'd find out and stop it if he was," he replied. "Don't look so innocent, because we both know that Richard's attracted to you. Hell, he'd have to be dead not to be. You're the type of woman who has men swarming around her like bees around a honey pot."

Richard had said much the same thing about Blake, she thought, and smiled sadly at how far they both were from the truth.

"I'm not seeing Richard," she said quietly. "Aside from the fact that he's married, when would I have time? I'm with you all day long, and I'm too tired at night to put forth the energy that sneaking around would take."

"Serena said that she saw you on the patio one night."

"She did. We were talking about you, not making love. I know that Richard's unhappy with Serena—"

"How do you know that?"

"I'm not blind. She's devoted the last two years to you and virtually ignored her husband, and naturally he resents it. Why do you think he was so determined to find a therapist for you? He wants you walking again so he can have his wife back." Perhaps she shouldn't have told him that, but it was time Blake realized that he'd been dominating their lives with his physical condition.

He sighed. "All right, I believe you. But just in case you start thinking how attractive Richard is, let me tell you now that the one thing I won't tolerate is for Serena to be hurt."

"She's a big girl, Blake. You can't run interference for her for the rest of her life."

"I can do it as long as she needs me, and as long as I'm able. When I think of how she was after our mother died...I swear, Dee, I think I'd kill to keep her from ever looking like that again."

At least she'd had a mother who loved her. The

words were on Dione's lips, but she bit them back. It wasn't Serena's fault that Dione's mother hadn't been loving. Her burden of bitterness was her own, not something to be loaded onto someone else's shoulders.

She pushed it away. "Do you think he really is seeing someone else? In a way, I can't see it. He's so besotted with Serena that no one else registers."

"*You* register with him," Blake insisted.

"He's never said anything to me," Dione replied honestly, though she was still stretching the truth a little. "How do you know? Male intuition?"

"If you want to call it that," he murmured, leaning back against her as he tired. Her soft breasts supported his weight. "I'm still a man, even if I couldn't chase a turtle and catch it. I can look at you and see the same thing he sees. You're so damned beautiful, so soft and strong at the same time. If I could chase you, lady, you'd have the race of your life."

The soft words alarmed her in a way that was different from the panic she normally felt when faced with a prowling, hunting male. Her hands were still on his shoulders, and his weight was resting on her; his body was as familiar to her as her own, the texture of his skin, even the smell of him. It was as if he were a part of her, because she was building him, remaking him, shaping him into the gorgeous man he'd been before the accident. He was her creation.

She suddenly wanted to rest her cheek on his shaggy head, feel the silky texture of his hair. Instead she denied the impulse, because it was so foreign to her. Yet his head beckoned, and she moved her hand from his shoulder to touch the dark strands.

"You're beginning to look like a sheepdog," she told

him, her voice a little breathless and tinged with the laughter that they shared so often now.

"Then cut it for me," he said lazily, letting his head find a comfortable position on her shoulder.

"You'd trust me to cut your hair?" she asked, startled.

"Of course. If I can trust you with my body, why not my hair?" he reasoned.

"Then let's do it now," she said, slapping his shoulder. "I'd like to see if you have ears. Come on, get off me."

A shudder rippled down him, and he turned his eyes to her, eyes as blue as the deepest sea, and as primal. She knew what he was thinking, but she turned her gaze away and refused to let the moment linger.

A nameless intimacy had enfolded them. She was jittery, yet she couldn't say that she was really frightened. It was...*odd,* and her forehead was furrowed with a pensive frown as she plied the scissors on his thick hair. He was a patient, and she'd learned not to be afraid of her patients. He'd gotten closer to her than she'd ever allowed anyone else to get, even the children who had tugged the most strongly at her heartstrings. He was the challenge of her career; he'd become so much to her, but he was still a man, and she couldn't understand why she didn't get that icy, sick feeling she normally got when a man got close to her. Blake could touch her, and she couldn't tolerate the touch of any other man.

Perhaps, she decided, it was because she knew that she was safe with him. As he'd pointed out, he wasn't in any condition to do any chasing. Sexually, he was as harmless as the children she'd hugged and comforted.

"You look like Michelangelo, agonizing over the final touches to a statue," he said provokingly. "Have you cut a big gap in my hair?"

"Of course not!" she protested, running her fingers through the unruly pelt. "I'm a very good barber, for your information. Would you like a mirror?"

He sighed blissfully. "No, I trust you. You can shave me now."

"Like heck I will!" With mock wrath she practically slapped the loose hair off his shoulders. "It's time for your session on the rack, so stop trying to stall!"

In the days that followed nothing else was said about the situation between Serena and Richard, and though the couple continued to have dinner with Blake and Dione, the coolness between them was obvious. Richard treated Dione with a warmth that never progressed beyond friendliness, though Dione was certain that Serena wasn't convinced that the situation between them was innocent. Blake watched everything with an eagle eye and kept Dione close by his side.

She understood his reasons for doing so, and as it suited her to be with him, she let him be as demanding of her company as he wanted. She liked being with him. As he grew stronger his rather devilish personality was coming out, and it took all her concentration to stay one step ahead of him. She had to play poker with him; she had to play chess with him; she had to watch football games with him. There were a million and one things that took his interest, and he demanded that she share them all. It was as if he'd been in a coma for two years and had come out of it determined to catch up on everything he'd missed.

He pushed himself harder than she ever would have. Because she could lift more weigh than he could, he worked for hours with the weights. Because she could swim longer and faster than he could, he pushed himself to do lap after lap, though he still couldn't use his legs. And every week they had a rematch at arm wrestling. It was their fifth match before he finally defeated her, and he was so jubilant that she let him have blueberry waffles for breakfast.

Still, she was nervous when she decided that it was time for him to begin using his legs. This was the crux of the entire program. If he couldn't see some progress now in his legs, she knew that he'd lose hope and sink into depression again.

She didn't tell him what she had planned. After he'd done his sets on the weight bench she got him back into the wheelchair and guided the chair over to the parallel bars that he would use to support himself while she reeducated his legs in what they were expected to do. He looked at the bars, then at her, his brows lifted in question.

"It's time for you to stop being so lazy," she said as casually as possible, though her heart was pounding so loudly it was a miracle he couldn't hear it. "On your feet."

He swallowed, his eyes moving from her to the bars, then back to her.

"This is it, huh? D day."

"That's right. It's no big deal. Just stand. No trying to walk. Let your legs get accustomed to holding your weight."

He set his jaw and reached out for the bars. Bracing his hands on them, he pulled himself out of the wheelchair.

The weight lifting came in handy as he pulled himself up, using only the strength in his shoulders and arms. Watching him, Dione noted the way his muscles bunched and played. He had real muscles now, not just skin over bone. He was still thin, too thin, but no longer did he have the physique of a famine victim. Even his legs had responded to the forced exercises she gave him every day by forming a layer of muscle.

He was pale, and sweat dripped down his face as Dione positioned his feet firmly under him. "Now," she said softly, "let your weight off your hands. Let your legs hold you. You may fall; don't worry about it. Everyone falls when he reaches this phase of therapy."

"I won't fall," he said grimly, throwing his head back and clenching his teeth. He was balancing himself with his hands, but his weight was on his feet. He groaned aloud. "You didn't say it would hurt!" he protested through his teeth.

Dione's head jerked up, her golden eyes firing with excitement. "Does it hurt?"

"Like hell! Hot needles—"

She let out a whoop of joy and reached for him, drawing back as she remembered his precarious balance. Unbidden, her eyes moistened. She hadn't cried since she was a child, but now she was so proud she was helpless against the tears that formed. Still, she blinked them back, though they shimmered like liquid gold between her black lashes as she offered him a tremulous smile. "You know what that means, don't you?"

"No, what?"

"That the nerves are working! It's all working! The massages, the exercises, the whirlpool...*your legs!* Don't you understand?" she shrieked, practically jumping up and down.

His head jerked around to her. All the color washed

out of his face, leaving his eyes glowing like blue coals. "Say it!" he whispered. "Spell it out!"

"You're going to walk!" she screamed at him. Then she couldn't control the tears any longer and they trickled down her face, blurring her vision. She brushed them away with the back of her hand and gave a watery chuckle. "You're going to walk," she said again.

His face twisted, contorted by an agony of joy; he let go of the bars and reached for her, falling forward as his body pitched off-balance. Dione caught him, wrapping her arms tightly around him, but he was too heavy for her now, and she staggered and went down under his weight. He had both arms around her, and he buried his face in her neck. Her heart gave an enormous leap, her blood turned by icy terror into a sluggish river that barely moved. "No," she whispered, her mind suddenly blanking, and her hands moved to his shoulders to push him off.

There was an odd quivering to his shoulders. And there was a sound...it wasn't the same sound of her nightmares.

Then, like someone throwing a light switch and changing a room from dark to light, she knew that this was Blake, not Scott. Scott had hurt her; Blake never would. And the strange sound was the sound of his weeping.

He was crying. He couldn't stop the tears of joy any more than she'd been able to a moment before; the heaving sobs that tore out of him released two long years of torment and despair. "My God," he said brokenly. "My God."

It was like a dam bursting inside her. A lifetime of holding her hurts inside, of having no one to turn to for comfort, no one to hold her while *she* cried, was suddenly too much. A great searing pain in her chest rose into her throat and burst out in a choked, anguished cry.

Her body shuddered with the force of her sobs, and her enormous golden eyes flooded with tears. For the first time in her life she was being held close in someone's arms while she cried, and it was too much. She couldn't bear the bittersweet pain and joy of it, yet at the same time she felt as if something had changed inside her. The simple act of weeping together had torn down the wall that kept her isolated from the rest of the world. She had existed on only a surface level, never letting anything get too close to her, never letting herself feel too deeply, never letting anyone know the woman behind the mask, because the woman had been hurt so badly and feared that it could happen again. She'd developed quite a defense mechanism, but Blake had somehow managed to short circuit it.

He was different from every other man she knew. He was capable of loving; he was at once a laughing daredevil and a hard-hitting businessman. But most of all, he needed her. Other patients had needed her, but only as a therapist. Blake needed *her,* the woman she was, because only her personal strengths had enabled her to help him with her trained skills and knowledge. She couldn't remember anyone ever needing *her* before.

She cuddled him close to her, stunned by the slowly increasing warmth inside her that was gradually melting the frozen pain that had dominated her for so long. She wanted to weep some more, because she was both frightened and excited by her new freedom to touch and be touched. Her hand stroked his hair, her fingers lacing themselves in the silky waves, as his tears finally stopped and he lay sweetly, limply against her.

He lifted his head to look at her. He wasn't ashamed

of the tears that wet his face and glittered in his blue eyes. Very gently he rubbed his wet cheek against hers, a subtle caress that mingled their happiness as well as their tears.

Then he kissed her.

It was a slow, wondering kiss, a gentle touch that sought but didn't pursue, a delicate tasting of her lips that lacked any aggressive, masculine need. She quivered in his arms, her hands automatically moving to his shoulders to shove him away if he progressed beyond the still-guarded borders of intimacy that she could accept. But he didn't try to deepen the kiss. He raised his mouth and instead touched his nose to hers, rolling his head back and forth in a light, brushing movement.

After a long moment he drew back slightly and let his gaze roam over her face with a certain curiosity. Dione couldn't look away from his eyes, watching the irises expand until they had almost swallowed the blue. What was he thinking? What caused that sudden flash of desperation that startled her, the shadow that crossed his face? His eyes lingered on the soft, trembling fullness of her lips, then slowly lifted to meet her gaze and lock in place. They stared at each other, so close that she could see her reflection in his eyes and knew that he could see himself in hers.

"Your eyes are like melted gold," he whispered. "Cat eyes. Do they shine in the dark? A man could get lost in them," he said, his voice suddenly rough.

Dione swallowed; her heart seemed to be rising to stick in her throat. Her hands were still on his shoulders; beneath the warmth of his flesh she could feel the flexing of his muscles as he levered himself up on his elbows, the weight of his body still pressed into hers from the waist down. She shivered, faintly alarmed by their posture, but too bemused by the emotional intimacy quivering between them to push him away.

"You're the loveliest thing I've ever seen," he murmured. "As exotic as Salome, as graceful as a cat, as simple as the wind…and so damned mysterious. What goes on behind those cat eyes? What are you thinking?"

She couldn't answer; instead she shook her head blindly as fresh tears made her eyes glitter. He sucked in his breath, then kissed her again, this time parting her lips and slowly penetrating her mouth with his tongue, giving her the time to decide if she would accept the caress. She was trembling in his arms, afraid to let herself be tempted by the gentle touch, yet she *was* tempted, terribly so. Her tongue moved hesitantly and touched his, withdrew, returned for another shy taste, and finally lingered. He tasted marvelous.

He deepened the kiss, exploring the ridges of her teeth, the softness of her mouth. Dione lay quietly beneath him, unaware of the growing force of his passion until suddenly his mouth turned hard and demanding, asking for more than she could give, reminding her abruptly and with chilling clarity how it had been with Scott—

The black pit of her nightmares loomed before her, and she squirmed under him, but he didn't feel the sudden tension in her body. His hands grasped her with the roughness of desire, and the last thread holding her control snapped.

She tore her mouth from his with a raw cry. "No!" she shrieked, sudden fear giving her strength. She shoved him away with all the considerable power of her arms and legs, and he rolled across the floor, bumping into the wheelchair and sending it flying across the room.

He pulled himself into a sitting position and seared her with a scathing, furious look. "Don't bother screaming," he snapped bitterly. "It's a cinch that nothing's going to happen."

"You can bet on it!" she snapped in return, scrambling to her feet and straightening her blouse and shorts, which had somehow become twisted. "I'm a therapist, not a...a convenience!"

"Your professional integrity is safe," he muttered. "From me, at any rate. You might want to try someone like Richard if you're really serious with your kisses, though I warn you right now, all of his parts are in working order and he might not be so easy to throw off!"

It was evident that his ego had been bruised, because she'd tossed him off so easily; he hadn't even noticed the wild expression that had touched her face. She gave silent thanks, then calmly retrieved the wheelchair and placed it beside him. "Stop feeling sorry for yourself," she said curtly. "We have work to do."

"Sure, lady," he snarled. "Anything you say. You're the therapist."

He pushed himself so hard for the rest of the day that Dione had to lose her temper with him that afternoon to make him stop. He was in the foulest mood she'd ever seen him in, surly and bleak. Even Serena was unable to coax him into a better mood that night over dinner, and he excused himself shortly afterward, uttering that he was tired and going to bed.

Serena's brows lifted, but she didn't protest. Richard got to his feet and said, "Let's go into the study for a minute, Blake. There are some things that I need to talk over with you; it won't take long."

Blake nodded briefly, and the two men left the room.

Silence fell between Dione and Serena, who had never had much to say to each other.

Serena was apparently engrossed with the strappy white sandal she was dangling from her toes. Without looking up from it, she asked casually, "What's wrong with Blake tonight? He's like a hornet."

Dione shrugged. She wasn't about to tell Serena about the kisses that day, or the reason for Blake's ill humor. Instead she passed along the encouraging news that Blake, for some reason, hadn't. "He stood today. I don't know why he's so grouchy; he should be on top of the world."

Serena's eyes lighted up, and her pretty face glowed. "He stood?" she cried, dropping the sandal to the floor and sitting upright. "He actually stood?"

"He had his weight on his legs, yes, and he could feel it," Dione clarified.

"But that's wonderful! Why didn't he tell me?"

Again Dione shrugged.

Serena made a rueful face. "I know; you think I make too much of a fuss over him. I do; I admit it. I...I'm sorry for my attitude when you first came. I didn't think you'd be able to help him, and I didn't want him to get his hopes up, only to be disappointed again. But even if he doesn't walk again, I can see that therapy has been good for him. He's gained weight; he's looking so healthy again."

Surprised by the apology, Dione didn't know what to say beyond the conventional disclaimer, "That's all right."

"No, it isn't all right. Richard's barely speaking to me, and I can't say that I blame him. I've treated him like the invisible man for the two years since Blake had the accident. God knows how he's been as patient as he has. But now I can't get close to him again, and it's all my fault. Still, I'm irrational where Blake's concerned. He's my security, my home base.''

''Perhaps Richard wants that distinction,'' Dione murmured, not really wanting to get into a discussion of Serena's marital problems. She hadn't forgotten that Serena thought Richard might be seeing another woman, namely herself, and she didn't think that involving herself with them would be smart. She liked Richard enormously, and Serena had behaved remarkably well since their bad beginning, but still, she felt uneasy discussing Richard as if she knew him a lot better than she actually did.

''Oh, I know he does! The trouble is, Blake's such a hard act for any man to follow. He was the perfect older brother,'' she sighed. ''Strong, affectionate, understanding. When Mother died he became my rock. Sometimes I think that if anything happened to Blake, I'd die on the spot.''

''Not a very considerate thing to do,'' Dione commented, and Serena looked at her sharply before giving a laugh.

''No, it wouldn't be, would it?''

''I've been jealous of you,'' Serena continued after a moment, when Dione showed no signs of picking up the conversational threads. ''I'd been with Blake almost constantly since the accident; then you practically forbade me to come over except at a time *you* decided would be all right. I was livid! And almost from the beginning, Blake has been engrossed with his therapy, which has taken his attention away from me even when I am with him. He was so close to you, so obviously taken with you; you could get him to do all the things the other therapists couldn't even get him to think about.''

Dione shifted uncomfortably, afraid that Serena was going to start talking about Richard. It looked as if there was nothing she could do to prevent it, so she decided she might as well hold up her end of the conversation. Lifting her head, she turned somber golden eyes on the other woman.

''I knew you felt that way. I regretted it, but there was nothing I could do about it. Blake had to come first; you were interfering, and I couldn't let you do that.''

Serena arched her dark brows in a manner so like Blake's that Dione stared at her, taken by their similarities. ''You were entirely right,'' Serena said firmly. ''You were doing what you were supposed to do. It took about two weeks before I began to see the difference in Blake, and then I had to admit that I was resenting you on *my* behalf, not his. If I really loved Blake, then I had to stop acting like a spoiled brat. I'm sorry, Dione; I'd really like to be friends with you.''

Dione was startled again; she wondered briefly if Serena's apology had any ulterior motive, but decided to take the younger woman at face value. When all was said and done, she herself was there only temporarily, so anything Serena said wouldn't affect Dione beyond the moment. Lifelong friendships didn't come Dione's way, because she'd learned not to let anyone get too close to her. Even Blake—however close they might be right now, no matter how well she knew him or how much he knew about her—when this was all over, she would be gone and very probably never see him again. She didn't make a habit of keeping in touch with her ex-patients, though she did sometimes receive cards from some of them at Christmas.

"If you'd like," she told Serena calmly. "An apology really wasn't necessary."

"It was for *me*," Serena insisted, and perhaps it had been. She was Blake's sister, and very like him. Blake didn't back down from anything unpleasant, either.

Dione was tired after the emotional impact of the day, and she didn't look in on Blake before she went to bed. The mood he'd been in, he was probably lying awake waiting for her to stick her head in so he could bite it off. Whatever was bothering him, she'd worry about it in the morning. She fell into a deep sleep, untroubled by dreams.

When she was jerked awake by her name being called, she had the feeling that the sound had been repeated several times before it penetrated her sleep. She scrambled out of bed as it came again. "Dione!"

It was Blake, and from the horse strain in his voice, he was in pain. She ran to his room and approached the bed. He was writhing, trying to sit up. What was wrong with him? "Tell me," she said insistently, her hands on his bare shoulders, easing him back.

"Cramps," he groaned.

Of course! She should have realized! He'd pushed himself far too hard that day, and now he was paying the price. She ran her hands down his legs and found the knotted muscles. Without a word she got on the bed with him and began to knead the cramps away, her strong fingers working efficiently. First one leg relaxed, then the other, and he sighed in relief. She kept massaging his calves, knowing that a cramp could return. His flesh was warm under her fingers now, the skin roughened by the hair on his legs. She pushed the legs of his pajamas up over his knees and continued with her massage. Perhaps he would go back to sleep under the soothing touch....

Abruptly he sat up and thrust her hands away from his legs. "That's enough," he said curtly. "I don't know what kind of a thrill you get out of handling cripples, but you can play with someone else's legs. You might try Richard; I'm sure he could do you more good than I can."

Dione sat there astonished, her mouth open. How could he *dare* to say something like that? She'd pulled her nightgown up to give her legs more freedom of movement when she'd climbed on his bed, and now she thrust the cloth down to cover her long legs. "You need slapping," she said, her voice shaking with anger. "Damn it, what's wrong with you? You know I'm not seeing Richard, and I'm sick of you throwing him up to me! *You* called *me*, remember? I didn't sneak in here to take advantage of you."

"You'd have a hard time doing that," he sneered.

"You're pretty sure of yourself since you've gotten stronger, aren't you?" she said sarcastically. It made her doubly angry that he'd act like that after what they'd shared earlier. He'd kissed her. Of course, he couldn't possibly know that he was the only man to have touched her since she was eighteen, which had been twelve years before, but still...the injustice of it made her get to her knees on the bed, leaning forward as she jabbed a finger at him.

"You listen to me, Mr. Grouch Remington! I've been driving myself into the ground trying to help you, and you've fought me every step of the way! I don't know what's eating you and I don't care, but I won't let it interfere with your therapy. If I think your legs need massaging, then I'll do it, if I have to tie you down first! Am I getting through that hard head of yours?''

"Who do you think you are? God?" he roared, his face darkening so much that she could see it even in the dim light that came through his windows. "What do you know about what *I* want, what *I* need? All you think about is that damned program you've mapped out. There are other things that I need, and if I can't—''

He stopped, turning his head away. Dione waited for him to continue, and when he didn't she prompted, "If you can't...what?''

"Nothing," he muttered sullenly.

"Blake!" she said in utter exasperation, reaching out and grasping his shoulders and shaking him. "What?''

He shrugged away from her grip and lay back down, his expression bleak as he turned his face back to the windows. "I thought that learning to walk again would be the answer," he whispered. "But it's not. My God, woman, you've been around me for weeks now, running around in almost nothing sometimes, and those see-through nightgowns of yours the rest of the time. Haven't you noticed yet that I can't...''

When his voice trailed off again Dione thought she'd explode. "Can't what?" she tried again, forcibly keeping her tone level.

"I'm impotent," he said, his voice so low that she had to lean closer to hear him.

She sat back on her heels, stunned.

Once he'd said the words aloud, the rest poured out of him in a torrent, as if he couldn't control it. "I didn't think about it before, because what was there to arouse me? It didn't matter, if I couldn't walk, but now I find that there's an opposite side of the coin. If I can't live life as a man instead of a sexless gelding, then it doesn't matter if I walk or not."

Dione's mind went blank. She was a physical therapist, not a sex therapist. It was ironic that he should even mention the subject to *her*, of all people. She was in the same boat he was in; perhaps she'd sensed that from the beginning, and that was why she hadn't been frightened of him.

But she couldn't let this prey on his mind, or he'd give up. Desperately she tried to think of something to tell him.

"I don't see why you'd even think you should be aroused by me," she blurted. "I'm a therapist; it's totally unethical for there to be any sort of relationship except a professional one between us. I certainly haven't been trying to seduce you, or even interest you! You shouldn't think of me like that! I...I'm more of a mother figure than I am anything else, so I'd think it was odd if you responded physically to me."

"You *don't* remind me of my mother," he said heavily.

Again she searched for something to say. "Did you really expect all of your capabilities to return immediately, just because you put your weight on your legs today?" she finally asked. "I would've been surprised if you had been...er, responding like that. You've had a lot on your mind, and you've been in terrible physical shape."

"I'm not in terrible physical shape now," he pointed out tiredly.

No, he wasn't. Dione considered him as he lay there, wearing only the bottoms of his pajamas. He'd started leaving off the tops several weeks ago. He was still lean, but now it was the leanness of a hard layer of muscle.

Even his legs had fleshed out some as he gained weight, and thanks to the rigorous program he'd been following, he even had muscles in his legs, despite his inability to command movement from them yet. He was a natural athlete anyway, and his body had responded promptly to the training. His arms and shoulders and chest were showing the benefits of weight lifting, and the hours in the pool had given his skin a glowing bronze color. He looked incredibly healthy, all things considered.

What could she say? She couldn't reassure him that his mind and body would recover and let him respond normally, because recovery hadn't happened yet for her. She couldn't even say that she wanted to "recover." Perhaps she missed out on a great deal of human warmth by living the way she did, but she also avoided the pain of human cruelty. Until the accident, Blake had led a charmed life. He had loved, and been loved, by more women than he could probably remember. To him, life wasn't complete without sex. To her, life was much safer without it. How could she even begin to convince him of something she didn't believe in herself?

At last she said cautiously, "You're better, yes, but you're not in top physical condition yet. The body is a series of complementary systems; when any part of it is hurt, all the systems cooperate in helping to speed healing. With the therapy program you've been following, you've focused your mind and body on retraining your muscles. It's part of the recovery process, and until you've progressed enough that such intense concentration isn't needed, I think you're being unrealistic to expect any sexual responses. Let things happen in their own time." After considering him for another minute, she tilted her head sideways. "I estimate that you're at about sixty-five percent of your normal strength. You're expecting too much.''

''I'm expecting what any normal man expects in his life,'' Blake said harshly. ''You were bubbling over with self-confidence when you promised me that I'd walk again, but you're not sure about this, are you?''

''I'm not a sex therapist,'' she snapped. ''But I do have common sense, and I'm trying to use it. There's no physical reason why you shouldn't be able to have sex, so I'd advise you to stop worrying about it and concentrate on walking. Nature will take care of everything else.''

''Stop worrying!'' he muttered under his breath. ''Lady, it's not the weather we're talking about! If I can't function as a man, what's the use in living? I'm not talking about just sex; there'd be no marriage for me, no children, and while I've never wanted to marry anyone yet, I've always thought that I'd like to have a family someday. Can't you understand that? Haven't you ever wanted a husband, children?''

Dione winced, physically shrinking away from him. He had an uncanny knack of hitting her where she was most vulnerable. Before she could stop herself, she blurted out thickly, ''I've always wanted children. And I *was* married. It just didn't work out.''

His chest rose and fell as he drew in a deep breath, and she could feel his gaze searching her face in the darkness. Surely he couldn't see anything more than an outline, since she was sitting out of the dim light coming through the windows, so why did she feel as if he could tell exactly how her lower lip was trembling, or see the sudden pallor of her cheeks?

''Damn,'' he said softly. ''I've done it again, haven't

I? Every time I say something, I stick my foot in my mouth.''

She shrugged, trying not to let him know how thin her armor was. ''It's all right,'' she murmured. ''It was a long time ago. I was just a kid, too young to know what I was doing.''

''How old were you?''

''Eighteen. Scott—my ex-husband—was twenty-three, but neither of us was ready for marriage.''

''How long did it last?''

A harsh laugh tore from her throat. ''Three months. Not a record-setting length of time, was it?''

''And since then? Haven't you been in love with anyone else?''

''No, and I haven't wanted to be. I'm content the way I am.'' The conversation had gone on long enough; she didn't want to reveal any more than she already had. How did he keep chipping away at the wall she'd built around her past? Most people never even realized it was there. She uncoiled her legs and crawled off the bed, tugging her nightgown down when it tried to crawl up to her hips.

Blake said a harsh expletive. ''You're running, Dee. Do you realize how long you've been here without receiving a single phone call or a letter, without even going shopping? You've sealed yourself in this house with me and shut the world out. Don't you have any friends, any boyfriends on a string? What is it out there that you're afraid of?''

''There's nothing out there that frightens me,'' she said quietly, and it was true. All of her terrors were locked within herself, frozen in time.

''I think everything out there frightens you,'' he said, stretching out his arm and snapping on the bedside lamp. The soft glow drove away the shadows and illuminated her as she stood there in her white gown with her long, black hair streaming down her back. She looked medieval, locked away in a fortress of her own making. His blue eyes seared over her as he said softly, "You're afraid of life, so you don't let anything touch you. You need therapy as much as I do; my muscles won't work, but you're the one who doesn't feel."

Chapter Six

She didn't sleep that night; she lay awake, feeling the seconds and minutes ticking away, becoming hours. He was right; she _was_ afraid of life, because life had taught her that she would be punished if she asked for too much. She had learned not to ask for anything at all, thereby risking nothing. She had denied herself friends, family, even the basic comfort of her own home, all because she was afraid to risk being hurt again.

It wasn't in her character to deny the truth, so she looked it in the face. Her mother wasn't a typical example of motherhood; her husband hadn't been a typical husband. Both of them had hurt her, but she shouldn't shut everyone else out because of them. Serena had made an overture of friendship, but Dione had backed away from it, doubting the other woman's motives. Those doubts were just an excuse for her own instinctive reaction to withdraw whenever anyone got too close to her. She had to take risks, or her life would be just a mockery, no matter how many patients she helped. She needed help just as much as Blake did.

But facing the truth and dealing with it were two very different things. Just the thought of lowering her defenses and letting anyone get close to her gave her a sick feeling. Even the little things were more than she had ever had, and more than she could handle. She'd never giggled with a girl friend far into the night, never gone to a party, never learned *how* to be with people in the normal manner. She'd had her back to the wall for her entire life, and self-protection was more than a habit: it was a part of her, branded into her cells.

Perhaps she was beyond changing; perhaps the bitter horror of her childhood had altered her psyche so drastically that she'd never be able to rise above the murky pit of her memories. For a moment she had a vision of her future, long and bleak and solitary, and a dry sob wrenched at her insides. But she didn't cry, though her eyes burned until her lids felt scorched. Why waste tears on years that stretched away emptily for as far as she could see? She was used to being alone, and at least she had her work. She could touch people through her work, giving them hope, helping them; perhaps it wasn't enough, but surely it was better than the sure destruction that awaited her if she allowed someone to hurt her again.

Suddenly a memory of Scott flashed into her mind and she almost cried out, her hands rising in the dark to push him away. The sickness in her changed to pure nausea, and she had to swallow convulsively to control it. For a moment she wavered on the edge of a black abyss, memories rising like bats from a rancid cave to dart at her; then she clenched her teeth on the wild cry that was welling up in her and reached out a trembling hand to turn on the lamp. The light drove away the horrors, and she lay staring at the shadows.

To combat the memories she deliberately pushed them aside and called up Blake's face as a sort of talisman against the evils of the past. She saw his blue eyes, burning with despair, and her breath caught. Why was she lying there worrying about herself, when Blake was teetering on the edge of his own abyss? *Blake* was the important one, not her! If he lost interest now, it would wreck his recovery.

She'd trained herself for years to push her personal interests and problems aside and concentrate entirely on her patient. Her patients had reaped the benefits, and the process had become a part of her inner defenses when things threatened to become too much for her. She used it now, ruthlessly locking out all thoughts except those of Blake, staring at the ceiling so intently that her gaze should have burned a hole in it.

On the surface the problem seemed to be simple: Blake needed to know that he could still respond to a woman, still make love. She didn't know why he couldn't now, unless it was because of the common-sense reasons she'd given him just a few hours before. If that were the case, as his health improved and he gained strength, his sexual interest would reawaken naturally, if he had someone to interest him.

That was a problem Dione chewed on her lower lip. Blake obviously wasn't going to start dating now; his pride wouldn't allow him to be helped in and out of cars and restaurants, even if Dione would allow him to disrupt his schedule so drastically, which was out of the question. No, he *had* to stay in therapy, and they were just now getting into the toughest part of it, which would require more time and effort, and pain, from him.

There simply was a shortage of available women in his life right now, a necessary shortage, but there nevertheless. Besides Serena, Alberta and Angela, there was only herself, and she automatically discounted herself. How could she attract anyone? If any man made a move toward her, she reacted like a scalded cat, which wasn't a good start.

A frown laced her brows together. That was true with

all men...except Blake. Blake touched her, and she wasn't frightened. She had wrestled with him, romped on the floor with him...kissed him.

The idea that bloomed was, for her, so radical that when it first entered her consciousness she dismissed it, only to have it return again and again, boomeranging in her mined. Blake needed help, and she was the only woman available to help him. If she could attract him...

A shudder rose from her toes and flowed upward to shake her entire body, but it wasn't from revulsion or fear, except perhaps fear at her own daring. Could she do it? How could she do it? How could she possibly manage such a thing? It wouldn't do Blake any good if he made a pass at her and she ran screaming from the room. She didn't think she would do that with him, but just the thought of trying to attract a man was so foreign to her that she couldn't be sure. Could she tempt him enough to prove to him that he was a man?

She couldn't let the situation progress into anything concrete; she knew that not only was it something she wasn't ready for, but an affair with a patient was totally against her professional integrity. Besides, she wasn't Blake's type, so there was little chance of anything serious happening. She tried to decide if he would find her so lacking in expertise that she wouldn't appeal to him at all, or if his isolation for the past two years would blind him to her inexperience. He was fast leaving behind his morose preoccupation with his invalidism, and she knew that she wouldn't be able to fool him for long. Every day he became more himself—the man in the photo that Richard had shown her, with a biting intellect and a driving nature that swept everyone along with him like the force of a tidal wave.

Could she do it?

She trembled at the thought, but she was so shaken by what he'd said that night that she didn't push the idea away as she would have before. For the first time in her life Dione decided to try to attract a man. It had been so long since she'd cut herself off from sexual contact with anyone that she had no idea if she could do it without looking obvious and silly. She was thirty years old, and she felt as inexperienced and awkward as any young girl just entering her teens. Her brief marriage to Scott didn't count at all; far from trying to attract Scott, after her wedding night she'd gone out of her way to avoid him. Blake was a mature, sophisticated man, used to having any woman he wanted before the accident had robbed him of the use of his legs. Her only advantage was that she was the only available woman in his life right then.

She just didn't know how to arouse a man.

That unusual problem, one she'd never thought she'd face, was the reason she was standing hesitantly before the mirror the next morning, long past the time when she usually woke Blake. She hadn't even dressed; she was staring at herself in the mirror, chewing on her lower lip and frowning. She knew that men usually liked the way she looked, but were looks enough? She wasn't even blond, as Blake preferred his women to be. Her thick black hair swirled over her shoulders and down her back; she'd been about to braid it out of her way when she'd paused, staring at herself, and she still held the brush in her hand, forgotten, as she intensely surveyed the ripe figure of the woman in the mirror. Her breasts were full and firm, tipped with cherry nipples, but perhaps she was too bosomy for his tastes.

Perhaps she was too athletic, too strong; perhaps he liked dainty, ultrafeminine women.

She groaned aloud, twisting around to study herself from the back. So many ifs! Maybe he was a leg man; she had nice legs, long and graceful, smoothly tanned. Or maybe... Her bottom, covered only by wispy, pink silk, was curvy and definitely feminine.

Her clothes were another problem. Her everyday wardrobe consisted mostly of things that were comfortable to work in: jeans, shorts, T-shirts. They were neat and practical, but not enticing. She did have good clothes, but nothing that could be worn while working and be practical, too. Her dresses weren't sexy, either, and her nightgowns were straight out of a convent, despite Blake's comment about her "running around in see-through nighties." She needed new clothes, things that were sexy but not transparently so, and definitely a real see-through nightie.

She was so preoccupied that she hadn't heard the sounds of Blake in his bedroom; when his rumbling, early-morning voice broke into her thoughts with an ill-tempered, "Lazybones, you overslept this morning!" she whirled to face the door as it swung open and Blake rolled his wheelchair through the doorway.

They both froze. Dione couldn't even raise her arms to cover her bare breasts; she was stunned by the shock of his entrance, so lost in her thoughts that she was unable to jerk herself back to reality and take any action. Neither did Blake appear capable of moving, though good manners demanded that he leave the room. He didn't; he sat there with his blue eyes becoming even bluer, a dark, stormy expression heating his gaze as it raked down her almost naked body, then rose to linger over her breasts.

"Good Lord," he whispered.

Dione's mouth was dry, her tongue incapable of moving. Blake's intent look was as warm as a physical touch, and her nipples shrank into tiny points, thrusting out at him. He sucked in an audible breath, then slowly let his eyes dip lower, down the curve of her ribcage, the satiny smoothness of her stomach; his gaze probed the taut little indentation of her navel and finally settled on the juncture of her thighs.

An unfamiliar curling sensation low in her stomach frightened her, and she was finally able to move. She whirled away from him with a low cry, belatedly raising her arms to cover herself. Standing rigidly with her back to him, she said in a voice filled with mortification, "Oh, no! Please, get out!"

There was no obedient whir of an electric motor as he sent the wheelchair into motion, and she knew that he was still sitting there.

"I've never seen anyone blush all over before," he said, his voice deep and filled with an almost tangible male amusement. "Even the backs of your knees are pink."

"Get out" she cried in a strangled voice.

"Why are you so embarrassed?" he murmured. "You're beautiful. A body like that just begs for a man to stare at it."

"Would you please just leave?" she begged. "I can't stand here like this all day!"

"Don't hurry on my account," he replied with maddening satisfaction. "I like the back view as well as I did the front. It's a work of art, the way those long legs of yours sweep up into that perfect bottom. Is your skin as satiny as it looks?"

Embarrassment finally turned to anger and she

stomped her foot, although it was largely a wasted effort, as the thick carpet muffled any sound her bare foot might have made. "Blake Remington, I'll get back at you for this!" she threatened, her voice trembling with anger.

He laughed, the deep tone vibrating in the quiet morning air. "Don't be such a sexist," he taunted. "You've seen me in only a pair of undershorts, so why be shy about my seeing you wearing only panties? You don't have anything to be ashamed of, but you have to know that already."

He evidently wasn't going to leave; he was probably enjoying himself, the wretch! She sidled around until she could reach her nightgown, where she had thrown it across the bed. She was careful to keep her back to him, and she was so fiercely preoccupied with reaching that nightgown that she didn't hear the soft whir of the wheelchair as it came up behind her. Just as she touched the nightgown a much larger hand appeared from behind and anchored the garment to the bed.

"You're beautiful when you're angry," he jibed, returning the teasing compliment she'd given him the day he'd become enraged when he had discovered that she lifted weights.

"Then I must be the world's most beautiful woman right now," she fumed, then added, "because I'm getting madder by the minute."

"Don't waste your energy," he crooned, and she jumped as his hard hand suddenly swatted her on the bottom, then lingered to mold the round, firm cheek with his long fingers. He finished with an intimate pat, then removed his hand from the nightgown.

"I'll be waiting for you at breakfast," he said

smoothly, and she heard him chuckling as he left the room.

She wadded up the nightgown and threw it at the closed door. Her face felt as if it were on fire, and she pressed her cold hands to her cheeks. Furiously she considered ways of paying him back, but she had to stop short of physical harm, and that left out all the most delicious schemes she could imagine. It would probably be impossible to embarrass him in return; since he was in so much better condition now, she doubted if it would bother him if she saw him stark naked. In fact, from the way he'd acted that morning, he'd probably enjoy it and proudly let her look all she wanted!

She was seething, until the thought came to her that her scheme to attract him couldn't have gotten off to a better start. He hadn't been thinking about sex, really; he'd been indulging a streak of pure devilry, but the end result was that he'd become aware of her as a woman. There was the added advantage of the entire scene being totally spontaneous without any of the stiffness that would probably result from any effort she deliberately made.

That thought enabled her to get through the day, which was a difficult one. He watched her like a hawk, waiting for her to betray by either action or word that she was still embarrassed by the morning's incident. She was as cool and impersonal as she knew how to be, deliberately working him as hard as her conscience would allow. He spent more time than the day before at the bars, balancing himself with his hands while his legs bore his weight. He kept up a continuous stream of cursing at the pain he endured, but he didn't want to stop, even when she decided to go on to other exercises. She moved his feet in the first walking motions they'd made in two years; sweat poured off of him at the pain in his muscles, unaccustomed to such activity.

That night the cramps in his legs kept him awake for hours, and Dione massaged him until she was so weary she could hardly move. There were no intimate discussions in the dark that night; he was in pain, barely getting relaxed after one cramp was relieved before another one would knot in his legs. Finally she took him down and put him in the whirlpool, which relieved the cramps for the night.

She really did oversleep the next morning, but she had been careful to lock her door before she went to bed, so she wasn't afraid of an interruption. When she did wake, she lay there with a smile on her face as she relished how he would react to the interruption in his route that she planned.

Over breakfast she said casually, "May I borrow one of your cars? I need to do some shopping today."

Startled, he looked up; his eyes narrowed thoughtfully. "Are you doing this because of what I said the other night?"

"No, of course not," she lied with admirable ease. "I do need some things, though. I'm not much on shopping, but like every woman I have necessities."

"Do you know anything about Phoenix?" he asked, reaching for the glass of milk that he now drank without protest at every meal.

"Nothing," she admitted cheerfully.

"Do you even know how to get downtown?"

"No, but I can follow signs and directions."

"No need to do that; let me give Serena a call. She loves shopping, and she's been at loose ends lately."

At first the thought of shopping in Serena's company dampened Dione's enthusiasm for her project, but she realized that she would probably need another woman's opinion, so she agreed to his suggestion. Serena did, too; he'd barely mentioned it to her over the phone before he hung up the receiver, a wry smile tugging at his chiseled mouth. "She's on her way." Then the smile gave way to a sharply searching look. "You didn't seem very enthusiastic," he remarked. "Did you have some other plans?"

What did he mean by that? "No, it's just that I had something else on my mind. I'm glad you thought of asking Serena; I could use her opinion on some things."

The searching look disappeared, to be replaced by one of lively curiosity. "What things?"

"Nothing that concerns you," she replied promptly, knowing that her answer would drive him crazy. He wanted to know the whys and wherefores of everything. He'd probably dismantled every toy he'd received as a child, and now he was trying to do the same thing to her. He probably did it to everyone. It was one of the characteristics that had made him such an innovative engineer.

As she quickly dressed for her shopping trip, she realized that lately Blake had shown signs of becoming more interested in his work again. He talked to Richard on the phone more than he had before, and designing the pulley system at the pool and in the gym had piqued his interest even more. Every night after dinner he made some mysterious doodles on a pad in his study, random drawings that resembled nothing Dione recognized, but Richard had seen the pad one evening and made a comment on it. The two men had then embarked on a highly technical conversation that had lasted until Dione put an end to it by signaling that it was time for Blake to go to bed. Richard had caught the signal and understood it immediately, giving her a quick wink.

The Phoenix heat prompted her to wear the bare minimum of clothing: a white sundress; the necessary underwear, which wasn't much; and strappy sandals. The weeks had slipped away, taking the summer with it, but the changing season wasn't yet reflected by any dip in the temperature. When she went downstairs to meet Serena, Blake gave her a quick comprehensive look that seemed to take inventory of every garment she had on. Dione shivered at the fleeting expression in his eyes. He knew what she looked like now, and every time he saw her he was imagining her without any clothes. She should probably be glad, as that was what she wanted, but it still made her uneasy.

Serena drove, as Dione knew absolutely nothing about Scottsdale or Phoenix. The pale blue Cadillac slipped as silently as oiled silk past the array of expensive millionaires' homes that decorated Mount Camelback. Overhead, a sparkle of silver in the pure blue of the sky, one of the innumerable jets from the air bases in the Phoenix area, painted a white streak directly above their path.

"Blake said you had shopping to do," Serena said absently. "What sort of shopping? Not that it matters; if it exists, I know a shop that carries it."

Dione gave her a wry glance. "Everything," she admitted. "Dresses, underwear, sleepwear, bathing suits."

Serena arched her slim, dark brows in an astonished movement. "All right," she said slowly. "You asked for it."

By the time they'd had lunch several hours later, Dione firmly believed that Serena knew the location of every shop in Arizona. They had been in so many that she couldn't keep straight just where she had bought what, but that didn't really matter. What mattered was the steadily growing mound of bags and packages, which they made regular trips to the car to stow in the trunk.

Dione systematically tried on dresses that made the most of her dark coloring and tall, leggy build. She bought skirts that were slit up the side to showcase her long, slender legs; she bought real silk hosiery and delicate shoes. The nightgowns she chose were filmy, flimsy pieces of fabric that were held on her body more by optimism than any other means. She bought sexy lace panties and bras, wickedly seductive teddies, shorts and T-shirts that clung to her body, and a couple of bikinis that stopped just short of illegal.

Serena watched all of this in amazed silence, offering her opinion whenever Dione asked it, which was often. Dione couldn't quite decide if a garment was sexy without being blatant, so she yielded to Serena's taste. It was Serena who chose the bikinis, one a delicate shell pink and the other a vibrant blue, both of which glowed like jewels on Dione's honey-tanned body.

"You know," Serena mused as she watched Dione choose a skin-toned teddy that, from a distance, made her look as if she had nothing on at all, "this looks like war."

Dione was feeling a little frantic and out of touch by that time, and she merely gave Serena a blank look.

"I could almost pity Blake for being the target of such firepower," the other woman continued, laughing a little. "Almost, but not quite. From the effort you're making, Dione, I think you're out for unconditional surrender. Are you in love with Blake?"

That got Dione's attention with the force of a punch

in the jaw. In love? Of course not! It was impossible. Blake was her patient; falling in love with him would be against every professional ethic that she had. Not only that, how could she be in love with him? Couldn't Serena see that it was totally out of the question? she wondered distractedly. It was just that Blake's was such a demanding case. She'd rebuilt him almost literally, molded him from a basket case into a strong, healthy man; she couldn't let him give up now, couldn't let all of that sweat and effort go to waste.

But suddenly, seeing through Serena's eyes the staggering amount of clothing she'd bought in one day, she realized what a hopeless effort it was. How could she ever have imagined that she'd be able to physically attract Blake Remington? Not only did she not know how to do it, but she'd probably go into screaming hysterics if she succeeded!

She sagged into a chair, crumpling the flesh-colored teddy in her lap. "It's no use," she muttered. "It'll never work."

Serena eyed the teddy. "If he's human, it will."

"All of these props are useless, if the actors can't perform," Dione said in self-disgust. "I don't know how to seduce anyone, least of all a man who's been around as much as Blake has!"

Serena's eyes widened. "Are you serious? The way you look, you don't *have* to seduce anyone; all you have to do is stand still and let him get to you."

"Thanks for the pep talk, but it's not that easy," Dione hedged, unable to tell Blake's sister the entire story. "Some men like my looks, but I know that Blake's always preferred blondes. I'm not his type at all."

"How you can look in a mirror and still worry about

not being blond is more than I can understand,'' Serena said impatiently. ''You're...sultry. That's the only word I can think of to describe the way you look. If he hasn't made a pass at you yet, it's because you haven't given him a go-ahead signal. Those clothes will do it for you. Then just let things develop naturally.''

If only they would! Dione thought as she paid for the teddy and a bottle of heady perfume that the saleswoman had sworn drove her husband mad with lust.

She didn't want Blake mad with lust, just aroused. What a dilemma for her to be in! Life was just full of little ironies, but she couldn't find this one very amusing.

Blake wasn't in evidence when they arrived back at the house, and Dione could only be thankful for that. She didn't want him to have any idea of the extent of her shopping trip. Angela silently helped Dione and Serena carry all the packages up to Dione's room, and when asked about Blake's whereabouts, the woman smiled shyly and murmured, ''In the gym,'' before quickly walking out.

Serena gave a little laugh after Angela had left the room. ''She's something, isn't she? I think Blake picked his entire staff on the basis of how much they talk, or rather, don't talk.'' Before Dione could make any comment, Serena changed the subject. ''Do you mind if I stay for dinner? I know you probably want to start your campaign, but Richard told me this morning that he'd be late coming home tonight, and I'm at loose ends.''

Far from being anxious to begin her ''campaign,'' Dione was dreading it, and gladly asked Serena to stay. As she usually had dinner with them, Blake might think something was off if all of a sudden she stopped the practice.

While Serena went to the den to entertain herself, Dione made her way down to the pool and entered the gym. She stopped abruptly. Blake was on the bars, balancing himself with his hands, while Alberta was on her knees, moving his feet in walking motions. From the looks of him, he'd been hard at it since she'd left with Serena that morning, and poor Alberta was frazzled, too. Blake wore only a brief pair of blue gym shorts, and he'd tied his shirt around his forehead to keep the sweat from getting into his eyes. He was literally dripping as he strained, trying to force his muscles to do his bidding. Dione knew that he had to be in a great deal of pain; it was revealed in the rigid set of his jaw, his white lips. The fact that he'd enlisted Alberta's help instead of waiting for her to return said something about his determination, but she was afraid that he'd tried to do too much. He'd paid for his excesses the night before with agonizing cramps, and she had the feeling that tonight would be a repeat.

"Time for the whirlpool," she said easily, trying not to sound anxious. Alberta looked up with an expression of acute relief, and achingly got to her feet. Blake, on the other hand, shook his head.

"Not yet," he muttered. "Another half hour."

Dione signaled to Alberta, who quietly left the room. Taking a towel from the stack she always kept handy, she went up to him and wiped his face, then his shoulders and chest. "Don't push it so hard," she advised. "Not yet. You can do yourself more harm than good at this stage. Come on, into the whirlpool; give your muscles a rest."

He sagged against the bars, panting, and Dione quickly brought the wheelchair over to him. He levered himself into it; he seldom needed her help moving himself around now, since he was so much stronger. She switched the whirlpool on and turned around to find that he'd been staring at her bottom as she bent over. Wondering how much she'd exposed in the unaccustomed dress, she flushed pink.

He gave her a wicked little smile, then grasped the pulley and swung himself over the pool, letting himself down expertly in the water. He sighed in relief as the pulsing water eased his tired, strained muscles.

"I didn't expect you to be gone all day," he said, closing his eyes wearily.

"I only shop once a year." She lied without compunction. "When I shop, it's an endurance event."

"Who won, you or Serena?" he asked, smiling as he lay there, his eyes still closed.

"I think Serena did," she groaned, stretching her tight muscles. "Shopping uses an entirely different set of muscles than weight lifting does."

He opened one eye a slit and surveyed her. "Why not join me?" he invited. "As the old saying goes, 'Come on in, the water's fine.'"

It was tempting. She looked at the swirling water, then shook her head regretfully as she thought of the many things that she needed to do. She didn't have time to relax in a whirlpool.

"Not tonight. By the way," she added, changing the subject, "how did you talk Alberta into helping you with your exercises?"

"A mixture of charm and coercion," he replied, grinning a little. His gaze slipped over the bodice of her dress; then he closed his eyes again and gave himself up to the bliss of the whirlpool.

Dione moved around the room, putting everything in place and preparing for the massage she'd give him when he left the whirlpool, but her actions were purely automatic. Their conversation had been casual, even trivial, but she sensed an entirely different mood under the cover of their words. He was looking at her, he was seeing her, as a woman, not a therapist. She was both frightened and exhilarated at her success, because she'd expected it to take much longer before she got his attention. The intent way he stared at her was sending messages that she wasn't trained to interpret. As a therapist, she knew instinctively what her patient needed; as a woman, she was completely in the dark. She wasn't even completely certain that he wasn't staring at her with derision.

"All right, that's enough," he said huskily, breaking her train of thought. "I hope Alberta's not going to hold a grudge against me, because I'm hungry. Do you think she'll feed me?"

"Serena and I will let you have our scraps," Dione offered generously, earning a wryly appreciative glance from him.

A few minutes later he lay on his stomach on the table with a towel draped over his hips, sighing in contentment as her strong fingers worked their magic on his flesh. He propped his chin on his folded arms, the look on his face both absent and absorbed, a man concentrating on his inner plans. "How long before I'll be able to walk?" he asked.

Dione continued manipulating his legs as she considered the answer. "Do you mean until you take your first steps, or walk without aid?"

"The first steps."

"I'll take a stab and say six weeks, though that's only a rough guess," she warned him. "Don't hold me to it. You could do it in four or five, or it could be two months. It really depends on how well I've planned your therapy program. If you push too hard and injure yourself, then it'll take longer.''

''When will the pain ease?''

''When your muscles are accustomed to your weight and the mechanics of movement. Are your legs still numb?''

''Hell, no,'' he growled feelingly. ''I can tell when you're touching me now. But after those cramps last night, I'm not certain I want to feel.''

''The price to pay,'' she taunted gently, and slapped him on the bottom. ''Time to turn over.''

''I like that dress,'' he said when he was lying on his back and could stare at her. Dione didn't glance up, consciously keeping the flexing of her fingers in an unbroken rhythm. When she failed to comment he pushed a little harder. ''You've got great legs. I see you every day, dressed in next to nothing, but I hadn't realized how good your legs are until I saw you in a dress.''

She quirked one eyebrow. That statement alone verified her suspicion that he hadn't been aware of her as a woman, not really. She half-turned her back to him as she rubbed her hands down the calf of his right leg, hoping that the vigorous massage would lessen any cramps he might have. When the warm touch of his hand rested on her bare thigh, under her skirt, she gave a stifled half scream and jerked up straight.

''Blake!'' she yelped, pushing frantically at his hand in an effort to dislodge it from under her dress. ''Stop it! What are you doing?''

''You're playing with *my* legs,'' he retorted calmly. ''Turnabout's fair play.''

His fingers were between her legs while his thumb was on the outside of her thigh, and she flinched from the feel of his hand as her other leg instinctively pressed against him to halt the upward movement. Her face flushed brightly.

"I like that," he said huskily, his eyes bright. "Your legs are so strong, so sleek. Do you know what you feel like? Cool satin."

She twisted, trying to loosen his grip, and to her dismay his fingers slid even higher. She sucked in a lungful of air and held it, going still, her eyes wide and alarmed as she tried to still the flare of panic in her stomach. Her heart lurched drunkenly in her chest.

"Let me go, please," she whispered, hoping that the trembling of her voice wouldn't be as noticeable if she didn't try to talk loudly.

"All right," he agreed, a little smile moving his lips. Just as she began to sag in relief, he added, "If you'll kiss me."

Now her heart was slamming so wildly that she pressed her hand to her chest in an effort to calm it. "I...just one kiss?"

"I can't say," he drawled, staring at her lips. "Maybe, maybe not. It depends on how well we like it. For God's sake, Dee, I've kissed you before. You won't be violating any sacred vow not to become involved with a patient. A kiss isn't what I'd term an involvement."

Despite her efforts to hold her legs together and trap his wandering hand, he somehow moved a little higher.

"It's only a kiss," he cajoled, holding his left hand out to her. "Don't be shy."

She wasn't shy, she was terrified, but she could still hold on to the thought that Blake wasn't Scott. That alone gave her the courage to lean down and touch her

lips to his as lightly, as delicately, as a breath of air.
She drew back and stared down at him. His hand remained on her leg.

"You promised," she reminded him.

"That wasn't a kiss," he replied. The expression in
his eyes was intent, watchful. "A real kiss is what I
want, not a child's kiss. I've been a long time without
a woman. I need to feel your tongue on mine."

Weakly she leaned against the table. I can't handle
this, she thought wildly, then stiffened as the thought
formed in her brain. Of course she could; she could
handle anything. She'd already been through the worst
that could happen to her. This was just a kiss, that was
all...

Though her soft, generous mouth trembled against
his, she gave him the intimate kiss he'd requested, and
she was startled to feel him begin to shake. He removed
his hand from her leg and placed both arms around her,
but he held her without any real force, only a warm sort
of nearness that failed to alarm her. The hair on his bare
chest was tickling her above the fabric of her sundress;
the faintly musky smell of him filled her lungs. She
became aware of the warmth of his skin, the roughness
of his chin against her smooth skin, the light play of
his tongue against hers. Her eyes had been open, but
now they slowly closed, and she became lost in a world
of sensation, the light only a redness against her lids,
her senses of touch and smell intensified by the narrowing of her concentration.

That was what she wanted, she reminded herself
dimly. She hadn't thought she would enjoy herself in
the process, but the excitement that was beginning to
course through her veins brought with it a warmth that
could only be pleasure.

"God, you smell good," he breathed, breaking the kiss to nuzzle his face in the soft hollow of her throat. "What perfume is that?"

Giddily she remembered all the perfumes she'd tried. "It's a mixture of everything," she admitted in a bemused tone.

He chuckled and turned his head to claim her mouth again. This time the kiss was deeper, harder, but she didn't protest. Instead she kissed him back as strongly as he kissed her, and he finally fell back onto the table, gasping.

"You're taking advantage of a starving man," he groaned, and she gave a spurt of laughter.

"I hope Alberta doesn't feed you anything," she told him, and turned away to hide the color that she knew still tinted her cheeks. She fussed over several insignificant details, but when she turned back he wasn't paying attention to her. She disciplined her face into smoothness and helped him to dress, but there was a sense of determination about him that bothered her. It nagged at her all during dinner, where Serena entertained Blake with a wholly fictitious tale of their shopping trip.

What was he up to? She'd agonized over her scheme, gone to ridiculous lengths to put it into action, but somehow she still had the feeling that he was the one who was scheming, not her.

Chapter Seven

"Dione, may I talk to you? In private, please." Richard's face was tight with strain, and Dione looked at him sharply, wondering at the bitterness that was so evident in his expression. She looked past him to the study door, and he read her mind.

"She's playing chess with Blake," he said heavily, thrusting his hands into his pockets and moving to the doors that opened onto the courtyard.

Dione hesitated only a moment, then followed him. She didn't want anything to be said about her being in his company, but on the other hand, she knew that Richard wasn't going to make a pass at her, and she resented feeling guilty for being friendly to him. Serena had continued her efforts at friendship, and Dione found that she really liked the younger woman; Serena was a lot like Blake, with his directness, his willingness to accept challenges. Sometimes Dione had the uneasy thought that Serena could check on her more easily under the guise of friendship, but more and more it seemed that the thought came from her own wariness, not any premeditated action on Serena's part.

"Aren't things going well?" she asked Richard quietly.

He gave a bitter laugh, rubbing the back of his neck. "You know they're not. I don't know why," he said wearily. "I've tried, but it's always in the back of my mind that she'll never love me the way she loves Blake, that I'll never be as important to her as he is, and it makes me almost sick to touch her."

Dione chose her words carefully, picking them like wildflowers. "Some resentment is only natural. I see this constantly, Richard. An accident like this really shakes up everyone connected to the patient. If it's a child who's injured, it can cause resentment between the parents, as well as the other children. In circumstances like these, one person gets the lion's share of the attention, and others don't like it."

"You make me sound so small and petty," he said, one corner of his stern mouth curving upward.

"Not that. Just human." Her voice was full of warmth and compassion, and he stared at her, his eyes moving over her tender face. "It'll get better," she reassured him.

"Soon enough to save my marriage?" he asked heavily. "Sometimes I almost hate her, and it's damned peculiar, because what I'm hating her for is not loving me the way I love her."

"Why make her take all the blame?" Dione probed. "Why not put some of that resentment on Blake? Why not hate him for taking her attention?"

He actually laughed aloud. "Because I'm not in love with him," he chuckled. "I don't care what he does with his attention...unless he hurts you with it."

Shock rippled through her, widening her enormous eyes. In the dimness of twilight they gleamed darkly gold, as deep and bottomless as a cat's. "How can he hurt me?" she asked, her voice husky.

"By making you fall in love with him." He was too astute, capable of summing up a situation in a glance. "I've been watching you change these last couple of weeks. You were beautiful before, God knows, but now you're breathtaking. You…glow. Those new clothes of yours, the look on your face, even the way you walk…all of that has changed. He needs you now so intensely that everyone else is wiped out of his mind, but what about later? When he can walk again, will he still watch you as if his eyes are glued on you?''

"Patients have fallen in love with me before," she pointed out.

"I don't doubt that, but have you ever fallen in love with a patient before?" he asked relentlessly.

"I'm not in love with him." She had to protest the idea, had to thrust it away from her. She couldn't be in love with Blake.

"I recognize the symptoms," Richard said.

As sticky as the conversation was when they were discussing Serena, Dione infinitely preferred it to the current line, and she moved jerkily away. "I don't have any sandcastle built," she assured him, clenching her hands into fists in an effort to keep herself from trembling. "When Blake's walking, I'll move on to another job. I know that; I've known it from the beginning. I *always* get personally involved with my patients," she said, laughing a little. That was all it was, just her normal intense concentration on her patient.

Richard shook his head in amusement. "You see so clearly with everyone else," he said, "to be so blind about yourself."

The old, blind panic, familiar in form but suddenly unfamiliar in substance, clawed at her stomach. *Blind.* That word, the one Richard had used. No, she thought painfully. It wasn't so much that she was blind as that she deliberately didn't see. She had built a wall between herself and anything that threatened her; she knew it was there, but as long as she didn't have to look at it, she could ignore it. Blake had forced her on two occasions to face the past that she'd put behind her, never realizing what the ordeal had cost her in terms of pain. Now Richard, though he was using his coolly analytical brain instead of the gut instincts Blake operated on, was trying to do the same.

"I'm not blind," she denied in a whisper. "I know who I am, and what I am. I know my limits; I learned them the hard way."

"You're wrong," he said, his gray eyes thoughtful. "You've only learned the limits that other people have placed on you."

That was so true that she almost winced away from the thrust of it. Instinctively she pushed the thought away, drew herself up, marshaling her inner forces. "I think you wanted to talk to me about Serena," she reminded him quietly, letting him know that she wasn't going to talk about herself any longer.

"I did, but on second thought, I won't bother you with it. You have more than enough on your mind now. In the end, Serena and I will have to settle our differences on our own, so it's useless to ask anyone else's advice."

Walking together, they reentered the house and went into the study. Serena was sitting with her back to them, though her posture of concentration told them exactly what expression was on her face. She hated to lose, and she poured all her energies into beating Blake. Although she was a good chess player, Blake was better. She was usually wild with jubilation whenever she managed to beat him.

Blake, however, looked up as Richard and Dione

came in together, and a hard, determined expression pulled his face into a mask. His blue eyes narrowed.

Later that night, when she poked her head into his bedroom to tell him good-night, he said evenly, "Dee, Serena's marriage is hanging by a thread. I'm warning you: don't do anything to break that thread. She loves Richard. It'll kill her if she loses him."

"I'm not a home wrecker or a slut," she retorted, stung. Anger brought red spots to her cheeks as she stared at him. He had left the lamp on, evidently waiting until she told him good-night, as she usually did, so she could see exactly how forbidding he looked. Bewildered pain mingled with her anger to make her tremble inside. How could he even think... "I'm not like my mother," she blurted, her voice stifled, and she whirled, slamming the door behind her and fleeing to her own room despite the sound of her name being called demandingly.

She was both hurt and furious, but years of self-discipline enabled her to sleep dreamlessly anyway. When she woke hours later, just before her alarm went off, she felt better. Then she frowned. It seemed as if her subconscious could hear the echo of her name being called. She sat up, tilting her head as she listened.

"Dee! Damn it to hell!"

After weeks of hearing that particular note in his voice when he called her, she knew that he was in pain. Without her robe, she ran to his room.

She turned on the light. He was sitting up, rubbing his left calf, his face twisted in a grimace of pain. "My foot, too," he gritted. Dione seized his foot and forcefully returned his toes to their proper positions, digging her thumbs into the ball of his foot and massaging. He fell back against his pillow, his chest rising and falling swiftly as he gulped in air.

"It's all right," she murmured, moving her soothing hands up his ankle to his calf.

She devoted her attention to his leg, unaware of the fixed way he watched her. After several minutes she straightened out his leg and patted his ankle, then pulled the sheet over him. "There," she said, smiling as she looked up, but the smile faded as she met his gaze. Those dark blue eyes were as fierce and compelling as the sea, and she faltered in the face of his regard, her soft lips parting. Slowly his eyes dipped downward, and she was abruptly aware of her breasts, thrusting against the almost transparent fabric of her nightgown. A throbbing ache in her nipples made her fear that they had hardened, but she didn't dare glance down to confirm it. Her new nightgowns didn't hide a lot; they merely veiled.

Suddenly she couldn't withstand the force of his gaze, and she averted her eyes, her thick lashes dropping to shield her thoughts. His body was in her line of vision, and abruptly her eyes widened. She almost gasped, but controlled her reaction at the last second.

Jerkily she got to her feet, forgetting about how much the nightgown revealed. She'd accomplished her aim, but she didn't feel smug about it; she felt stunned, her mouth dry, her pulses hammering through her veins. She swallowed, and her voice was too husky to be casual when she said, "I thought you said you were impotent."

It was a moment before her words registered. He looked as stunned as she felt, then he glanced down at himself. His jaw hardened and he swore aloud.

A hot blush suddenly burned her face. It was ridiculous to stand there, but she couldn't move. She *was* fascinated, she admitted, completely bewildered by her reaction, or rather, her lack of it. As fascinated as a bird before a cobra, and that was a Freudian simile if ever she'd heard one.

"I must be psychic," he whispered rawly. "I was just thinking that that little bit of nothing you have on would rouse the dead."

She couldn't even smile. Abruptly, though, she was able to move, and she left the room as swiftly as she could without actually running.

That disturbing dryness was still in her mouth as she dressed, pulling out her old clothes rather than the clinging new garments she'd been wearing. There was no need to dress seductively now; that particular milestone was behind him, and she knew better than to play with fire.

The only problem was, she discovered as the days passed, that Blake didn't seem to notice that she'd reverted to her old clothes, her modest nightgowns. He didn't say anything, but she could always feel the blue fire of his gaze on her when they were together. In the course of therapy she was constantly touching him, and she gradually became accustomed to the way he'd wrap his fingers around her leg while she massaged him, or the frequency with which their bodies rubbed together when they were swimming.

Much sooner than she'd expected, he stood alone, not using his hands. He swayed for a moment, but his legs held and he regained his balance. He worked harder than any patient she'd had before, determined to end his dependency on the wheelchair. He paid for his determination every night with the torturous cramps that he suffered, but he didn't let up the killing pace he'd set for himself. Dione no longer organized his therapy; he pushed himself. All she could do was try to prevent him from doing so much that he harmed himself, and soothe his muscles at the end of every workout with massages and sessions in the whirlpool.

Sometimes she got a lump in her throat as she watched him straining himself to the limit, his teeth clenched, his neck corded with effort. It would soon be over, and she'd move on to another patient. He was already an entirely different man from the one she'd first seen almost five months before. He was as hard as a rock, tanned the color of teak, his body rippling with lean muscles. He'd regained all of his weight, and possibly more, but it was all muscle, and he was as fit as any professional athlete. She couldn't analyze the emotions that quivered through her when she watched him. Pride, of course, even some possessiveness. But there was also something else, something that made her feel warm and languid; yet at the same time she was more alive now than she'd ever been. She watched him, and she let him touch her, and she felt closer to him than she'd ever thought possible. She *knew* this man, knew his fierce pride, the daredevil in him that thumbed his nose at danger and laughingly accepted any challenge. She knew his swift, cutting intelligence, the blast of his temper, his tenderness. She knew the way he tasted, the strength of his mouth, the texture of his hair and skin beneath her hesitant fingers.

He was becoming so much a part of her that, when she allowed herself to think about it, it frightened her. She couldn't let that happen. Already he needed her less and less, and one day in the near future he would return to his work and she would be gone. For the first time the thought of moving on was painful. She loved the huge, cool hacienda, the smooth tiles underfoot, the serene expanses of white wall. The long summer days she'd spent in the pool with him, the laughter they'd shared, the hours of work, even the sweat and tears, had forged a bond that linked him to her in a way she didn't think she could bear.

It wasn't easy admitting that she loved him, but as the gilded fall days slipped past, she stopped trying to hide it from herself. She'd faced too much in the past to practice self-deception for long. The knowledge that at last she loved a man was bittersweet, because she didn't expect anything to come of it. Loving him was one thing; allowing him to love her was quite another. Her golden eyes were haunted as she watched him, but she threw herself into their remaining time together with a single-minded determination to gather all the memories she could, to let no shadows darken the time she had left. Like pieces of gold, she treasured his deep chuckles, the blistering curses he used whenever his legs wouldn't do as he wanted, the way the virile groove in his cheek deepened into a dimple when he would look up at her, elated, at every triumph.

He was so vitally alive, so masculine, that he deserved a woman in every sense of the word. She might love him, but she knew that she wouldn't be able to satisfy him in the way that was most important to him. Blake was a very physical man; that was a part of his character that became more and more evident with each passing day as he regained command of his body. She wouldn't burden him with the tangle of somber memories that lay just under the calm exterior she presented to the world; she wouldn't make him feel guilty that she'd come to love him. If it killed her, if it tore her to pieces inside, she'd keep their relationship on an even keel, guide him through the last weeks of his therapy, celebrate with him when he finally took those first, all-important steps, then quietly leave. She'd had years of practice in doing just that, devoting herself body and soul to her patient…no, the relentlessly honest side of her corrected. Never before had she devoted herself *body* and soul to anyone else, only to Blake. And he'd never know. She would smilingly say good-bye, walk away, and he'd pick up his life again. Perhaps sometimes he'd think of the woman who'd been his therapist, but then again, perhaps he wouldn't.

Her eyes were cameras, hungrily catching images of him and etching them permanently into her brain, her dreams, the very fiber of her being. There was the morning she went into his room and found him lying on his back, staring at his feet with fierce concentration. "Watch," he grunted, and she watched. Sweat beaded on his face, his fists clenched…and his toes moved. He threw his head back, giving her a blinding smile of triumph, and her built-in shutter clicked, preserving another memory; there was the scowl he gave her one night when she bested him in a long-fought game of chess, and he acted as outraged as he had when he'd discovered that she lifted weights. Laughing or frowning, he was the most beautiful thing that had ever happened to her, and she watched him constantly.

It simply wasn't fair that one man should be so rich with all the treasures of manhood, tempting her with his strength and laughter, when she knew that he was forbidden to her.

The depths of her fey golden eyes held a world of silent suffering, and though she was very controlled whenever she thought anyone was looking at her, in repose her features reflected the sadness she felt. She was so engrossed with the discovery of her love, and regret for what could never be, that she failed to notice the sharp blue eyes that watched her in return, read the pain she felt and determined to find the cause.

As the early days of November brought the sizzling Phoenix heat down into the comfortable mid-seventies, the milestone that she had dreaded, yet worked for so determinedly, was finally reached. He'd been on the bars all morning, literally dragging his feet along, and he was so wet with sweat that his dark blue shorts were soaked and clinging to him. Dione was exhausted by the effort of crouching beside him, moving his feet in the proper motions, and she sank to the floor.

"Let's rest a minute," she said, her voice muffled by fatigue.

His nostrils flared, and he made a sound that was almost a snarl. With his hands clenched around the bars, his teeth bared with determination, he flexed his muscles and bore down with the strain. His right foot moved erratically forward. A feral cry tore itself from deep in his chest and he sagged on the bars, his head falling forward. Trembling, Dione scrambled to her feet and reached out for him, but before she could touch him, he pulled his shoulders back and began the agonizing process with his left foot. His head arched back and he gulped in air; every muscle in his body stood out from the strain he was subjecting himself to, but at last the left foot moved, dragging more than the right foot had, but it moved. Dione stood rooted beside him, her face wet with silent, unnoticed tears as she watched him.

"Damn it," he whispered to himself, shuddering with the effort it cost him as he tried to take another step. "Do it again!"

She couldn't take it any longer; with a choked cry she hurled herself at him, wrapping her arms around his taut waist and burying her face in the sweaty hollow of his shoulder. He wavered, then regained his balance, and his sinewed arms locked around her, holding her so tightly that she moaned from the exquisite pain of it.

"You witch," he muttered thickly, burrowing his fingers under her tumbled mane of hair and twisting his hand in the black mass of it. He exerted just enough pressure to lift her face out of his shoulder and turn it up to him so he could see her wet cheeks, her drowning, glittering eyes and trembling lips. "You stubborn, beautiful witch, you all but jerked me out of that wheelchair by the hair on my head. Shhh, don't cry," he said, his tone changing to one of rustling tenderness. He bent his head and slowly kissed the salty tears from her lashes. "Don't cry, don't cry," he crooned, his lips following the tracks of her silvery tears down her cheek, sliding to her lips, where his tongue licked them away. "Laugh with me, lady; celebrate with me. Let's break out the champagne; you don't know what this means to me...lady...no more tears," he whispered, sighing the words against her face, her lips, and as the last one became sound he settled his mouth firmly over hers.

Blindly she clung to him, hearing the tone of his voice, though the words didn't make any sense. His arms were living shackles, holding her to him, his long, bare legs pressing against hers, her breasts crushed into the dark curls that decorated his chest, and she wasn't afraid. Not of Blake. The taste of him was wild and heady, his tongue strong and insistent as it moved into her mouth and tasted her deeply, possessively. Instinctively she kissed him in return, making her own discoveries, her own explorations. He bit gently at her tongue, then sucked it back into his mouth when she began a startled withdrawal. Dione's knees buckled and she sagged against him, which was enough to upset his precarious balance. He lurched sideways, and they stumbled to the floor in a tangle of arms and legs, but not once did he release her. Again and again his mouth met hers, demanding things that she didn't know how to give, and giving her a wild, alien pleasure that set her to trembling like a tree in a hurricane.

Her nails dug into his shoulders and she strained against him, mindlessly seeking to intensify the contact with him. Not once did she think of Scott. Blake filled her world. The sweaty male scent of him was in her nostrils, the slippery texture of his hot skin under her hands; the unbearably erotic taste of his mouth lay sweetly on her tongue. At some unknown point his kisses had slipped past celebration and become intensely male, demanding, giving, thrilling. Perhaps they'd never been celebration kisses at all, she thought fuzzily.

Suddenly he removed his mouth from hers and buried his face in the curve of her neck. When he spoke his voice was shaky, but husky with an undertone of laughter. "Have you noticed how much time we spend rolling around on the floor?"

It wasn't that funny, but in her sensitized state it struck her as hilarious, and she began to chuckle helplessly. He propped himself up on his elbow and watched her, his blue eyes lighted by a strange light. His hard, warm hand went to her stomach and slid under the thin fabric of her T-shirt top, resting lightly but soothingly on her bare flesh. The intimate but unthreatening touch calmed her almost immediately, and she quieted, lying there and watching his face with huge, fathomless eyes, in which her tears still glittered.

"This definitely calls for champagne," he murmured, leaning over to crush his lips lightly over hers, then withdrawing before the contact could start anew the searing fire of discovery.

Dione was under control again, and the therapist in her began to take over. "Definitely champagne, but first let's get off the floor." She rolled gracefully to her feet and extended her hand to him. He used his hands to place his feet in a secure position, then placed his forearm against hers, his hand cupping her elbow. She stiffened her arm, and he used the leverage to pull himself up, swaying for a moment before he found his balance.

"What now?" he asked.

Someone else might have thought he was asking about the immediate future, but Dione was so attuned to him that she knew he was asking about his progress. "Repetition," she replied. "The more you do it, the easier it'll be. On the other hand, don't push yourself too hard, or you could hurt yourself. People get clumsy when they're tired, and you could fall, break an arm or a leg, and the lost time would really hurt."

"Give me a time," he insisted, and she shook her head at his persistence. He didn't know how to wait; he pushed things along, impatient even with himself.

"I'll be able to give you a ballpark figure in a week," she said, not letting him push *her*. "But I'll definitely be able to keep my promise that you'll be walking by Christmas."

"Six weeks," he figured.

"With a cane," she threw in hastily, and then he glared at her.

"Without a cane," he insisted. She shrugged. If he set his mind to walking without a cane, he probably would.

"I've been thinking of going back to work," he said, startling her. She looked up and was tangled in the web of his blue gaze; it captured her as surely as a spider caught a helpless fly. "I could do it now, but I don't want to interfere with my therapy. What do you say about the first of the year? Will I be far enough along that working won't interfere with my progress?"

Her throat clogged. By the first of the year she'd be gone. She swallowed and said in a low but even voice, "You'll be out of therapy by then and can resume your normal schedule. If you want to continue your exercise program, that's up to you; you have all of the equipment here. You won't have to work as hard as you have, because I was building you up from a very low point. All you have to do now, if you want to continue, is maintain the level you're at now, which won't require such intensive training. If you'd like, I'll draw up a program for you to follow to stay in your present shape."

Blue lightning suddenly flashed from his eyes. "What do you mean, for me to follow?" he demanded harshly, his hand darting out to grip her wrist. Despite her strength, her bones were slender, aristocratic, and his long fingers more than circled her flesh.

Dione could feel her insides crumbling; hadn't he realized that when his therapy was completed, she'd be leaving? Perhaps not. Patients were so involved with themselves, with their progress, that the reality of other responsibilities didn't occur to them. She'd been living for weeks with the pain of knowing that soon she'd have to leave him; now he had to realize it, too.

"I won't be here," she said calmly, straightening her shoulders. "I'm a therapist; it's what I do for a living. I'll be on another case by then. You won't need me anymore; you'll be walking, working, everything you did before…though I think you should wait a while before climbing another mountain.''

"You're *my* therapist," he snapped, tightening his grip on her wrist.

She gave a sad laugh. "It's normal to be possessive. For months we've been isolated in our own little world, and you've depended on me more than you have on any other person in your life, except your mother. Your perspective is distorted now, but when you begin working again, everything will right itself. Believe me, by the time I've been gone a month, you won't even think about me.''

A dark red flush ran up under his tan. "Do you mean you'd just turn your back on me and walk away?" he asked in a disbelieving tone.

She flinched, and tears welled in her eyes. She'd gone for years without crying, having learned not to when she was a child, but Blake had shattered that particular control. She'd wept in his arms…and laughed in them. "It…it's not that easy for me, either," she quivered. "I get involved, too. I always…fall a little in love with my patients. But it passes…. You'll pick up your life and I'll move on to another patient—"

"I'll be damned if you're going to move in with some other man and fall in love with him!" Blake interrupted hotly, his nostrils flaring.

Despite herself, Dione laughed. "Not all of my patients are men; I have a large percentage of children.''

"That's not the point." His flesh was suddenly taut over his cheekbones. "*I* still need you.''

"Oh, Blake," she said in a half sob, half chuckle. "I've been through this more times than I can remember. I'm a habit, a crutch, nothing more, and I'm a crutch that you don't even need now. If I left today, you'd do just fine.''

"That's a matter of opinion,'' he snapped. He shifted his grasp on her wrist and brought her hand up, cradling it to his beard-roughened cheek for a moment before touching his mouth to her knuckles. "You shoved your way into my life, lady, took over my house, my routine, *me....* Do you think people forget volcanoes?''

"Maybe you won't forget me, but you'll discover, one day soon, that you don't need me anymore. Now,'' she said briskly, deliberately inserting cheer into her voice, "what about that champagne?''

They had champagne. Blake rounded up everyone, and between them they drank the entire bottle. Angela received the news of Blake's progress by gently crying; Alberta forgot herself so far as to give Dione a smile of self-satisfied complicity and drank three glasses of champagne; Miguel's dark face suddenly lighted, the first smile Dione had ever seen from him, and he toasted Blake with a silently raised glass, the two men's eyes meeting and communicating as memories flashed between them.

There was another bottle of champagne at dinner that night. Serena hurled herself into Blake's arms when he broke the good news to her, wrenching sobs of relief shaking her body. It took some time to quiet her; she was almost wild with the joy of it. Richard, whose face had become more and more strained as the weeks passed, suddenly looked as if the weight of the world had been lifted from his shoulders. "Thank God,'' he said with heartfelt sincerity. "Now I can have that nervous breakdown I've been putting off for two years.''

Everyone laughed, but Blake said, "If anyone deserves a long vacation, it's you. As soon as I get back into harness, you're relieved of duty for at least a month.''

Richard moved his shoulders tiredly. ''I won't refuse it,'' he said.

Serena looked at her husband with determined cheerfulness. ''How about Hawaii?'' she asked. ''We could spend the whole month lying on the beach in paradise.''

Richard's mouth thinned. ''Maybe later. I think I just need to be by myself for a while.''

Serena drew back as though he'd slapped her, and her cheeks paled. Blake looked at his sister, reading the dejection in her, and anger brightened the dark blue of his eyes. Dione put her hand on his sleeve to restrain him. Whatever problems Richard and Serena were having, they had to work them out by themselves. Blake couldn't keep smoothing the path for Serena; that was a large part of the trouble. He was so important to her that Richard felt slighted.

In only a moment Serena gathered herself and lifted her head, smiling as though Richard's comment had completely missed her. Dione couldn't help but admire her grit. She was a proud, stubborn woman; she didn't need big brother to fight her battles for her. All she had to do was realize that for herself, and make Blake realize it, too.

Dinner was an astonishing melange of items that weren't normally served together, and Dione suspected that Alberta was still celebrating. When the cornish hen was followed by fish, she knew that the three glasses of champagne had been too much. She made the mistake of glancing at Blake, and the barely controlled laughter on his face was too much for her. Suddenly everyone at the table was laughing, effectively banish-

ing the silence that had fallen after Richard's rejection
of Serena.

To keep from hurting Alberta's feelings, they made
a valiant effort at eating everything placed before them,
though she'd evidently gotten carried away and prepared much more than she normally did. If she hadn't
been such a good cook, even when she was tipsy, it
would have been impossible.

They could hear occasional bursts of song from the
kitchen, and just the thought of Alberta, of all people,
singing, was enough to bring on fresh bouts of hilarity.
Dione laughed until her stomach muscles were sore.
The champagne was having its effect on them, too, and
she suspected that anything would have made them
laugh at that point.

It was much later than usual when Serena and Richard left, and if nothing else, the champagne had destroyed the distance between them. Richard had to support his wobbly wife for the short distance to the car,
and Serena was frankly hanging on him, laughing like
a maniac. Dione was still sober enough to be glad that
Richard handled his alcohol well, since he was driving,
but she was also tipsy enough to fall into gales of laughter at the thought that it was a good thing Blake was
still in a wheelchair; he'd never have made it up the
stairs if he'd been walking.

He insisted that she help him undress, and she put
him to bed as if he were a child. As she leaned over
him to adjust the sheet, he caught her hand and pulled
it. After the champagne, her balance wasn't the best it
had ever been, and she tumbled across him. He stopped
her giggles by kissing her slowly, sleepily, then settling
her in his arms. "Sleep with me," he demanded, then
closed his eyes and fell immediately to sleep himself.

Dione smiled a little sadly. The lights were still blazing, and she was dressed in the royal-blue dress she'd put on to celebrate the occasion. She hadn't had *that* much to drink. After a few moments she gently extricated herself from his sleep-relaxed grip and slid from the bed. She turned out the lights, then made her way to her own room and removed the dress, dropping it carelessly on the floor. She, too, slept deeply, and woke the next morning with a headache that tempted her to just stay in bed.

With admirable, if painful, self-discipline, she got out of bed and showered, then went about her normal activities. The champagne hadn't affected Blake as much as it had her, and he was as clear-eyed as usual, ready to begin his exercises. After helping him to warm up, she left him to it and went to take a couple of aspirin.

Serena came in just as she was about to go downstairs—a radiant Serena, whose mouth seemed curved in a permanent smile. "Hi," she said cheerfully. "Where's Blake?"

When Dione told her, she said, "Good, I came to see you, not him. I just wanted to ask you how the chase is going."

It took a moment before Dione realized what she meant; her "scheme" to attract Blake had been so short-lived that, in retrospect, it seemed silly that she'd gotten so upset over something so trivial. Other worries had taken over her time and attention. "Everything's fine," she said, forcing herself to smile. "I think everything's fine with you, too. You look better than I'd expected you to look this morning."

Serena gave her a wink. "I hadn't had that much to drink," she admitted without a hint of shame. "It just seemed like too good an opportunity to pass up. You inspired me; if you could go after the man you wanted, why couldn't I? He's my husband, for heaven's sake! So I seduced him last night.''

Despite her headache Dione chuckled. Serena grinned. ''The war isn't won yet, but I've recaptured some lost territory. I've decided that I'm going to get pregnant.''

''Is that wise?'' So many things could go wrong. If the marriage failed, then Serena would be left to raise the child alone. Or Richard might stay because of the child, but that seemed like a hellish situation for all concerned.

''I know Richard,'' said Serena with confidence. ''I've offended him, and it'll take him a while to forgive me, but I really think that he loves me. Having his baby will show him how much I love him, too.''

''What he really needs is to know that you love him more than you love Blake,'' Dione said. She felt a little uneasy at giving advice; what did she know about handling a love life? Her own brief experience with marriage had been disastrous.

''I *do!* I love Richard in an entirely different way from the way I love Blake.''

''If you were faced with a situation where you could save one of them, but not both of them, which one would you save?''

Serena paled, staring at her.

''Think it over,'' Dione said gently. ''That's what Richard wants. Your wedding vows were to forsake all others.''

''You're telling me that I have to let Blake go, to cut him out of my life.''

''Not entirely; just change the amount of time that you devote to him.''

"I shouldn't have dinner over here every night, should I?"

"I'm sure Richard wonders which house you consider your home."

Serena was a fighter; she absorbed Dione's words, and for a moment she looked frightened. Then her shoulders straightened and her chin went up. "You're right," she said forcefully. "You're a dear!" She startled Dione by giving her a fierce hug. "Poor Richard won't know what's hit him. I'm going to positively smother him with tender loving care! You can be the baby's godmother," she added with a wicked twinkle.

"I'll remember that," said Dione, but after Serena had left she wondered if Serena would remember. By that time, Dione would be long gone.

The next day, without mentioning it to anyone, Dione began making arrangements to take another case. She'd give herself time to recover from the pain of losing Blake, time to adjust to waking up without knowing that he was in the next room. She'd begin at the end of January, she thought. Blake would be returning to work after the first of January, and she'd probably leave sometime around then.

Now that success was in his grasp, Blake pushed himself harder. Dione gave up even trying to rein in his energy. She watched him force himself along the bars, sweating, cursing steadily as an antidote against the pain and weariness, and when he was too tired to continue she'd massage his exhausted body, put him in the whirl-pool, then give him another massage. She watched his diet more closely than ever, knowing how badly he needed extra nutrition now. When cramps knotted his legs in the night, she rubbed them out for him. There was no stopping him.

It was time for him to leave the wheelchair behind. She brought in a walker, a four-legged half cage that provided him with the balance and stability he needed, and the pleasure of getting around under his own power was so great that he gladly endured the slow pace, the strain.

He didn't mention Serena's sudden absence from the

dinner table, though Alberta immediately adjusted both her menus and the amount she cooked. The full dinners almost ceased; instead she began preparing small, light dinners, and Dione often found the table set with candles and a decanter of wine. The intimate atmosphere was another spike that crucified her heart, but as Blake welcomed the pain of therapy, she welcomed the hurt of his company. This was all she had, and the days were trickling away so swiftly that she felt as if she were grasping at shadows.

On Thanksgiving Day, following Blake's directions, she drove them to Serena's house for dinner. Except for being transferred from the hospital to home, it was the first time he'd been out since his accident, and he sat turned to stone, his entire body tense as his senses struggled to take everything in. In two years Scottsdale had changed, cars had changed, clothing had changed. She wondered if the desert sky seemed bluer to him, the sun brighter.

"When will I be able to drive?" he asked abruptly.

"When your reflexes are fast enough. Soon," she promised absently. She seldom drove, and she had to concentrate on what she was doing. She jumped when his hand rested on her knee, then slid up under the skirt she was wearing to pat her thigh.

"Next week we'll start practicing," he said. "We'll go out in the desert, away from all the traffic."

"Yes, fine," she said, her voice taut with tension caused by the warm hand on her leg. He touched her constantly, bestowing kisses and pats, but somehow his hand seemed much more intimate when she had on a skirt.

A smile twitched at his lips. "I like that dress," he said.

She gave him a harried glance. He liked every dress she wore, evidently. He was definitely a leg man. He slid closer and bent his head to inhale the perfume she'd used in honor of the occasion, his warm breath caressing her collarbone just before he pressed his lips into the soft hollow. Simultaneously his hand slid higher, and the car wobbled dangerously before Dione straightened it.

"Stop it!" she fumed, pushing uselessly at his hand. "You're making me nervous! I don't drive that well anyway!"

"Then put both hands on the wheel," he advised, laughing. "I'm in the same car, remember? I'm not going to do anything that'll cause you to crash."

"You wretch!" she shouted as his fingers began stroking back and forth over her thigh. "Damn it, Blake, would you stop it! I'm not a doll for you to play with!"

"I'm not playing," he murmured. His fingers circled higher.

Desperately Dione released the wheel and grabbed his wrist with both hands. The car veered sideways, and with a curse he finally moved his hand, grabbing the steering wheel and bringing the car back under control. "Maybe I'd better start driving *now*," he panted.

"You're going to be walking to Serena's!" she yelled, her face scarlet.

He threw his head back and laughed. "You don't know how good that sounds, lady! It would take me a while, but I could do it! God, I feel like a human being again!"

Abruptly she realized that his spirits were sky-high, the natural result of his victory and the experience of being away from the house. He was delirious with pleasure, drunk on his newfound freedom from the prison of his own body. Still, she was driving, and she was afraid that he was going to make her run into something.

"I mean it, stop fooling around!" she said sharply.

He gave her a lazy smile, a heart-stopping smile. "Lady, if I decided to fool around, you'd be the first to know."

"Why don't you go back to work tomorrow?" she demanded in sudden exasperation.

"We're closed for the holidays. I wouldn't have anything to do."

"I'm going to give you something to do," she muttered.

"Like what?"

"Picking your teeth up off the pavement," she said.

He threw his hands up in mock alarm. "All right, all right! I'll be good. Next thing I know, you'll be sending me to bed without my supper. I wouldn't really mind, though, because you always come to tuck me in, and I get to watch you running around in those thin nightgowns of yours that you think are so modest.... Serena's house is the solar redwood and rock one.'

He threw in the last sentence just as she opened her mouth to blast him again, and she maneuvered the Audi up the steep drive to where the house nestled against the mountain. By the time she'd gotten out of the car and gone around to help Blake wrestle with the walker, Serena and Richard had come out to greet them.

The steps were a problem for Blake, but he mastered them. Serena watched, an anxious look on her face, but she didn't run to help him. Instead she stayed firmly by Richard's side, her arm looped through his. Dione remained a step behind Blake, not out of servitude but to catch him in case he started to tumble. He looked over his shoulder at her and grinned. "Not bad, huh?"

"A regular goat," she replied, and only he caught her hidden meaning.

He gave her another of his breathtaking smiles. "Don't you mean mountain goat?"

She shrugged. "A goat is a goat is a goat."

His eyes promised retribution, but she felt safe from him for the time being. If he started anything on the drive back home, *she'd* get out and walk!

The traditional dinner had all of them groaning before it was over. Blake and Richard then retired to talk business, and Dione helped Serena clear the table. Serena had a cook, but she told Dione that everything had been prepared the day before and she'd given the cook the rest of the week off. "I don't mind being alone in the house with Richard," she said, laughing a little.

"Is Operation Manhunt going well?" asked Dione.

"At times." Serena laughed. "Sometimes I…ah… undermine his resistance. Then he'll freeze up on me again. But I think I'm winning the battle. He noticed that I've stopped going to Blake's every day."

"Did he ask you about it?"

"Richard? Not a chance! But he calls me almost every afternoon about some little something, as if he's checking on me."

They traded a few comments on the mule-headedness of men in general and finished cleaning the kitchen. When they finally emerged they discovered that the men were still deep in conversation about the company, with Richard going over some sort of electronic blueprint with Blake. Dione looked at Serena, and they both shrugged. Kicking off their shoes, they sat down, and Serena used the remote control to turn on the television set, which revealed two football teams tearing into each other.

Within ten minutes the men had left their technical conversation and were sitting beside the women. Dione liked football, so she didn't mind watching the game, and evidently Serena shared the same fondness for it. At first Dione didn't pay attention to the hand that touched her shoulder, lying absently over it so that the fingers touched her collarbone. Gradually the touch firmed, shifted and exerted pressure. Without quite knowing how it had happened, she suddenly realized that she was leaning back in the circle of Blake's arm, resting against his chest while his arm kept her firmly anchored there.

The startled movement of her body brought a knowing smile to his lips, but he merely held her more closely than before. "Shhh. Just watch the game," he murmured.

She was so rattled that nothing sank into her consciousness, but eventually the warmth of his body began to relax her. He would behave himself here, so she was free to enjoy the sensation, let herself drown in the heady scent of his skin. All too soon she would have only the memories of him to take out and savor.

The time passed swiftly. Incredibly they became hungry again, so everyone raided the refrigerator and constructed enormous sandwiches of turkey, lettuce, tomato and anything else they could find. Blake's sweet tooth demanded feeding, and he devoured what was left of the strawberry pie. The atmosphere was easy, comfortable, and he commented on it when they were driving home late that night.

"Serena and Richard seem to have patched up their differences," he said, watching her sharply in the dim light from the dash.

"I think they're well on their way," she said, carefully keeping her tone bland. She wasn't about to divulge anything Serena had told her.

When they got home Dione looked him squarely in the eye and smiled. "I really don't think there's any need for me to tuck you in any longer," she said sweetly. "You're perfectly mobile now. I'll see you in the morning. Good night."

As she let herself into her room she heard him doing a perfect imitation of a chicken clucking, and she had to bite her lip to stifle her laughter. The monster!

But when he called her several hours later, jerking her out of a sound sleep, she didn't hesitate. She hurried to his room and flipped on the light switch. He was lying on his stomach, hopelessly tangled in the sheet as he tried to reach his left leg.

"Easy," she crooned, finding the cramp and briskly rubbing the muscle of his calf between her hands. He went limp with relief as the pain eased away.

"How much longer will this go on?" he muttered into his pillow.

"Until your muscles are used to the demands you're making on them," she said. "It's not as bad as it was. You seldom have a cramp in your right leg now."

"I know. My left leg drags more than the right. I'll always limp, won't I?"

"Who knows? It won't matter, though. You'll look smashing with a cane."

He laughed and rolled over on his back, tangling the sheet even more. Despite what she'd said earlier, Dione bent over him and automatically began straightening the sheet. "You managed to make a disaster area of your bed," she complained.

"I was restless tonight," he said, his voice suddenly strained.

Dione glanced up, and her hands froze at their task. He was staring at her, his gaze locked on her breasts. A look of such raw hunger was in his eyes that she would have flinched away if she'd had any strength in her limbs. But she continued to sit on the side of his bed, mesmerized by the way his gaze moved lovingly, longingly, over her female curves.

"Lady, what you do to me is almost criminal," he groaned in a shaky voice.

An odd tightening in her breasts made her close her eyes. "I've got to go," she said weakly, but for the life of her she couldn't make herself move.

"No, don't go," he pleaded. "Let me touch you... my God, I've got to touch you!"

Dione caught her breath on a sob as she felt his fingertips trace lightly over her breast, and she squeezed her eyes shut even more tightly than before. For a moment the awful unfamiliarity of a man's touch on her breast brought back a nightmare of pain and humiliation, and she made a choked sound of protest.

"Dee, honey, open your eyes. Look at me; look at how I'm shaking. Touching you makes me dizzy," he whispered fiercely. "I get drunk on the very smell of you."

Dione's eyes fluttered open, and she found that he'd moved closer, until his face was filling her vision. It was Blake's face, not Scott's, and his blue eyes were as dark and stormy as the sea, full of incredible hunger. His trembling fingers were still moving only lightly over her breasts, though the heat of his hand burned her even through her nightgown.

"That...that's enough," she said, her voice thin, wavering out of control. "This isn't right."

"I need you," he cajoled. "It's been so long...can't

you tell how much I need you? Please. Let me touch you, really touch you. Let me unbutton this granny gown and see you.''

Even as the words were tumbling harshly from his lips, his agile fingers were slipping the tiny buttons of her nightgown free of the buttonholes. The buttons ran down to her waist, and he undid every one of them while she sat helplessly transfixed by the primitive call of his need. Slowly, with rapt attention, he opened the gown and pushed it off her smoothly tanned shoulders, dropping the cloth around her arms and baring her to the waist.

"I've dreamed of this," he whispered harshly. "I saw you, that morning.... You were so perfect, so damned *female,* that you took my breath away." Gently he cupped a breast in his palm, curving his fingers over its ripe curve as if he were measuring the heft of it.

Dione began to tremble, wild little tingles of sensation shooting through her body. She didn't know what to do, how to handle him. She had no experience with men other than her husband, and that had been a horror from start to finish, nothing that compared to the sweet pain of Blake's touch. Sweet, yes...and not really pain. Incredible. Unknown. A primitive exultation raced along her veins, heating her blood, making her feel stupidly, happily weak. She wanted to sink down beside him on the bed, but she couldn't do that. Despite the joy her body was feeling, her mind was still locked away from even the possibility of it.

Now both of his hands were on her, holding her breasts together. His head bent, and she sucked in a convulsive breath, staring down at his dark hair with terrified fascination. His tongue darted out and washed a cherry nipple, then he blew his warm breath across it, watching with delight as it tightened and thrust out at him. "That's beautiful," he breathed, and tasted the other one.

At last she could move, and her fingers threaded through his hair. She thought dimly that she'd pull his head away, but instead her palms pressed against his warm skull and held him to her, held his mouth to the tender flesh he was suckling as fiercely as any starving infant.

He released her nipple from his mouth and lay back, his hands sliding to her ribs and drawing her with him, pulling her down until she lay half-across him. He began kissing her with short, hard kisses that stung her lips. "I need you," he panted. "Please. I want you so much. Let me make love to you."

Dione moaned, a high, keening sound that reflected both the tumult he'd stirred in her and her fear of going any further. "I can't," she cried, tears suddenly stinging her eyes. "You don't know what you're asking of me."

"Yes, I do," he whispered, moving his mouth down to the line of her jaw, nipping at her with his teeth. "I'm asking you to let me love you. I want you so much that I'm aching all over. I can't sleep for dreaming about you. Let me be a man with you; let me bury myself in you and forget about the past two years. Make me whole again," he pleaded.

She'd spent too long nurturing this man, agonized over him too much, felt his pain, celebrated his triumphs, loved him. How could she refuse him now? She'd be leaving soon, and she'd never know the heady taste of him again. But she was shaking, almost convulsed with the fear of what he'd do to her. For him, she'd bear it, this one last time. The scars that Scott had left on her mind had ruined her forever, kept her from feeling the total pleasure of a man, and when Blake rolled, deftly placing himself above her, the nauseating panic that beat its wings in her stomach threatened to overtake her.

He saw the fixed expression in her enormous golden eyes and began to speak softly to her, making her realize his identity. With silent desperation she stared at him, her nails digging into his shoulders.

"It's all right," he murmured soothingly. "You know I won't hurt you; I'd never hurt you. Let's get you out of this," he said as he began thrusting the bunched cloth at her waist down over her hips, then stroking it away from her thighs. He leaned on his elbow and looked at her, drinking in and savoring all the details that he'd only dreamed about before. He steadied his shaking hand by flattening his palm on her stomach and sliding it over her satiny skin. One finger dipped into the tight little hollow of her navel, and she gasped again, but though her nails were digging so deeply into his shoulders that she'd broken the skin, the blind fear had left her face. Her eyes were locked on him, letting him know that for him, she would do this. Though she was afraid, she trusted him, and she would give him this one last gift, the pleasure of her body.

His hand slid lower, insinuating itself between her thighs and exploring, as he'd tried to do so many times before. She clenched her teeth in shock and tried to control her body's instinctive movement, but her thighs tightened as she tried to dislodge the alien touch.

"Honey, don't!" he cried. "I won't hurt you, I swear."

Dione swallowed and slowly regained control of herself, forcing her legs to relax. He was shaking all over, his body dewed with sweat, the color in his face as florid as if he burned with fever; she felt the heat of his skin beneath her hands and wondered vaguely if he weren't really fevered after all. His blue eyes were glittering wildly, and his lips were red, swollen. She removed one trembling hand from his shoulder and touched his face, placing her fingertips on his lips. "It's all right," she whispered thinly. "I'm ready."

"Oh, God, no, you're not," he groaned, kissing her fingers. "I wanted to wait, but I don't think I can."

"It's all right," she repeated, and with a muffled cry he moved to lie fully over her.

All of the love she felt for him welled up and made her body pliable for his touch; with her eyes wide open and locked on his face, she knew that this was Blake, and that she would do anything for him. Though her heart was slamming against her ribs with almost shattering force, though her entire body shook, she clutched his shoulders and drew him tightly to her.

He tried to be gentle, but the years of celibacy had destroyed a great deal of his normal self-control. When he parted her legs and felt the silkiness of her thighs cradle his hips, he moaned deep in his chest and took her with a single strong movement.

Hot tears burned her lids, then slid down her cheeks. This wasn't the agony she'd expected, but her body had been untouched for twelve years, and the pain and shock of his entry were all too real. To her astonishment, her flesh didn't flinch from him; she still lay soft and willing beneath him. She began to weep in earnest, not from the pain, which was already fading, but because suddenly she realized that Blake had given her as much as he was taking. He'd given her back her womanhood. The years had wrought their healing miracle, after all; it had taken Blake to make her realize it, Blake to make her love enough to overcome the past.

He lifted his head from her throat and saw the tears, and he paled. "No," he croaked. "Dee, what have I done? I'll stop—"

Inexplicably the tears mingled with laughter, and she caught him tightly, preventing the removal of his body. "Don't stop!" she said joyously, the words clogging in her throat. "I didn't know...I had no idea! No, don't ever stop—"

He caught the babbling words in his mouth, kissing her wildly and deeply, relief making him drunk. "I'm going to have to stop," he panted, beginning to move rhythmically on her. "It's been over two years, darling. I don't think I can wait—"

"Then don't wait," she said softly, her eyes shining. "This is for you."

He kissed her again, even harder than before. "The next one's for you," he promised hoarsely, just before he slid over the edge of control. Dione hugged him to her, accepting his body and his desperate, almost violent movements, cradling him, soothing him, and in a moment the storm had passed and he sagged against her.

She could feel the heavy pounding of his heart as he lay on her in the silent aftermath, feel the heat of his breath on her shoulder, the trickle of sweat that ran from his side and slipped down her ribs. She smoothed his tousled dark hair, adjusted his head more comfortably on her shoulder. He murmured something and his hand came up to cover her breast. She waited, lying there pressed into the bed by his weight, as his body relaxed and he drifted slowly, easily into sleep.

She stared up at the light that still blazed brightly; turning out the light hadn't occurred to either of them.

Exhaustion made her body heavy, but she couldn't sleep. The night had been a major turning point in her life, but she didn't know what direction to take. Or was it such a major turning point? Blake had taught her that she no longer needed to fear the touch of a man, but what difference did it make? If the man weren't Blake, then she didn't want him. It was the love that she felt for him that had enabled her to tear down her prison of fear, and without that love she simply wasn't interested.

Nor, she realized suddenly, could it ever happen again. She couldn't afford to let it happen. She was a therapist, and Blake was her patient. She'd violated her own professional code, totally forgotten the rules and standards that she'd set for herself. This was the worst mistake she'd ever made and she felt sick with remorse.

Whatever happened, she had to remember that soon she'd be leaving, that she was only a temporary part of Blake's life. She'd have to be stupid to jeopardize her career for something that she knew was only a moment out of time. I should have seen it coming, she thought tiredly. Of course Blake had been attracted to her; she was the only woman available to him. But she'd been so engrossed in her own misery and attraction that she hadn't realized that his actions hadn't been meant merely to tease.

Gently she shifted him to one side, and he was sleeping so deeply that he didn't flicker an eyelash. With slow, careful movements she sat up and reached for her discarded nightgown, pulling it over her head before she got to her feet. As she stood she winced at the unfamiliar soreness of her body, but forced herself to walk silently to the door and leave, turning out the light as she passed the switch.

In her own room she stared at her bed, but realized

that it would be a waste of time to return to it. She'd never be able to sleep. Too many sensations, too many memories, were warring in her mind and body. Her bedside clock told her that it was a little after three; she might as well stay up the rest of the night.

She felt oddly empty, her regret candeling out the bittersweet pleasure she'd found in his embrace and leaving her with nothing. For a short while, in his arms, she'd felt wildly alive, as if all her fetters had fallen away. Reality was something less than that. Reality was knowing that the night meant nothing to him beyond the immediate satisfaction of his sex-starved body. She'd seen it coming from a mile away and still hadn't had the sense to duck; no, she'd taken the punch full on the jaw.

But mistakes were something to learn from, better textbooks than anything that ever got put into print. She'd picked herself up before and gone on, and she'd do it again. The trick was to remember that there was an end to everything, and the end of her time with Blake was coming at her with the speed of a jet.

She cringed inwardly at the thought, and in agitation walked out to the gallery. The desert air was cold, and she shivered when it touched her heated skin, but she welcomed the shock of it. The night had been an emotional roller coaster, a ride that had left her stunned, bewildered. She'd gone from fear to acceptance, then to joy, followed by regret and a rerun of acceptance, and now she was afraid again, afraid that she wouldn't be able to pick up the pieces, afraid that life after Blake would be so hollow that it would be useless. Afraid, even, of the possibility that the fear he'd destroyed had been her strongest defense.

_____ *Chapter Nine*

The sudden lancing of light across the dark gallery made her heart leap into her throat, and she turned her head to the left to wearily eye the sliding doors to Blake's room, where the light was coming from. What had awakened him? When the glass doors remained closed, she turned back to stare out again into the blackness of the garden. She hoped he wouldn't come looking for her; she didn't think she could face him right then. Perhaps in the morning, when she was dressed in her familiar "therapist uniform" of shorts and a T-shirt and they were involved in the routine of exercise. Perhaps then she'd have herself under control and could act as if nothing unusual had happened. But now she felt raw and bleeding, every nerve exposed. Wearily she leaned her head against the railing, not even feeling how cold she'd become.

A whirr came to her ears and she lifted her head, frowning. It was coming from her room...then it stopped just behind her, and she knew. Blake had used the wheelchair, because he could get around faster in it than he could using the walker. Her entire body tensed as she listened to him getting out of the chair, struggling for balance, but she didn't dare look around. She kept her forehead pressed against the cold metal of the railing, hoping without belief that he'd realize she didn't want to be disturbed and leave her alone.

First she felt his hands, gripping her shoulders, then the hard, warm press of his body against her back and the stirring of his breath in her hair. "Dee, you're freezing," he murmured. "Come inside. We'll talk there, and I'll get you warm."

She swallowed. "There's nothing to talk about."

"There's everything to talk about," he said, a hardness that she'd never heard before in his voice making her shudder in reaction. He felt the ripple of her muscles under his fingers and pulled her closer to him. "Your skin is icy, and you're coming in with me now. You're in shock, honey, and you need to be taken care of. I thought I understood, but you threw me for a loop tonight. I don't know what it is you're hiding, what you're afraid of, but I'm damned well going to find out before this night is over."

"The night *is* over," she told him thinly. "It's morning now."

"Don't argue with me. In case you haven't noticed, I don't have a stitch of clothing on and I'm freezing, but I'm staying right here with you. If you don't come inside I'll probably catch pneumonia and undo all the progress you've worked for. Come on," he said, his tone changing into one of cajolery. "You don't have to be afraid. We'll just talk."

She shook her head, her long hair flying wildly and striking him in the face. "You don't understand. I'm not afraid of you; I never have been."

"Well, that's something," he muttered, dropping his arm to her waist and urging her to turn. She gave up and dully let him guide her inside, with his using her for balance. His pace was slow but remarkably steady, and he didn't really put any of his weight on her. He stopped to close the sliding doors, then guided her to the bed.

"Here, get under the covers," he ordered as he bent down to switch on the lamp. "How long have you been out there? Even the room is cold."

She shrugged; it didn't really matter how long it had been, did it? She did as he said and crawled into the bed, pulling the thick comforter up to her neck. Blake studied her pale, set expression for a moment, and his lips pressed grimly together. He lifted the cover and slid into the bed next to her, and she stared at him in shock.

"I'm cold, too," he said, and it was only half a lie. He slid his arm under her neck and curved his other hand around her waist, pulling her into the cocoon of his body heat. At first she was rigid; then the warmth began to penetrate her chilled skin and she started to shiver. His hand exerted just the slightest pressure and she moved with it, unconsciously pressing more closely to him in search of extra heat. When he had her settled, her head cradled on his shoulder and her legs tangled with his, he stroked the heavy black hair away from her face and she felt the pressure of his mouth on her forehead.

"Are you comfortable?" he murmured.

Comfortable wasn't the word for it; she was so tired that her limbs lay heavily, without strength. But she nodded, as he seemed to want an answer. What did it matter? She was just so tired....

After a moment he said with misleading mildness, "I thought you said you'd been married."

Surprise made her lift her head and stare at him. "I was." What did he mean?

Gently he threaded his fingers through her hair and forced her head back to his shoulder. "Then why was it so…painful for you?" he asked, his voice a rumble under her ear. "I damned near fainted, thinking that you'd been a virgin."

For a moment her mind was blank, struggling to understand what he was saying; then realization came abruptly and a hot flush warmed her cold cheeks. "I wasn't a virgin," she assured him huskily. "It's just that I haven't…it's been a long time."

"How long?"

With rising alarm she heard the determination in his voice, barely masked by the quietness of his tone. He meant to know everything, to uncover all her secrets. Twice before he'd torn away the protection of her forgetfulness, forcing her to remember the pains and failures that she'd tried so hard never to think of again. Did he like causing her pain?

"How long?" he repeated inexorably. "Talk to me, honey, because you're not leaving this bed until I know."

Dione closed her eyes in despair, swallowing in an effort to relieve the dryness of her mouth. She might as well tell him and get it over with. "Twelve years," she finally admitted, the words muffled against his skin because as she said them, she turned her face into his throat.

"I see." Did he? Did he really see? Could any man really understand what goes through a woman's mind when her body is violated? A wild bitterness sprang out of the well of pain that she usually kept covered. He didn't care if he explored the clock's workings until it could no longer tick, as long as he discovered what had made it tick in the beginning. Her hands stiffened against him and she pushed, but now he was much stronger than she was, and held her welded tightly to him, his body hard and unyielding against hers. After a moment she gave up the futile effort and lay beside him in rigid rejection.

He curved his long fingers over her smooth shoulder and tucked her even closer to him, as if to shield her. "Twelve years is a long time," he began easily. "You had to be just a kid. How old are you now?"

"Thirty." She heard the ragged edge of panic in her voice, felt the way her heart began to skitter, the increased rhythm of air rushing in and out of her lungs. She'd already told him too much; he could put the pieces of the puzzle together now and read the whole ugly story.

"Then you had to be just eighteen.... You told me that you got married when you were eighteen. Haven't you been in love since then? I know men have been attracted to you. You've got a face and body that turn my insides into melted butter. Why haven't you let someone love you?"

"That's my business," she cried sharply, trying again to roll away from him. He held her without hurting her, gently subduing her with his arms and legs. Goaded, maddened by the bonds that held her, she shrieked, "Men don't *love* women! They hurt them, humiliate them, then say, 'Whatsamatter? You frigid?' *Let me go!*"

"I can't," he said, his voice catching oddly. She was in no state to pay any attention to how her words had affected him; she began to fight in earnest, kicking at his legs, trying to scratch his face, her body arching wildly in an effort to throw herself off the bed. He snatched her hands away from his cheeks before she could do any damage, then wrestled her around until she was beneath him, his weight holding her captive.

"Dione, stop it!" he yelled. "Damn it, talk to me! *Were you raped?*"

"Yes!" she screamed, a sob tearing out of her throat. "Yes, yes, yes! Damn you! I didn't want to remember! Can't you understand that? It kills me to remember!" Another tearing, aching sob wrenched its way out of her chest, but she wasn't crying. Her eyes were dry, burning, yet still her chest heaved convulsively and the awful sounds, like someone choking on a pain too large to be swallowed, continued.

Blake's head fell back and he ground his teeth in a primal snarl, his neck corded with the rage that surged through him. His muscles trembled with the need to vent his fury physically, but a despairing whimper from the woman in his arms made him realize the need to control himself, to calm her. He held her and stroked her, sliding his palms down her body and feeling the marvelous tone of her sleek muscles even through the fabric of her gown. His lips nuzzled into her hair, moved on to discover the softness of her eyelids, the satin stretch of skin over her exotic cheekbones, the intoxicating bloom of her soft, generous mouth. He whispered to her, crooned endearments, reassured her with broken phrases that told her how lovely she was, how much he wanted her. He promised her with his words and his body that he wouldn't hurt her, reminding her over and over of the hour not long past when she'd trusted him enough to let him make love to her. The memory of that joining burned over his skin, but his need for her could wait. *Her* needs came first, the needs of a woman who had known too much pain.

Gradually she calmed; gradually she reached out to him, by slow degrees curling her arms around his muscular back. She was tired, so worn out from the emotional strain of the night that she was limp against him, but he had to know, so he said again, "Tell me about it."

"Blake, no," she moaned, turning her head weakly away from him. "I can't...."

"You can; you have to. Was that why you got divorced? Couldn't your husband handle what had happened to you?" His questions fell on her like rocks, bruising her, and she flinched in his arms. He caught her chin and turned it back to him so he could read the nuances of her expression. "What kind of bastard was he, to turn his back on you when you needed him most? Did he think it was your fault?"

A high, strained peal of laughter escaped her, and she shut it off abruptly by clapping her hand over her mouth, afraid of the rising hysteria in her. "He...oh, this is funny! He didn't have any trouble handling what happened to me! *He* did it. My husband was the one who raped me!"

Blake went rigid, stunned both by her words and the way she began to laugh, gasping shrieks of laughter that again she shut off, visibly clenching herself in an effort to regain control. She attained it, but she used all of the inner strength she possessed, and as she lay in his arms she could feel the emotion draining away from her, leaving her heavy, spent...

"Tell me," he insisted, his voice so hoarse that she didn't recognize it.

Her heartbeat had changed from a frantic sledgehammer pounding to a ponderous rhythm; dimly she wondered at it, but what did it really matter? What did anything really matter? She'd had all she could bear tonight....

"Dione," he prodded.

"I don't know why I married him," she said dully. "I don't think I ever loved him. But he was handsome and he had money, something I'd never had. He dazzled me with it. He bought me things, took me places, told me how much he loved me. I think that was it; he told me that he loved me. No one had ever told me that before, you see. But I was still standoffish with him, and Scott couldn't stand that. I don't think anyone had ever said no to him before. So he married me."

Blake waited a moment for her to resume, and when she didn't he jostled her lightly. "Go on."

Her eyelids lifted slowly. She stared at him with half-veiled eyes, the glimmering, mysterious golden pools darkened to amber by the shadow of her lashes. "On our wedding night, he hurt me," she said simply. "He was so rough...I started fighting him. I was strong even then, and I knocked him off of me. He went wild.... He forced me to have sex with him, and he wasn't gentle. It was my first time, and I thought I was dying.

"I knew then that the marriage was an awful mistake, that I wanted out, but he wouldn't let me go. Every night I'd fight him again, and he'd force me again. 'He was going to teach me how to be a woman if he had to break every bone in my body,' he said. I couldn't stop fighting him," she muttered to herself. "I never could just lie there and let him get it over with. I *had* to fight back, or I felt like something in me would die. So I fought, and the more I fought, the rougher he got. He started...hitting me."

Blake cursed violently and she jumped, throwing her arm up to cover her face. She was so deep inside her bitter memories that she was reacting as she had then, defending herself. His curse changed into a groan and he cuddled her, coaxing her to lower her arm. "I'm sorry, darling, I didn't mean to startle you," he panted. "When he started hitting you, why didn't you turn him into the police?"

"I didn't know that he couldn't do that," she said tiredly. "I was so dumb; I read a lot of things about it afterward, but at the time I thought he had a legal right to do what he wanted with me, short of murder. He got worse and worse; he almost stopped wanting sex. He'd just start right in hitting me. Sometimes he'd go ahead and rape me, as roughly as he could, but most of the time he didn't."

"You stayed with him for three months? Isn't that how long you told me your marriage lasted?"

"Not even that long. That I stayed with him, I mean. I can't remember.... He pushed me down the steps one night, and I landed in the hospital with a broken arm and a concussion. I was there for several days, and a nurse figured out that I hadn't simply tripped while going down the steps. She talked to me, and a counselor talked to me. I didn't go back to Scott. When I was released from the hospital, the nurse let me stay with her."

She was calmer now, the memories easier to bear. In her normal voice she said, "Scott's family was horrified by what had happened, they were good people, and when I filed for divorce they forced Scott to go along with it. They gave me a lot of support, paid for my training as a therapist, kept Scott away from me, even got him into psychiatric counseling. It must have worked; he's remarried now, and they seem very happy. He has two daughters."

"Have you kept in touch with him?" Blake asked incredulously.

"Oh, no!" she denied, shaking her head. "But while

his mother was alive she kept track of me, sort of looked after me like a guardian angel. She never got over what had happened to me, as if it were her fault because Scott was her son. She told me when he remarried, and when her grandchildren were born. She died a couple of years ago.''

"So he lived happily ever after, and you've been dragging a ball and chain around with you for all these years," he said angrily. "Afraid to let anyone touch you, keeping people pushed away at a safe distance…only half-alive!"

"I haven't been unhappy," she said wearily, her lashes sweeping down. She was so tired…. He knew all of it now, and she felt so empty, as if all the terror that had filled her for so long had seeped away, leaving her hollow and lost. The warmth of Blake's body was so comforting in the chilly room; the steady rumble of his heartbeat in his strong chest was so reassuring. She could feel the iron in the bands of flesh that wrapped around her, feel the security of his strength. She'd given him that strength; it was only right that she rely on it now. She turned her face against him, inhaling and tasting on her tongue the heady scent of his body. He smelled of man, of sweat, of a clean grassy scent that eluded her when she tried to search it out. He had the musky smell of sex, a reminder of the incredible night. With a slow, gentle sigh, she slept, all of her senses filled with him.

When she woke she was alone in the bed and the brightness of the room told her that the morning was almost over. She wasn't fortunate enough to forget, even for a moment, the events of the night. Her eyes went to the gallery, but the wheelchair was gone, and she wondered how Blake could have left her bed and taken the wheelchair without waking her; she was normally the lightest of sleepers, coming awake at any unusual noise. But she'd been so tired…she was still tired, her body heavy and clumsy feeling, her reactions slow.

She eased out of bed, wincing at the unfamiliar soreness of her body. How could she have been so stupid that she'd let Blake make love to her? She was trying to get through these last days with him with the least amount of emotional damage, and she'd made it impossibly complicated. She should never have tried to arouse him; she didn't know anything about handling men, or handling herself, if it came to that. He'd said, ''I need you,'' and she'd melted. A real pushover, she told herself contemptuously. He must have seen her coming a mile away. Then, to top it all off, she'd told him about Scott.

She writhed inwardly with embarrassment. She'd managed for years to control herself, to keep herself from wallowing in the slimy pool of the past. So she hadn't been comfortable with men; what of it? A lot of women managed very well without men. When she thought of the way she'd clung to him, weeping and moaning, she wanted to die of shame. Her solitary nature hated the thought of displaying so much of herself to anyone, even the man who had taken up her days and nights for months.

Willpower had a lot to say for itself; it steadied her nerves, gave her the courage to shrug her shoulders and step into the shower as if there was nothing unusual about that morning. She dressed as she normally did, then went straight to the gym, where she knew she'd find Blake. There was no point in putting off their meeting, because time wouldn't make it any easier. It was best to face him and get it over with.

When she opened the door he glanced at her but didn't say anything; he was lying on his stomach, lifting weights with his legs, and he was counting. He was totally engrossed in the demands he was making of his body. With a slow but steady rhythm he lifted each leg in turn.

"How long have you been doing that?" Dione asked sternly, forgetting her discomfort as her professional concern surfaced.

"Half…an…hour," he grated.

"That's enough. Stop right now," she ordered. "You're overdoing it; no wonder your legs give you fits! What are you trying to do, punish your legs for the years they didn't work?"

He relaxed with a groan. "I'm trying to get away from the walker," he said irritably. "I want to walk alone, without leaning on anything."

"If you tear a muscle you're going to be leaning on something for a lot longer than necessary," she snapped back. "I've watched you push yourself past the bounds of common sense, but no more. I'm a therapist, not a spectator. If you're not going to follow my instructions, then there's no use in my staying here any longer."

His head jerked around, and his eyes darkened to a stormy color. "Are you telling me that you're leaving?"

"That's up to you," she returned stonily. "If you'll do as you're told and follow your training program, I'll stay. If you're going to ignore everything I say and do what you want, there's no point in my wasting my time here."

He flushed darkly, and she realized that he still wasn't used to giving in to anyone. For a moment she expected him to tell her to pack her bags, and she pulled herself up, braced for the words that would end her time with him. Then he clenched his jaw and snapped, "All right, lady, you're the boss. What's the matter with you today? You're as touchy as a rattler."

Absurd relief washed over her, at both her reprieve from exile and the familiar, comforting ill-temper apparent in his words. She could handle that; but she knew beyond a doubt that she wouldn't have been able to handle the situation if he'd made any reference to the intimacy of the night, if he'd tried to kiss her and act like a lover.

She was so determined to regain the therapist-patient relationship that during the day she resisted his teasing and efforts to joke with her, turning a cold face to his laughing eyes. By the time they had finished they were snarling at each other like two stray dogs. Dione, having eaten nothing all day, was so hungry that she was almost sick, and that only added to the hostility she felt.

Her body was rebelling against her misuse of it when it was finally time for dinner. On wobbly legs she made her way down the stairs, her head whirling in a nauseating manner that made her cling to the banisters. She was so preoccupied with the task of getting down the stairs in one piece that she didn't hear Blake behind her, didn't feel his searing blue gaze on her back.

She made it to the dining room and fell into her chair with relief at not having sprawled on the floor. After a moment Blake made his way past her and went into the kitchen; she was too sick to wonder at that, even though it was the first time she'd seen him enter the kitchen in the months she'd been living there.

Alberta came out promptly with a steaming bowl of soup, which she placed before Dione. "Eat that right now," she ordered in her gruff, no-nonsense voice.

Slowly Dione began to eat, not trusting her queasy stomach. As she ate, though, she began to feel better as her stomach settled; by the time she'd finished the soup the trembling in her body was subsiding and she wasn't as dizzy. She looked up to find Blake seated across from her, silently watching her eat. A wave of color heated her face, and she dropped her spoon, embarrassed that she'd begun eating without him.

"Lady," he said evenly, "you give the word *stubborn* a whole new meaning."

She lowered her eyes and didn't respond, not certain if he were talking about how hungry she'd been or something else; she feared it was the "something else," and she just couldn't carry on a calm, ordinary conversation about what had happened between them.

She made an effort to call a truce between them, though without lowering her guard an inch. She couldn't laugh with him; her nerves were stretched too tightly, her emotions were too ravaged. But she did smile and talk, and generally avoided meeting his eyes. In that manner she made it safely through the evening until it was time to go to bed and she could excuse herself.

She was already in bed, staring at the ceiling, when she heard him call. It was like an instant replay of the night before and she froze, a film of perspiration breaking out on her body. She couldn't go in there, not after what had happened the last time. He couldn't have cramps in his legs, because she'd heard him come up not five minutes before. He wasn't even in bed yet.

She lay there telling herself fiercely that she wouldn't go; then he called her name again and years of training rose up to do battle with her. He was her patient, and he was calling her. She could just check and make certain that he was all right, and leave again if there was nothing wrong.

Reluctantly she climbed out of bed, this time reaching for her robe and belting it tightly around her. No more going into his room wearing only her nightgown; the thought of his hands on her breasts interfered with the rhythm of her breathing, and an odd ache began in the flesh that he had touched.

When she opened the door to his bedroom she was surprised to see that he was already in bed. "What did you want?" she asked coolly, not leaving her position by the door.

He sighed and sat up, stuffing his pillows behind his back. "We have to talk," he said.

She froze. "If you like to talk so much, maybe you should join a debating team," she retorted.

"I made love to you last night," he said bluntly, going straight to the heart of the issue and watching as she flinched against the door. "You had a rough deal with your ex-husband, and I can understand that you're wary, but last night wasn't a total disaster for you. You kissed me, you responded to me. So why are you acting today as if *I'd* raped you?"

Dione sighed, shaking her long hair back. He'd never understand something that she didn't really understand herself; she only knew that, in her experience, caring led to pain and rejection. It wasn't so much a physical distance she wanted from him as an emotional one, before he took everything she had and left her only a shell, empty and useless. But there was something he *would* understand, and at last she met his eyes.

"What happened last night won't happen again," she said, her voice low and clear. "I'm a therapist, and you're my patient. That's the only relationship that I can allow between us.''

"You're closing the barn door after the horse is already out," he said with maddening amusement.

"Not really. You had doubts about your ability to have sex after the accident, and that was interfering with your training. Last night removed those doubts. That was the beginning and end of anything sexual between us.''

His face darkened. "Damn it," he growled, all amusement gone. "Are you telling me that last night was just a therapeutic roll in the hay?''

Her lips tightened at his crudity. "Bingo," she said, and stepped out of his room, closing the door firmly behind her.

She returned to bed, knowing it was useless to think of sleep, but making the effort anyway. She had to leave. She simply couldn't stay until the first of the year, not with things as strained as they were now. Blake was almost fully recovered; time and practice would accomplish the rest of it. He didn't need her any longer, and there were other people who did.

Her bedroom door opened and he stood there, without the walker, moving slowly and carefully as he closed the door and crossed the room to her.

"If you want to run, I can't catch you," he said flatly.

She knew that, but still she lay where she was, watching him. He was nude, his tall, perfect body shamelessly exposed to her gaze. She looked at him and couldn't help feeling a thrill of pride at the ripple of muscles, the fluid grace of his body. He was beautiful, and she'd created him.

He lifted the sheet and got into bed beside her, immediately enveloping her in the warmth of his body.

She wanted to sink into his flesh, but instead she made one more effort to protect herself. "This can't work," she said, her voice cracking with pain.

"It already has; you just haven't admitted it yet." He put his hand on her hip and pulled her to him, nestling her against him down the entire length of his body. She sighed, her soft breath tickling the hairs on his chest; her body relaxed in traitorous contentment.

He tilted her chin up and kissed her, his lips gentle, his tongue dipping into her mouth briefly to taste her, then withdrawing. "Let's get one issue settled right now," he murmured. "I've been lying to you, but I thought it best to keep from frightening you. I wanted you since...hell, it seems like from the first time I saw you. Definitely since I threw my breakfast at you, and you laughed the most beautiful laugh I'd ever heard."

Dione frowned. "Wanted me? But you couldn't—"

"That's what I've been lying about," he admitted, kissing her again.

She jerked back, her cheeks going scarlet. "What?" she gasped, mortified when she thought of the effort she'd made to arouse him, and the money she'd spent on seductive clothes.

Wryly he surveyed her furious face, but braved the wildcat's claws and pulled her back into his arms. "Several things you did made me think that you might have been mistreated," he explained.

"So you decided to show me what I'd been missing," she exploded, pushing at his chest. "Of all the sneaky, egotistical snakes in the world, you're at the top of the heap!"

He chuckled and gently subdued her, using the strength that she'd given him. "Not quite. I wanted you, but I didn't want to frighten you. So I pretended that I couldn't make love to you; all I wanted was for you to get to know me, learn to trust me, so I'd have a chance at least. Then you started dressing in those thin shirts and shorts, and I thought I'd go out of my mind. You damn-near killed me!'' he said roughly. ''You touched me constantly, driving me so wild I'd almost exploded out of my skin, and I'd have to hide my reaction from you. Didn't you wonder why I'd been working like a maniac?''

She sucked in a shaky breath. ''Is that why?''

''Of course it is,'' he said, touching her lip with his finger. ''I tried to get you used to my touch, too, and that only made my problem worse. Every time I kissed you, every time I touched your legs, I was driving myself crazy.''

Closing her eyes, she remembered all the times when he'd stared at her with that peculiar, hot light in his eyes. A woman with any real experience would have known immediately that Blake wasn't impotent, but she'd been the perfect, all-time sucker for that line. ''You must have laughed yourself sick at me,'' she said miserably.

''I haven't been in any shape to laugh, even if it had been a laughing matter. Which it wasn't,'' he said. ''The thought that someone had hurt you made me so furious I wanted to tear the guy apart. Whoever he was, *he* was the reason you were frightened of me, and I hated that. I'd have done anything to make you trust me, let me love you.''

She bit her lip, wishing that she could believe him, but how could she? He made it sound as if he'd been so concerned for her, and all he'd really been concerned with was his own sexual appetite. She knew how touchy he'd been about letting even Serena see him while he was less than perfect; he wouldn't want to make love to a woman who might pity him for the effort it took him to walk, or, even worse, might want him because of a morbid curiosity. Dione was the one safe female of his acquaintance, the one who knew everything about him already and was neither shocked, curious, nor pitying. "What you're saying is that you wanted sex, and I was handy," she said bitterly.

"My God, Dee!" He sounded shocked. "I'm not getting through to you, am I? Is it so hard for you to believe that I want *you*, not just sex? We've been through a lot together; you've held me when I hurt so much I couldn't stand it any longer, and I held you last night when you were afraid, but trusted me with yourself anyway. You're not just a sexual outlet for me; you're the woman I want. I want all of you: your temper, your contrariness, your strength, even your downright bitchiness, because you're also an incredibly loving woman."

"All right, I absolve you," she said wearily. "I don't want to talk about it now; I'm tired and I can't think straight."

He looked down at her, and impatience flickered across his face. "There's no reasoning with you, is there?" he asked slowly. "I shouldn't have wasted my time talking to you. I should have just shown you, like I'm going to do now."

Dione drew back sharply, her golden eyes flashing. "Do all men use force when a woman isn't willing?" she said between clenched teeth. "I warn you, Blake, I'll fight. Maybe I can't stop you, but I can hurt you."

He laughed softly. "I know you can." He lifted one of her fists and carried it to his lips, where he kissed each knuckle in turn. "Darling, I'm not going to force you. I'm going to kiss you and tell you how lovely you are, and do everything I can think of to give you pleasure. The first time was for me, remember, but the second time is for you. Don't you think I can show you?"

"You're trying to seduce me," she snapped.

"Mmmm. Is it working?"

"No!"

"Damn. Then I'll have to try something else, won't I?" He laughed again, and pressed his warm lips to her wrist. "You're so sweet, even when you're mad at me."

"I am not!" she protested, practically insulted by his compliment. "There's not a 'sweet' bone in my body!"

"You're sweet smelling," he countered. "And sweet tasting. And the feel of you is sweet torment. Your name should be Champagne instead of Dione, because you make me so drunk I barely know what I'm doing."

"Liar."

"What did I do for excitement before I met you?"

he asked wryly. "Fighting with you makes mountain climbing pale in comparison."

The amusement in his voice was more than she could bear; she was so confused and upset, but he seemed to think it was funny. She turned her head away to hide the tears that welled up. "I'm glad you're getting such a kick out of this," she muttered.

"We'll talk about that later," he said, and kissed her. She lay rigidly in his arms, refusing to let her mouth soften and mold itself to his, and after a moment he drew back.

"Don't you want me at all?" he whispered, nuzzling her hair. "Did I hurt you last night? Is that what's wrong?"

"I don't know what's wrong!" she shouted. "I don't understand what I want, or what *you* want. I'm out of my depth, and I don't like it!" The frustration she felt with herself and with him came bubbling out of her, but it was nothing less than the truth. Her mind was so muddled that nothing pleased her; she felt violent, but without a safe outlet for that violence. She'd been violated, hurt, and though years had passed, only now was the anger breaking out of the deep freeze where she'd locked her emotions. She wanted to hurt him, hit him, because he was a man and the symbol of what had happened to her, but she knew that he was innocent, at least of that. But he had dominated her last night, manipulated her with his lies and his truths, and now he was trying to dominate her again.

Furiously she shoved at him, rolling him over on his back. Before he could react she was astride him, her face pagan with the raw force of her emotions. "If there's any seducing to be done, I'll do it!" she raged at him. "Damn you, don't you dare move!"

His blue eyes widened, and a rich understanding crossed his face. "I won't," he promised, a little hoarsely.

With a sensual growl she assaulted him, using her mouth, her hands, her entire body. A man's sexuality had always been denied to her, but now this man offered himself in spread-eagled sacrifice, and she explored him with voracious hunger. Much of his body she already knew; the sleek strength of his muscles under her fingers; the roughness of the hair on his chest and legs; the male scent that made her nostrils flare. But now she learned the taste of him as she nibbled at his ears, his chin, his mouth; she pressed her lips against the softness of his temple and felt his pulse hammering madly. She kissed his eyes, the strong column of his throat, the slope of his shoulder, the sensitive inside of his elbow.

His palms twitched as her tongue traced across them, and he groaned aloud when she sucked on his fingers. "Hush!" she said fiercely, crouching over him. She didn't want any break in her concentration. As she learned him, her body was coming alive, warming and glowing like something long frozen and slowly beginning to thaw. She moved upward, licked the length of his collarbone, then snaked her tongue downward through the curls of hair until she found the little nipples that hid there. They were tight, as hard as tiny diamonds, and when she bit them he shuddered wildly.

His flat stomach, ridged with muscles that were now writhing under her touch, beckoned her marauding mouth. She traced the arrow of downy hair, played a wet game of sneak attack with his navel, then slithered downward. Her silky hair draped across him as she kissed his legs from thigh to foot, biting the backs of his knees, dancing her tongue across his instep, then working her way back up.

He was shaking in every muscle, his body so taut that only his heels and shoulders were touching the bed. He was gripping the bedposts, his arms corded as he writhed in tormented ecstasy. "Please...please!" he begged hoarsely. "Touch me! Damn it, I can't take any more!"

"Yes, you can!" she insisted, panting for breath. She touched him, her hand learning him, stroking him, and something close to a howl broke from his throat.

Suddenly she knew. For such vital strength, for such tender power, there was only one resting place, and that was the mysterious depth of her femininity. Male and female, they had been created to join together, the two halves to make a whole. She felt breathless, stunned, as if suddenly the world had shifted and nothing was the same as it had been.

His body was a bow, taut and aching. "Take...me!" he rasped, both in plea and demand, and Dione smiled a radiant, mysterious smile that almost blinded him with the joy of it.

"Yes," she said, and with aching tenderness moved over him. She accepted him easily. He cried out, but lay still, letting her move as she wished. She looked at him, and golden eyes met blue, communicating wordlessly. She was awed by the rightness of their union, by the heated flares of pleasure that shot through her body. All the barriers were gone now; the fears and nightmares that had prevented her from letting herself enjoy the magic of giving herself to the man she loved had disappeared. She was sensual by nature, but events had taught her to deny that part of herself. No longer. Sweet heaven, no longer. He freed her, not only allowing her to be herself, but glorying in the woman she was. It was evident in the lost, rapt look he wore, the mindless undulating of his body.

She reveled in him. She adored him, she used him, she sank deeply into the whirlpool of the senses and welcomed the drowning. She was burning alive in the heat of her own body as the pleasure intensified and became unbearable, but still she couldn't stop. The moans and gasping cries that kept forcing themselves from his throat as he fought for control were matched by her own sounds of pleasure, until that pleasure became wildfire and she was consumed by it. She heard a wordless cry lingering in the night air and didn't recognize it was hers, or realize that it was joined by a deeper cry as Blake finally released himself from his sweet torture. She sank down, a long, long way, and sprawled weakly on him. His arms swept up and held her safely, securely in place.

He was kissing her, his mouth all over her face before finally settling on her lips and drinking deeply. She met his tongue with her own, and they lay together for a long time exchanging tired, leisurely kisses.

"You took me apart," he murmured.

"I put you together again," she said sleepily.

"I'm not talking about Humpty Dumpty, lady bird, I'm talking about what you did to me."

"Didn't you like it?"

"I loved it." A deep chuckle rumbled through his chest. "As if you had to ask." Then he sobered and pushed her hair away from her face so he could read her eyes. "Was it good for you?"

She smiled and ducked her head against him. "As if you had to ask."

"No bad moments?"

"None," she said, and yawned.

"Wretch, are you going to sleep on me?" he demanded in mock indignation, but his hands were tender as he stroked her. "You're tired, aren't you? Then sleep, darling. I'll hold you. Just don't move; I want to stay inside you all night."

She would have blushed, but she was too tired, too satisfied, and he made a wonderful bed. She was boneless, draped over him, protected by him. She eased into sleep with the steady throb of his heartbeat in her ear.

He woke her at dawn with his slow, tender movements. The room was chilled, but they were warm, heated by the excitement that began to curl inside. There was no urgency, no need to hurry. He talked to her and teased her, told her jokes that made her laugh, and her laughter somehow increased her inner heat. He knew her body as well as she knew his, knew how to touch her and make her writhe with pleasure, knew how to gradually move her up the plane to satisfaction. Her trust was a tangible thing between them, evident in her clear, shining eyes as she allowed him to handle her as he pleased. Even when he rolled her onto her back and pinned her with his weight, no shadow of ancient fear darkened her joy. He had earned her trust the night before when he had offered his own body for her enjoyment. How could she deny him the pleasure of hers?

There was pleasure for her, too, a deep and shining pleasure that took her breath away. It was so intense that she almost cried out her love for him, but she clenched her teeth on the words. The time with him was golden but transient, and there was no need to burden him with an emotion that couldn't be returned.

"I'd like to stay in bed with you all day," he whispered against her satiny skin. "But Alberta will be up here soon if we don't put in an appearance. She was worried about you yesterday, almost as much as I was."

She buried her hands in his thick, dark hair. "Why were you worried? You knew why I was upset."

"Because I never meant to upset you. I didn't want to remind you of anything that had hurt you, but I did. You were so pale and cold." He kissed the enticing slope of her breast and smiled at the ripple of response that was evident under her skin.

They showered together; then he sprawled on the bed and directed her dressing. He wanted her to wear the slinky, seductive shorts she'd worn before, and his eyes glittered as he watched her pull them on. He had to return to his room to dress, as he'd come to her stark naked, and stark naked he walked down the hall, moving slowly but with increasing confidence and grace. Tears of pride stung her eyes as she watched him.

"It's a beautiful day," Alberta said with an odd smugness as she served breakfast, and it was so unusual for Alberta to make small talk that Dione glanced at her sharply, but could read nothing in the woman's stoic face.

"Beautiful," Blake echoed gravely, and gave Dione a slow smile that started her blood racing.

Their workouts were leisurely and remarkably short; Blake seemed more interested in watching her than in lifting weights or walking on the treadmill. He was relaxed, satisfaction lying on him like a golden glow. Instead of trying to slow him down, Dione scolded him for doing so little. "I'm going to have to cut down on the amount you're eating if you aren't going to work any more than this."

"Whatever you say," he murmured, his eyes on her legs. "You're the boss."

She laughed and gave up. If he weren't going to work out, he might as well be walking. It was warmer out than it had been recently, so they walked around the grounds; the only support he used was his arm around her waist. She noticed that he was limping less; even his left leg moved without dragging as badly as it had.

"I've been thinking," he announced as they returned to the house. "There's no use in waiting until the first of the year before I go back to work. I'm going back Monday; I'll get myself accustomed to the place and what's going on, before Richard takes off."

Dione stopped and stared at him, her cheeks paling. He saw her expression and misunderstood it; he laughed as he hugged her to him. "I'm not going to hurt myself," he assured her. "I'll just work in the mornings. Half a day, I promise. Then I'll come home and put myself in your hands again, and you can work me until I drop if that's what you want."

She bit her lip. "If you're capable of returning to work, then there's no need for me to stay at all," she said quietly.

He frowned, his hands tightening on her. "There's all the need in the world. Don't even think about leaving me, honey, because I won't let you. You're part of me. We've already been through this once, and it's settled. You're staying here."

"Nothing's settled," she denied. "I have to work, to support myself—"

"By all means, work if you want," he interrupted. "But you don't *have* to. I can support you."

She jerked back, indignant color staining her face. "I'm not a call girl," she snapped. "Or a lap dog."

He put his hands on his hips. "I'll agree with that, but I'm not talking about either of those," he said, his own temper rising. "I'm talking about marriage, lady, the 'till death do us part' bit."

She couldn't have been more startled if he'd turned green before her eyes. She stared at him. "You can't mean that."

"Why can't I mean it?" he demanded irritably. "This is a hell of a reception for the only marriage proposal I've ever made."

She couldn't help it; she laughed at the anger in his tone, even though she knew inside that he would soon forget her. He was still involved in their intense, isolated therapist-patient relationship, with the added complication of their physical involvement. She'd known that making love with him was a mistake, but she hadn't suspected that he would carry it as far as considering marriage.

"I can't marry you," she said, shaking her head to reinforce her refusal.

"Why not?"

"It wouldn't work."

"Why wouldn't it work? We've been living together for almost half a year, and you can't say that we don't get along. We've had some great times. We fight, sure, but that's half the fun. And you can't say that you don't love me, because I know you do," he finished tightly.

Dione stared at him in silent dismay. She'd tried so hard not to let him know, but he'd seen through her pitiful defenses anyway. He'd demolished every wall that she'd built. She couldn't stay. She'd have to leave immediately, get away from him while she still could. "There's no sense in dragging this out," she said, pulling away from him. "I'll leave today."

Once she was free of his grip she knew that he wouldn't be able to keep up with her. Her conscience twinged at leaving him alone to make his way back to the house—what if he fell? But needs must when the devil drives, and her devil was driving her mercilessly. She went straight to her room and began pulling out her clothes. She was swift and efficient; she had all the clothes lying on the bed in neat stacks when she realized that the new clothes she'd bought made it impossible for her to fit everything into her two suitcases. She'd either have to leave them there, or buy another suitcase. If she bought another suitcase, she'd have to beg a ride from someone…no, where was her brain? She could always call a taxi. She didn't have to beg for anything.

"Dee, you're not leaving," Blake said gently from the doorway. "Put everything back and calm down."

"I have to leave. I don't have any reason to say." It had been a waste of breath for him to tell her to calm down. She was utterly calm, knowing what she had to do.

"I'm not reason enough to stay? You love me. I've known for quite a while. It's in your eyes when you look at me, your touch, your voice, everything about you. You make me feel ten feet tall, darling. And if I still needed proof, I had it when you let me make love to you. You're not a woman to give herself to any man without love. You love me, even if you're too stubborn to tell me the words."

"I told you," she said, her voice muffled with pain. "I always fall in love with my patients. It's practically required."

"You don't go to bed with all of your patients, do you?"

He already knew the answer to that. He didn't need

the miserable little shake of her head, or the whispered, "No," to reassure him.

"It's not one-sided," he murmured, coming up behind her to wrap his arms around her middle. "I love you, so much I hurt. You love me, and I love you; it's only natural that we get married."

"But you *don't* love me!" she shouted, driven beyond control at hearing those precious words. It was unfair that she should be punished so much for loving him, but everything had to be paid for in coin. For daring to transgress, she would pay with her heart. She began to struggle against the bonds of flesh that held her, but he merely tightened his hold, not enough to hurt her, but she was securely restrained. After a moment of futile effort she let her head drop back against his shoulder. "You only think you love me," she wept, her voice thick with the tears lodged in her throat. "I've been through it before; a patient becomes so dependent on me, so fixated on me, that he confuses his feelings of need with love. It won't last, Blake, believe me. You don't really love me; it's just that I'm the only toy in your playground right now. When you go back to work you'll be seeing other women and everything will fall back into proportion. It would be awful if I married you and then you found out it had all been a mistake."

"I'm a man," he said slowly. "There have been other women who I wanted, other women who caught my interest, but give me credit for being intelligent enough to know the difference between the way I felt with them and the way I feel about you. I want to be with you, talk with you, fight with you, watch you laugh, make love with you. If that's not love, honey, no one will ever know the difference."

"I'll know the difference, and so will you."

He sighed impatiently. "You still won't listen to reason, will you? Then let's compromise. Are you willing to compromise?"

She eyed him warily. "It depends."

He smiled even as he shook his head. "You'd think I'm a mass murderer, the way you're looking at me. It's just a simple deal. You say that when I get out more and see other women to compare you to, I'll realize that I've just been infatuated with you. On the other hand, I say that I love you and I'll keep on loving you, regardless of how many other women I see. To settle the issue, all you have to do is stay until I've had a chance to make that comparison. Simple?"

She shrugged. "I see what's in the deal for you; you win, either way. I know that you're planning to sleep with me, and I'm honest enough to know that if I stay, that's exactly how things will work out. If you decide that it was just a passing fancy after all, then you've lost nothing and had a bed partner while you thought about it."

"There's something in it for you, too," he said, grinning.

The wicked gleam in his eyes gave him away. She could have kicked him, but it seemed that he could always make her laugh no matter how upset she was. "I know, I know," she said, beginning to giggle. "*I* get to sleep with *you*."

"That's not such a bad deal," he said with blatant immodesty.

"You talk a good game, Mr. Remington," she said, still laughing despite all she could do to stifle it.

"That's not all I do well," he said, reaching for her and folding her against him. His lips found the slope of her throat and she shivered, her lashes falling to veil her eyes. "Think of it as therapy," he encouraged. "A sort of repayment for your own therapeutic knowledge. You gave me a reason to live, and I'll show you how to live."

"Egotistical."

"Truthful."

"I can't do it."

He shook her, then pulled her back to him and began to lay tender seige to her mouth, storming the barrier of her teeth and taking the treasure that lay beyond. "You will do it," he insisted softly. "Because you love me. Because I need you."

"Past tense: You needed me. That's in the past. You're on your own, and you're doing fine."

"I won't be doing fine if you leave me. I swear I'll put myself back in the wheelchair and not get out again. I won't go to work; I won't eat; I won't sleep. I need you to take care of me."

"Blackmail won't work," she warned him, trying not to laugh again.

"Then I'll have to try another tactic. Please. Stay for me. I love you, and you love me. What if *you're* wrong? What if I'm still as wild for you ten years from now as I am today? Are you going to throw that chance away just because you're afraid to believe it can happen?"

The pain that seared her heart told her that at last he'd hit on the real reason why she wanted to leave. She was afraid to believe in love, because no one had ever loved her. She stared at him intently, aware inside of herself that she had reached a personal milestone. She could play it safe and run but people who played it safe never knew the intoxication of going for it all, of putting their hearts on the line. They never risked anything, so they never won anything. Everything had to be paid for; she reminded herself of that once again. All she could do was try. If she won, if by some miracle she gained the golden apple, her life would be complete. If she lost, would she really be any worse off than she was now? She already loved him. Would leaving him now make the pain any less than leaving him later?

"All right," she said huskily, aware of the bridges burning behind her. She could feel the heat at her back. "I'll stay with you. Don't ask me to marry you, not yet. Let's see how it works out. An affair is a lot easier to recover from when it goes sour than a marriage is."

He quirked a dark eyebrow at her. "You're not over-confident, are you?"

"I'm…cautious," she admitted. "Marriage was traumatic for me. Let me take one hurdle at a time. If…if everything works out, I'll marry you whenever you want."

"I'll hold you to that," he murmured. "I'd like to marry you now. I'd like to make you pregnant right now, if I could. I was looking forward to our devoting a lot of time to that project, but now I'll have to take precautions. Our children will all come *after* we've been married for at least nine months. No one's going to count their fingers and smirk at our babies."

Her eyes were such wide, huge golden pools of wonder, that they eclipsed the rest of her face. The thought of children was so enticing that she was tempted to tell him that she would marry him right then. She'd always wanted children, wanted to be able to pour out the deep reservoir of love that was dammed up inside her. The care and nourishment that she'd never received from her own mother were there, waiting patiently for a child of her own. Blake's child: blue eyes; dark hair; that engaging grin that brought out his hidden dimple.

But a child was the one thing she couldn't gamble with, so she didn't argue with him. Instead she offered quietly, "I'll see a doctor and get a prescription."

"No," he refused, steel lacing his voice. "No pills. You're not taking any risks, however slight, with your body. I can handle it without any risk at all, and that's the way we'll do it."

She didn't mind; the thought that he was willing to take responsibility for their lovemaking was a warm, melting one. She put her arms around him and nestled against him, drinking in his scent.

"Tell me you love me," he demanded, cupping her chin in his palm and lifting her face to him. "I know you do, but I want to hear it."

A tremulous smile quivered on her lips. "I love you."

"That's what I thought," he said with satisfaction, and kissed her as a reward. "Everything will be all right, darling. Just wait and see."

She didn't dare to hope, but it seemed as if he might be right. He bought a slim black cane that looked more like a sexy prop than something that was actually used as support, and every morning Miguel drove him to work. At first Dione fretted every moment he was gone. She worried that he might fall and hurt himself, that he'd try to do too much and tire himself out. After a week she was forced to admit that he was thriving on the challenge of working again. Far from falling, every day he improved, walking faster and with less effort. Nor did she have to worry that he was pushing himself too hard; he was in excellent shape, thanks to her program.

She almost drove herself mad thinking of all the women he was in contact with every day; she knew herself how attractive he was, especially with that intriguing limp. When he came home the first day she all but held her breath, waiting for him to say cheerfully, "Well, you were right; it was just infatuation. You can leave now."

But he never said it. He returned home as eagerly as he went to work, and they spent the afternoons in the gym, or swimming if the day was warm. December was a pleasant month, with the afternoon temperatures often in the high sixties and low seventies, though at night it sometimes dipped close to freezing. Blake decided to have a heating unit put in the pool so they could swim at night, but he had so much on his mind that he kept putting it off. Dione didn't care if the pool was ever heated or not; why bother with swimming when the nights were better spent in his arms?

Whatever happened, whatever the ending that was eventually written to their particular story, she would always love him for freeing her from the cage of fear. In his arms she forgot about the past and concentrated only on the pleasure he gave her, pleasure which she joyously returned.

He was the lover who she had needed; he was mature enough to understand the rewards of patience, and astute enough to sometimes be impatient. He gave, he demanded, he stroked, he experimented, he laughed, he teased, and he satisfied. He was as happily fascinated with her body as she was with his, and that was the sort of open admiration that she needed. The events that had shaped her had made her wary of repressed emotion, even when that emotion was happiness, and the complete honesty with which Blake treated her gave her a secure springboard from which she launched herself as a woman, secure at last in her own femininity and sexuality.

The days of December were the happiest of her life. She had known peace and contentment, not a small accomplishment after the terror she'd survived, but with Blake she was truly happy. Except for the absence of a ceremony, she might already have been married to him, and each passing day the idea of being his wife became more firmly rooted in her mind, changing from impossible to implausible, then to chancy, then to a half-scared, hopeful "maybe." She refused to let herself progress beyond that, afraid of tempting the fates, but still she began to dream of a long stretch of days, even years, and she found herself thinking up names for babies.

He took her Christmas shopping, something she'd never done before in her life. No one had ever been close enough to her to either give or receive a gift, and when Blake learned this, he embarked on a crusade to make her first real Christmas one that would boggle the imagination. The house was decorated in a unique and not always logical blend of traditional and desert styles; every cactus found itself sporting gaily colored bows or even decorative glass balls, if the spines were large enough. He had holly and mistletoe flown in and kept in the refrigerator until it was time to put them up, and Alberta entered into the spirit of the season by scouring cookbooks for traditional Christmas recipes.

Dione realized that they were all going to so much trouble for her, and she was determined to throw herself into the preparations and the happiness. Suddenly it seemed that the world was full of people who cared, and those she cared for.

She'd been half-fearful that Blake would embarrass her by giving her a lot of expensive gifts, and she was both delighted and relieved when she began opening her gifts to find that they were small, thoughtful and sometimes humorous. A long, flat box that could have held a watch or an expensive bracelet instead yielded an array of tiny charms that made her laugh aloud: a miniature barbell, a track shoe, a sweatband, a Frisbee, a loving cup trophy and a little silver bell that actually gave a tinny little chime when she shook it. Another box held the charm bracelet that the charms were supposed to go on; a third gift was a best seller that she'd picked up in a bookstore just the week before, then replaced and forgotten to buy in the confusion of shopping. A lacy black mantilla drifted over her head and she looked up to smile at Richard, who was regarding her with an oddly tender look in his cool gray eyes. Serena's gift made her gasp and quickly stuff it back into the box, as Serena rolled with laughter and Blake immediately came over to wrestle the box away from her and hold up the contents: a very intimate garment with heart-shaped cutouts in strategic places.

"This was something you overlooked when you bought all those clothes to wage war in," Serena said innocently, her blue eyes as limpid as a child's.

"Ahhh, those clothes." Blake sighed in satisfaction.

Dione snatched the teddy...thing...whatever...away from him and replaced it in the box, her cheeks fiery red. "Why is everyone watching me?" she asked uncomfortably. "Why aren't you opening your own gifts?"

"Because you're so beautiful to watch," Blake replied softly, leaning down so only she could hear him. "Your eyes are shining like a little girl's. I have something else for you to...ah, unwrap later on tonight. Think you might be interested?"

She stared at him, her black pupils dilating until they almost obscured the golden rims. "I'm interested," she murmured, her body already quickening at the thought of the lovemaking they'd share later, when they were laying pressed together in his big bed.

"It's a date," he whispered.

The rest of the gifts were opened amid laughter and

thank-yous; then Alberta served hot buttered rum. Dione seldom drank, having an aversion to alcohol that dated back to her earliest childhood, but she drank the rum because she was happy and relaxed and suddenly the old restrictions no longer mattered so much. The rum slid smoothly down her throat, warming her, and when that was finished she drank another.

After Serena and Richard had left, Blake helped Dione up the stairs with a steadying arm around her waist. He was laughing softly, and she leaned into him, letting him take most of her weight. "What's so funny?" she asked sleepily.

"You are. You're half-drunk, and you're beautiful. Did you know that you've had the sweetest, sleepiest smile in the world on your face for the last fifteen minutes? Don't you dare go to sleep on me, at least until after you've kept our date."

She stopped on the stairs and turned fully into his arms, winding herself around him. "You know I wouldn't miss that for the world," she purred.

"I'll see that you don't."

She let him talk her into wearing the scandalous teddy that Serena had given her, and he made love to her while she had it on, then even that scrap of fabric seemed to get in his way and he stripped it off her. "Nothing's as lovely as your skin," he whispered, stringing kisses like popcorn across her stomach.

She felt drugged, her mind a little fuzzy, but her body was throbbing, arching instinctively to meet the rhythmic thrusts that took her to bliss and beyond when he left off kissing her all over and possessed her again. When they were finished she lay weak and trembling on the bed, protesting with a murmur when she felt him leave her side.

"I'll be right back," he reassured her, and he was, his weight pressing the mattress familiarly. She smiled and moved her hand to touch him lightly, all without opening her eyes.

"Don't go to sleep," he warned. "Not yet. You haven't unwrapped your last present."

She propped her lids open. "But I thought that you were...when we made love, I thought that..." she mumbled in confusion.

He chuckled and slid an arm behind her back, urging her into a sitting position. "I'm glad you liked that, but I have something else for you." He placed another long, slim box in her hand.

"But you've already given me so much," she protested, awakening at the feel of the box.

"Not like this. This is special. Go ahead, open it."

He sat with his arm still around her, watching her face and smiling as she fumbled with the elegant gold wrapping, her agile fingers suddenly clumsy. She lifted the lid off and stared speechlessly at the simple pendant that lay on satin lining like a cobweb of gold. A dark red heart, chiseled and planed, was attached to the chain.

"That's a ruby," she stammered.

"No," he corrected gently, lifting it from the box and placing it around her neck. "That's my heart." The chain was long, and the ruby heart slid down her chest to nestle between her breasts, gleaming with dark fire as it lay against her honeyed skin.

"Wear that forever," he murmured, his eyes on the

lush curves that his gift used as a pillow. "And my heart will always be touching yours."

A single, crystalline tear escaped the confines of her lashes, and rolled slowly down her cheek. He leaned over and caught it with his tongue. "An engagement ring wasn't good enough for you, so I'm giving you an engagement heart. Will you wear it, darling? Will you marry me?"

She stared at him with eyes so huge and deep that they drowned the entire world. For a month she'd shared his bed, trying to prepare herself for the day when she was no longer able to do so, savoring every moment with him in an attempt to store up pleasure as a squirrel stores acorns as insurance against a hard winter. She'd been certain that he would lose interest in her, but every day he'd turned to her and taken her in his arms, told her that he loved her. Perhaps the dream wasn't a dream, after all, but reality. Perhaps she could dare to believe.

"Yes," she heard herself say shakily as her heart and hungry yearnings overruled her head, and her head instantly tried to recover lost ground by adding, "but give me time to get used to the idea.... It doesn't seem quite real."

"It's real, all right," he muttered, sliding his hand along her ribcage until a warm, full breast filled his palm. He studied the sheer perfection of her softly veined flesh, the taut little cherry tip that responded instantly to his lightest touch, and his body began to tighten with the familiar need that he could never quite satisfy. Gently he began to ease her down into a supine position. "I don't mind a long engagement," he said absently. "Two weeks is plenty of time."

"Blake! I was thinking in terms of months, not weeks!"

He looked up sharply; then as he saw the frightened uncertainty in her face, his gaze softened and his mouth eased into a smile. "Then name the day, darling, as long as it's within six months and you don't pick either Groundhog Day or April Fool's Day."

She tried to think, but her mind was suddenly fuzzy, entirely preoccupied by the rough, wonderful rasp of his hard hands over her body. His finger slid between her legs and she gasped aloud, a hot twinge of pleasure shooting through her body. "May Day," she said, no longer really caring.

He was disconcerted, too, his senses caught by the rich beauty of the woman under his hand while he tried to make sense of her words. "Mayday?" he asked, puzzled and a little shocked. "You're asking for help?"

"No...May Day, not mayday," she explained, exaggerating the two words so he could hear the pause between them. "The first of May."

"What about it?" he murmured, dipping his head to taste the straining nipples that had been tempting him. He was rapidly losing all interest in the conversation.

"That's when we're getting married," she gasped, her body beginning a slow, undulating dance.

Those words made sense to him, and he lifted his head. "I can't persuade you to marry me before then?"

"I...don't know," she moaned. Her nails flexed into his shoulders. He could probably talk her into anything he wanted, the way she felt now. Though they had made love only a short while before, the need that was filling her was so urgent that it might have been years since he'd taken her. She turned to him, her sleek, soft body crowding him, and he knew without words what she wanted. He lay back, his hands guiding her as she flowed over him and engulfed him. She was wild when she loved him like that, her long black hair streaming down her back, falling across his face when she leaned forward. She worshipped him with the ancient, carnal dance of love, and the ruby heart lay on her breast like a drop of liquid fire.

For two days nothing intruded on the spell of happiness that held them enthralled. Everyone was pleased with the engagement, from the taciturn Miguel to a bubbling Serena. Alberta was as satisfied as if she'd arranged it all herself, and Angela hummed all day long. Serena passed along Richard's best wishes; evidently a wedding was just what everyone wanted, and Dione almost forgot why she'd been so cautious in the beginning.

On the third day Serena arrived for dinner, alone and pale, though she was composed. "I might as well tell you, before someone else does," she said quietly. "Richard and I are separated."

Dione stifled her gasp of shock. They had been getting along so much better for the past several weeks that she'd stopped being concerned with their situation. She looked swiftly at Blake, and was shocked again at the change in his expression. She had known him as laughing, loving, teasing, angry, even afraid, but never before had she seen him so deadly and intent. Suddenly she realized that she'd never really felt the force of his personality, because he'd always tempered his actions with consideration for her. Now the steel, the sheer power, was showing as he prepared to protect his sister.

"What do you want me to do?" he asked Serena in a calm, lethal tone.

Serena looked at him and even smiled, her eyes full of love. "Nothing," she said simply. "This is something I have to work out with Richard. Blake, please, don't let this interfere with your working relationship with him; this is more my fault than it is his, and it wouldn't be fair for you to take it out on him."

"How is it your fault?" he growled.

"For not growing up and getting my priorities straight until it was almost too late," she replied, a hint of the same steel lacing her sweeter voice. "I'm not giving up on him, not without a fight. Don't ask me any more questions, because I won't answer them. He's my husband, and this is a private matter."

He regarded her silently for a moment, then gave a brief nod. "All right. But you know that I'll do whatever I can, whenever you ask."

"Of course I do," she said, her face relaxing. "It's just that I have to do this on my own. I have to learn how to fight my own battles." As she spoke she flashed Dione a look that said, "See, I'm trying." Dione nodded in acknowledgement, then looked up to find that Blake had witnessed the little exchange and was also staring at her, a steel determination in his expression. Dione met his stare blandly; he could ask, but she didn't have to answer. If Serena wanted her brother to know that she was deliberately trying to put a distance between them, then she would tell him. If not, then he'd have to figure it out for himself. Richard and Serena didn't need any more interference in their marriage, and if Blake discovered that he was the basic cause of their separation, he was fully capable of taking it up with Richard.

Later that night, after he had made love to her with an intensity that left her dazed and sleepy, he said lazily, "What's going on between you and Serena? All those significant glances have to mean something."

It was a sneak attack, she realized, struggling to gather her wits. He'd made love to her as usual, waited until she was almost asleep, and caught her unaware. To make the situation more even, she cuddled against him and slid her hand down his side in a long, slow caress. When she reached his thighs she was rewarded by the clenching of his entire body.

"It was nothing," she murmured, pressing soft, hot kisses on his chest. "Just a conversation we had the day she took me shopping for all those sexy clothes that you liked so much. She must have a secret fetish for indecent underwear. She picked out most of those barely there nightgowns, and then she gave me that teddy for Christmas."

Hard fingers wrapped around her wrist, and he removed her hand from his body. Leaning over, he switched on the lamp and washed them with light. Dione watched him, knowing that he wanted to be able to read the nuances of expression that crossed her face. She tried to shield her thoughts, but an uneasy coldness began to creep over her skin as she stared into his piercing blue eyes.

"Stop trying to change the subject," he ordered sharply. "Was Serena warning you away from Richard?"

That again! She stiffened, both angered and hurt by the way he had continually accused her of seeing Richard on the sly. How could he possibly think that of her? She had agreed to marry him only two days before, but for some reason she couldn't get it out of his mind that she might be involved with another man. She sat up, the sheet falling to her waist, but she was too angry to care if she were nude.

"What's with you?" she demanded furiously. "You sound like a broken record. What is it that makes you so suspicious of me? Why am I always the cause of any trouble between Serena and Richard?"

"Because Richard can never take his eyes off you when you're together," he replied, his mouth a hard line.

"I'm not responsible for Richard's eyes!" The injustice of it made her want to scream.

"Aren't you?" he snapped. "Whenever you look at him, it's as if you're passing secret messages."

"You just accused me of doing the same thing with Serena. Am I having an affair with her, too?" Dione exploded. She clenched her fists in an effort to control the burgeoning fury in her. It would be stupid to lose her temper, so she forcibly sucked in a deep, calming breath and made her muscles relax.

Blake eyed her narrowly. "If you don't have anything to hide, then why won't you tell me what Serena meant by what she said?" he questioned.

Another sneak attack. She registered the hit and realized that again he'd caught her when her control was slipping. "If you're so curious, why don't you ask her?" she said bitingly, and lay down again, turning her back to him and pulling the sheet up to her chin.

She heard his breath hiss through his teeth a split second before the sheet was jerked away from her and thrown to the foot of the bed. An iron hand bit into her shoulder and turned her over, flat on her back. "Don't turn your back on me," he warned softly, and the cold uneasiness in her turned into icy dread.

Silently, her face white and set, she threw his hand off her shoulder. She had never, *never,* been able to passively endure, even when resistance cost her additional pain. She didn't think; she reacted instinctively, the automatic resistance of someone fighting for survival. When he reached for her, angered by her rejection, she eluded his grasp and slid from the bed.

It didn't matter that this was Blake. Somehow, that made it worse. His image blurred with Scott's, and she felt a stabbing pain that threatened to drive her to her knees. She had trusted him, loved him. How could he have turned on her like that, knowing what he did about her? The sense of betrayal almost choked her.

He sprang from the bed and reached her as she stretched her hand out for the doorknob. He grabbed her elbow and spun her around. "You're not going anywhere!" he growled. "Come back to bed."

Dione wrenched herself away from his grip and flattened her body back against the door. Her golden eyes were blind, dilated, as she stared at him. "Don't touch me," she cried hoarsely.

He reached for her again, then stopped abruptly when he looked at her and saw the fixed expression in her eyes. She was white, so pale that he expected her to slide into a faint at any moment, but she held herself tautly upright. "Don't touch me," she said again, and his arms dropped heavily to his sides.

"Calm down," he said soothingly. "It's all right. I'm not going to hurt you, darling. Let's go back to bed."

She didn't move, her eyes still locked on him as she measured every move he made, however slight. Even the expansion of his chest with every breath he took made an impact on her senses. She saw the slight flare of his nostrils, the flexing of his fingers.

"It's all right," he repeated. "Dee, we had an argument, that's all. Just an argument. You know I'm not going to hit you." He extended his hand slowly to her, and she watched as his fingers approached. Without moving her body somehow drew in on itself, shrinking in an effort to avoid his touch. Just before he would have touched her, she slid swiftly to the side, away from the threatening hand.

Inexorably he followed, moving with her but not coming any closer. "Where are you going?" he asked softly.

She didn't answer; her eyes were wary now, instead of blindly staring. Blake held out both his hands to her, palms up in supplication.

"Honey, give me your hands," he whispered, desperation threading through his veins, congealing his blood. "Please believe me; I'll never hurt you. Come back to bed with me and let me hold you."

Dione watched him. She felt odd, as if part of herself were standing back and watching the scene. That had happened before with Scott, as if she somehow had to separate herself from the ugliness of what was happening to her. Her body had reacted mindlessly, trying to protect itself, while her mind had exercised its own means of protection by drawing a veil of unreality over what was happening. Now the same scene was being replayed with Blake, but it was somehow different. Scott had never stalked her, never talked to her in a crooning, husky voice. Blake wanted her to put her hands in his and go with him back to that bed, lie beside him as if nothing had happened. But what *had* happened? He had been angry, and he had grabbed her shoulder, throwing her to her back...no, that had been Scott. Scott had done that once, but they hadn't been in bed.

Her brow knitted, and she brought both hands up, rubbing her forehead. God, would she never be free of Scott, of what he had done to her? Blake's anger had triggered the memory of the other time, and though she hadn't confused their identities, she had been reacting to Scott, not Blake. Blake hadn't hurt her; he had been angry, but he hadn't hurt her.

"Dee? Are you all right?"

His beloved, anxious voice was almost more than she could bear. "No," she said, her voice muffled behind her hands. "I wonder if I'll ever be all right."

Abruptly she felt his touch, his hands on her arms, slowly drawing her to him. She could feel the tension in him as he folded her into his arms. "Of course you will," he reassured her, kissing her temple. "Come back to bed with me; you're cold."

Abruptly she felt the cold, the chill of the night on the bareness of her body. She walked with him to the bed, let him put her between the sheets and draw the comforter up over her. He walked around to the other side, turned out the lamp and got into bed beside her. Carefully, as though he were trying not to startle her, he pulled her into his arms and held her tightly to his side.

"I love you," he said in the darkness, his low tones vibrating over her skin. "I swear, Dee, that I'll never again touch you in anger. I love you too much to put you through that again.''

Hot tears burned her lids. How could he apologize for something that was, essentially, a weakness in her? How long would it take before he began to resent the flaw in her nature? He wouldn't be able to act naturally with her, and the strain would tear them apart. Normal couples had arguments, yelled at each other, knowing that their anger didn't harm the love between them. Blake would hold himself back, fearing another scene; would he come to hate her because he felt restricted by her? Blake deserved someone whole, someone free, as he was free.

"It would probably be better if I left," she said, the words trembling despite all she could do to hold her tone level.

The arm under her neck tensed, and he rose up on his elbow, looming over her in the darkness. "No," he said, and he achieved the firmness that she had striven for but failed to obtain. "You're where you belong, and you're going to stay here. We're getting married, remember?''

"That's what I'm trying to say," she protested. "How can we have any sort of life together if you're constantly watching what you say and do, afraid of upsetting me? You'd hate me, and I'd hate myself!"

"You're worrying about nothing," he said shortly. "I'll never hate you, so forget that line."

The edge in his voice cut her like a razor, and she fell silent, wondering why she had ever been fool enough to actually believe that they could have a normal life together. She should have learned by now that love wasn't meant to be a part of her life. Blake didn't love her; hadn't her common sense told her that from the beginning? He was infatuated with her, lured by the challenge of seducing her and the hothouse atmosphere that his intense therapy program had generated. Hothouses produced spectacular blooms, but she should have remembered that those blooms wouldn't flourish in the real world. They had to have that protected atmosphere; they withered and died when exposed to the often unfriendly elements of normal life.

Already the bloom of Blake's infatuation was dying, killed not by the attraction to another woman as she had feared, but by daily exposure to reality.

Chapter Twelve

Knowing that it was happening was one thing; preparing herself for it was another. Every time she glanced up and caught Blake watching her broodingly she had to turn away to hide the pain that twisted inside her. She knew that he was regretting his marriage proposal, but his pride wouldn't allow him to back out of it. Probably he would never ask to be released from the engagement; she would have to do the severing. She sensed that he still wasn't ready to admit that he'd been wrong, so she didn't try to take any action to break their engagement now. When the time came she would know, and she would free him.

New Year's passed, and, as he had planned, he began working full time. She could tell that he was always eager to leave the house, and he began to bring home a briefcase crammed with papers. Dione wondered if he brought work home so he would have an excuse to shut himself in the study and escape her company; then he mentioned that Richard had taken his suggestion and indulged in a month of vacation, and she felt guilty. He really was buried in paperwork without Richard to take part of the load off him.

One night he came to bed after midnight and groaned wearily as his body relaxed. Dione turned over and touched his cheek, trailing her fingers over his skin and feeling the prickle of his beard. "Do you need a massage to relax?" she asked quietly.

"Would you mind?" he sighed. "My neck and shoulders have a permanent kink in them from leaning over a desk. My God, no wonder Richard and Serena are having problems; he's had two years of this, and that's enough to drive any man crazy."

He rolled over on his stomach, and Dione pulled her nightgown up to her thighs, straddling his back and leaning forward to work her magic on his tight muscles. As her kneading fingers dug into his flesh he made a muffled sound of pain, then sighed blissfully as the tension left him.

"Have you seen Serena lately?" he asked.

Her fingers paused for a moment, then resumed their movement. "No," she replied. "She hasn't even called. Have you talked to her?"

"Not since the night she had dinner here and told us she and Richard had separated. I think I'll call her tomorrow. Ahhh, that feels good. Right there. I feel as if I've been beaten."

She rolled her knuckles up and down his spine, paying particular attention to the spot that he had indicated needed extra work. He made little grunting noises every time she touched a tender area, and she began to laugh. "You sound like a pig," she teased.

"Who cares? I'm enjoying this. I've missed the massages; several times I've started to call you and ask you to come to the plant to give me a rubdown, but it didn't seem like such a smart thing to do in a busy day."

"Why not?" she asked tartly, a little irritated that he considered her to be a traveling massage parlor, and a lot irritated that he hadn't followed through on his idea.

He laughed and rolled over, deftly keeping his body

between her thighs. "Because," he murmured, "this is what usually happens to me during one of your massages. Let me tell you, I had a hell of a time keeping you from realizing what was going on when you thought I was impotent and were so sweetly trying to turn me on to prove that I wasn't."

She moved off him like a rocket, her entire body blushing. "What?" she yelled furiously. "You *knew* what I was doing, and you let me go ahead and make a fool of myself?"

He laughed uproariously, reaching out to pull her into his embrace. "It didn't take me long to figure it out," he admitted, still chuckling. "As if you needed sexy clothes to turn me on...but I couldn't let you know what you were doing to me without frightening you away. Honey, you weren't seducing me; *I* was seducing *you*, but I had to let you think it was the other way around."

She burned with embarrassment, thinking of the things she had done, the revealing clothes she had worn. Then she felt his hand on her breast, and the heat intensified, but no longer from shame. He hadn't made love to her for several days; he had been coming to bed late and falling asleep as soon as his head hit the pillow, and she had missed his touch.

"You don't really mind, do you?" he asked softly, pulling the nightgown over her head. "What are you doing with this thing on?"

"I get cold when you aren't in the bed," she explained, stretching her body in his arms, reveling in the rasp of his hair-roughed skin against hers.

With a growl he rolled her to her back and buried his face between her breasts. "I'm here now, so you don't need it," he said, his voice muffled by her flesh. He took her quickly, impatient after the days of abstinence.

She held him even after he was asleep, her doubts momentarily eased by the passion of his lovemaking.

Serena called the next morning. "I've just talked to Blake," she said, laughing a little. "He practically ordered me to take you out to lunch. He said that you're going a little stir crazy with him so tied up at work. Does he really think I believe that?"

Dione laughed. "He thinks you're sitting there alone, brooding, and he wants you to get out of the house for a while. Shall we make him happy and go out to lunch?"

"Why not? I'll pick you up at twelve."

"I'm not brooding," Serena said firmly a few hours later as she bit into a crisp radish. "Richard wanted some time to himself, and I gave it to him. We didn't have an argument or anything like that. He's in Aspen. He loves to ski, and I've never learned how; he hasn't been since we were married, because he wouldn't do anything that I couldn't enjoy. I'm not athletic," she explained, grinning.

"You're not upset at all?"

"Of course I'm upset, but I'm borrowing a page from your book and keeping it all under control." She shrugged lightly. "We had a long conversation before he left, got everything out in the open. That's a first for Richard. He's so good at keeping his thoughts to himself that sometimes I want to scream. We decided that he's been under so much stress that the best thing to do was to get away from each other, let him relax and catch up on his sleep, before we did any more talking."

"Have you talked to him since he left?"

"No. That was part of the bargain. When he comes back we'll settle things once and for all."

Serena had changed a lot in the months since they had met, becoming a self-assured woman. Things might not work out for her, but she was facing the future with her chin up; Dione only hoped that she could do the same. While Blake was making love to her, she could forget that he was growing away from her, but they couldn't spend the rest of their lives in bed. The ruby heart rested warmly in the valley between her breasts; he had said that it was his heart, and she wouldn't be selfish. She would give his heart back to him.

"I know what we can do," Serena said firmly. "Let's go shopping! We can look for your wedding dress."

Shopping was Serena's cure-all, and Dione went along with it, though she couldn't work up any enthusiasm for any of the dresses that they looked at. How could she be concerned with a dress for a wedding that would never take place?

Blake was so tired when he came home that night that his limp was more pronounced, but he cross-examined her over dinner, asking for a word-for-word repetition of everything Serena had said, how she had looked, if she had seemed worried. Dione tried to reassure him, but she could tell that he was anxious about his sister.

The passion of the night before wasn't repeated; when he finally came to bed he threw his arm over her and went to sleep before his mumbled "good night" was out of his mouth. She listened to his steady breathing for a long time, unwilling to sleep and miss a moment of her time with him.

With calm resignation she made plans the next day for her future; she contacted Dr. Norwood and accepted a case, then booked a flight to Milwaukee. Her next patient was still hospitalized, but in three weeks he would be able to begin therapy, so that gave her three weeks to spend with Blake.

Every day he became more distant from her, more involved in his work, needing less from her. In her weak moments she tried to tell herself that it was just because he had so much work to do, but she couldn't believe that for long. She responded by doing as she had always done, shoving her pain and misery into a dark corner of her mind and building a wall around them. If it killed her, she would still leave him with her shoulders straight and not distress him by crying all over him. He wouldn't like that, and she wasn't the weepy type, anyway. She wouldn't just hit him with it; she would tell him that she was having doubts about their marriage, and that she thought it would be a good idea for them to spend some time apart. She would tell him that she'd taken another case, and that when it was finished they would discuss their situation. His conscience wouldn't bother him if she did it that way; he would be relieved that it was her idea.

She learned that Richard was back in town when he called her and asked if he could talk to her privately. She hesitated, and he said wryly, "Serena knows that I'm here. She suggested that I talk to you."

Why would Serena want Richard to talk to Dione? What could she possibly tell him that Serena couldn't say just as well? But a third party could sometimes see more clearly than the ones involved, so she agreed.

He drove over early that afternoon. He looked younger than he had, tanned from his weeks in Aspen in the winter sun, and far more relaxed. The lines of strain that had been in his face were gone, replaced by a smile.

"You're even more beautiful than before," he said,

leaning down to kiss her cheek. She didn't shy away from him now; Blake had taught her that not all men were to be feared. She smiled up at him.

"You're pretty great looking yourself. I gather you've seen Serena?"

"We had dinner together last night. She sent me to you."

"But why?" Dione asked, bewildered. They walked out to the courtyard and sat down in the sun. With the walls of the house keeping any wind away from them, the cool January day was pleasant, and she didn't even need a sweater.

Richard leaned against the concrete back of the bench, crossing his ankle over his knee. She noticed idly that he was wearing jeans, the only time she'd ever seen him dressed so casually, and a blue pullover sweater that made his gray eyes seem blue. "Because she's a smart woman," he mused. "She's known from the beginning that I was attracted to you, and our marriage can't work if you're between us."

Dione's eyes widened. "What?" she asked weakly. "But…but Serena's been so friendly, so open…."

"As I said, she's a smart woman. She knew that you didn't return my interest. You've never been able to see anyone but Blake. How I feel about you is something that I have to work out."

She shook her head. "This is ridiculous. You don't love me; you never have. You're in love with Serena."

"I know," he admitted, and laughed. "But for a while I was pretty confused. Serena didn't seem to care if I was around or not, and there you were, so damned lovely that it hurt to look at you, so strong and sure of yourself. You knew what you wanted and didn't let anything stand in your way. The contrast was striking."

Was that how he had seen her? As strong and confident? Hadn't he realized that she was that way only in her profession, that privately she was crippled, afraid of letting anyone get close to her? It was strange that, as astute as Richard was, he hadn't seen her as she really was.

"And now?" she asked.

"I'll always admire you," he chuckled. "But this visit is just for Serena's peace of mind. You were right all along; I love her, and I've been punishing her because she relied on Blake instead of me. I freely admit to the illogic of it, but people in love aren't logical."

"She wanted you to be certain before you went back to her."

"That's right. And I am certain. I love skiing, but I spent the entire time I was in Aspen wishing that she was with me. You should hang out a shingle as a doctor in psychology," he said, laughing, and put his arm on her shoulder to hug her.

She walked him to the door and sent him on his way, glad that he'd ironed out his problems, but she was also depressed at the thought that she'd been involved in any way at all, however innocently. She walked back out to the courtyard and resumed her seat. She was tired, so tired of these months of emotional strain. She closed her eyes and lifted her face to the winter sun, letting her thoughts drift.

"How long had he been here?"

The harsh voice sliced through the air and she jumped, getting to her feet and whirling to face Blake. "You're early," she stammered.

"I know," he said, his voice as hard and cold as his face. "I haven't been able to spend much time with you lately, and when I managed to get everything cleared for today I decided to surprise you. I didn't mean to interrupt anything," he finished with a sneer.

A sick feeling in her stomach made her swallow before she answered. "You didn't," she said briefly, lifting her chin. Suddenly she knew that this was it, that he would use this as an excuse to break their engagement, and she couldn't bear to listen to him saying things that would break her heart. It would break anyway when she left, but she didn't want to have the memory of hard words between them.

"He hadn't been here over five minutes," she said remotely, lifting her hand to cut him off when he started to speak. "He and Serena have patched up their differences, and he wanted to talk to me. She sent him over, as a matter of fact, but you're welcome to call her if you don't believe me."

His eyes sharpened, and he took a step toward her, his hand reaching out. Dione backed away. It had to be now, before he touched her. He might not love her, but she knew that he desired her, and with them, touching led inevitably to sex. That was another thing she couldn't bear, making love with him and knowing it was the last time.

"Now is as good a time as any to tell you," she said, still in that remote voice, her face an expressionless mask. "I've accepted another case, and I'll be leaving in a few days. At least, those were my original plans, but now I think it would be best if I left tomorrow, don't you?"

His skin tightened over his cheekbones. "What are you saying?" he demanded fiercely.

"That I'm breaking our engagement," she said, fumbling with the delicate clasp at the back of her neck and finally releasing it. She took the ruby heart and held it out to him.

He didn't take it. He was staring at her, his face white. "Why?" he asked, grinding the word out through lips that barely moved.

She sighed wearily, rubbing her forehead. "Haven't you realized by now that you don't love me?"

"If you think that, why did you set a wedding date?" he rasped.

She gave him a thin smile. "You were making love to me," she said gently. "I wasn't in my right mind. I've known all along that you didn't love me," she burst out, desperate to make him understand. She couldn't hold out much longer. "I humored you, but it's time now for it to end. You've changed these past weeks, needing me less and less."

"Humored me!" he shouted, clenching his fists. "Were you also 'humoring me' when we made love? I'll be damned if you were!"

She winced. "No. That was real…and it was a mistake. I've never been involved with a patient before, and I'll never let it happen again. It gets too… complicated."

"Lady, I don't believe you!" he said in disbelief. "You're just going to waltz out of here as if nothing ever happened, aren't you? You're going to mark me down as a mistake and forget about me."

No, he was wrong. She'd never be able to forget him. She stared at him with pain-glazed eyes, feeling as if she were shattering inside. A sickening headache pounded in her temples, and when she held the necklace out to him again her hand was trembling. "Why are you arguing?" she asked raggedly. "You should be glad. I'm letting you off the hook. Just think how miserable you'd be, married to someone you don't love.''

He reached out and took the necklace, letting the tiny gold links drip over his fingers like metal tears. The sun pierced the ruby heart, casting a red shadow that danced over the white bench beside her. Savagely he shoved it into his pocket. "Then what are you waiting for?" he shouted. "Go on, get out! What do you want me to do, break down and beg you to stay?"

She swayed, then steadied herself. "No," she whispered. "I've never wanted you to beg for anything." She moved slowly past him, her legs weak and unwilling to work as they should. She would pack and go to a hotel, and try to get an earlier flight rather than waiting until her original flight was scheduled. She hadn't imagined that it would be so difficult, or that she would feel so battered. This was worse, far worse, than anything Scott had ever done to her. He had hurt her physically and mentally, but he had never been able to touch her heart. It was killing her to leave Blake, but she had to do it.

Her headache was worse; as she stumbled around the bedroom trying to gather her clothing she had to grab at the furniture several times to keep from falling to her knees. Her mind was muddied, her thoughts jumbled, and nothing made much sense except the overpowering need she had to be gone. She had to leave before she was hurt any more, because she didn't think she'd be able to live if anything else happened.

"Stop it," a low voice commanded, and a hand caught her wrist, pulling her fingers away from the lingerie that she had been tossing carelessly into her suitcase. "You can pack later, when you're feeling better. You have a headache, don't you?"

She turned her head to look at him and almost staggered when her vision swayed alarmingly. "Yes," she mumbled.

"I thought so. I watched you practically crawl up the stairs." He put his arm around her waist, a curiously impersonal touch, and led her to the bed where they had shared so many nights. "Come on, you need a nap. You surprise me; I didn't think you were the type who lived on nerves, but this is a tension headache if I've ever seen one." His fingers moved down the front of her blouse, slipping the buttons out of their holes, and he eased the garment off her.

"I'm almost never sick," she apologized. "I'm sorry." She let him unsnap her bra and toss it aside. No, it wasn't a matter of *letting* him do anything. The truth was that she didn't feel capable of struggling with him over who would remove her clothes, and she badly needed the nap he had suggested. It wasn't as if he hadn't already seen every inch of her body. He eased her down on the bed and unfastened her slacks, sliding an arm under her and lifting her so he could pull them down over her hips. Her shoes came off with the slacks; then his hands returned and made short work of the filmy panties that were her last remaining garment.

Gently he turned her on her stomach, and she sighed as he began to rub the tight muscles in her neck. "I'm returning the favor," he murmured. "Just think of all the massages you've given me. Relax and go to sleep. You're tired, too tired to do anything right now. Sleep, darling."

She did sleep, deeply and without dreaming, sedated by his strong fingers as they rubbed the aching tension from her back and shoulders. It was dark when she woke, but her headache was gone. She felt fuzzy and disoriented, and she blinked at the dark form that rose from a chair beside the bed.

"Do you feel better?" he asked.

"Yes," she said, pushing her heavy hair away from her face. He tuned on the lamp and sat down on the edge of the bed, surveying her with narrowed eyes, as if gauging for himself how well she was feeling.

"Thank you for taking care of me," she said awkwardly. "I'll pack now, and go to a hotel—"

"It's too late to go anywhere tonight," he interrupted. "You've slept for hours. Alberta left a plate warming for you, if you feel like eating. I think you should try to eat something, or you'll be sick again. I didn't realize what a strain you had been under," he added thoughtfully.

She was hungry, and she sat up, holding the sheet to her. "I feel as if I could eat a cow," she said ruefully.

He chuckled softly. "I hope you'll settle for something less than a whole cow," he said, untangling a nightgown from the jumble of clothing that still littered the bed. He plucked the sheet away from her fingers and settled the nightgown over her head as impersonally as if he were dressing a child. Then he found her robe, and she obediently slid her arms into the sleeves while he held it.

"You don't have to coddle me," she said. "I feel much better. After food, I want a shower, and then I'll be fine."

"I like coddling you," he replied. "Just think of how many times you helped me to dress, how many times you coaxed me to eat, how many times you've picked me up when I lay sprawled on the floor."

He walked downstairs with her and sat beside her while she ate. She could feel his steady gaze on her, but the anger that had been there earlier was gone. Had it been only pride that made him lash out at her; did he now realize that she was right?

When she went back upstairs he was right behind her. She looked at him questioningly when he entered the bedroom with her. "Take your shower," he said, taking her shoulders and turning her in the direction of the bathroom. "I'll wait out here for you. I want to make sure you're okay before I go to bed."

"I'm fine," she protested.

"I'll stay," he said firmly, and that was that. Knowing that he was waiting, she hurried through her shower. When she came out of the bathroom he was sitting in the chair he'd occupied before, and he got to his feet.

"Bedtime." He smiled, pushing the robe off her shoulders. She hadn't fastened it, knowing that she would be taking it right off again, and it slipped to the floor. He leaned down and lifted her off her feet, then deposited her on the bed. She gasped and clutched at his shoulder.

"What was that for?" she asked, looking up at him.

"For this," he answered calmly, and kissed her. It was a deeply intimate kiss, his mouth opening over hers and his tongue moving in to touch hers. She dug her nails into his shoulder in surprise.

"Let me go," she said, pulling her mouth way from his.

"I'll let you go tomorrow," he murmured. "Tonight is mine."

He bent down to her again, and she rolled her head away; denied the sweet bloom of her lips, he found the sensitive slope where her neck met her shoulder and nipped at it with his teeth, making her gasp again. He dipped his hand into the bodice of her nightgown, rubbing his palm over the rich globes that had lured him.

"Blake...don't do this," she pleaded achingly.

"Why? You love me to touch your breasts," he countered.

She turned her head to look at him, and her lips were trembling. "Yes," she admitted. "But I'm leaving tomorrow. This...will only make it more difficult. I've accepted another job, and I have to go."

"I understand," he murmured, still stroking her flesh. "I'll put you on a plane tomorrow, if that's what you want, but we still have tonight together, and I want to spend it making love to you. Don't you like what we do to each other? Don't you like making me go out of my skull? You do. You make me wild, with your body like hot silk on me. One more night, darling. Let us have this last night together."

It was exactly what she hadn't wanted, to make love to him and know that she never would again, but the sensual promise he was making her with his hands and body was a heady lure. One more night, one more memory.

"All right," she whispered, beginning to unbutton his shirt. His hot flesh beckoned her, and she pressed her lips to him, feeling the curling hair under her mouth and the shiver that rippled over him. The intoxicating excitement that always seized her at his touch was taking over again, and she unbuckled his pants, helped him kick them away. He parted her legs and fit himself between them, the fever of feeling so high that no more preparation was needed, no more loving required to make her ready for him.

With a slow, smooth thrust he took her, and she adjusted her body to his weight and motion, letting the excitement well up like a cresting wave and take her away.

One more night. Then it would be finished.

_____ *Chapter Thirteen*

It didn't get any better. She had thought that it would get easier, even if the wound never quite healed, but from the time Blake saw her onto the plane at Sky Harbor Airport, the hurting never peaked, then declined. It stayed with her, eating at her. If she could forget about it during the day while she worked with Kevin, who was her new patient, it returned full force at night when she went to bed and lay there alone.

Milwaukee was at the opposite end of the world from Phoenix, or seemed like it. In a matter of a few hours she had exchanged a dry desert for several feet of snow, and she couldn't seem to get warm. The Colberts were nice, friendly people, anxious to do what they could to help her with Kevin, and Kevin was a darling, but he wasn't Blake. The childish arms that hugged her so spontaneously didn't satisfy the need she felt for strong, masculine ones, nor did the wet, loving kisses that Kevin and his little sister, Amy, gave her every night make her forget the kisses that had drowned her in a sea of sexual pleasure.

She had never thought that she would miss the fights that she and Blake had had, the loud and boisterous arguments, but she did. She missed everything about him, from his early-morning grumpiness to the wicked smile that lighted his face when he was teasing her.

With foolish desperation, she hoped that the last night

they'd had together would result in a baby; he hadn't taken any precautions that night, and for almost three weeks she was able to dream, to pretend. Then she discovered that it wasn't to be, and her world turned that much darker.

When she received a large check in the mail, forwarded by Dr. Norwood, it was all she could do to keep from screaming aloud in pain when she saw his signature. She wanted to tear it up, but she couldn't. The check was for the agreed-upon money. She traced her fingertip over the bold, angular script. It was just as she had known it would be; once she was away from him, she became only a part of his past. She had done what was best for him, but she hadn't known that she would have to live the rest of her life on the fine edge of agony.

With grim determination she set about rebuilding the defenses that he had torn down. She had to have them, to push the pain and memories behind, to hold the darkness at bay. Someday, she thought, looking at the wintry gray sky, she would find pleasure in living again. Someday the sun would shine again.

She had been with the Colberts exactly one month when she was called to the telephone. Frowning in perplexity, she gave Kevin his coloring book and crayons to keep him occupied until she returned, then went out to the hall to answer the phone.

"It's a man," Francine Colbert whispered, smiling at her in delight; then she left to see what had happened to make Amy suddenly bellow as if she were being scalped.

Dione put the phone to her ear. "Hello," she said cautiously.

"I'm not going to bite you," a deep, rich voice said

in amusement, and she slumped against the wall as her knees threatened to buckle under her.

"Blake!" she whispered.

"You've been there a month," he said. "Has your patient fallen in love with you yet?"

She closed her eyes, fighting down the mingled pain and pleasure that made her throat threaten to close. Hearing his voice made her weak all over, and she didn't know if she wanted to laugh or cry. "Yes," she gulped. "He's madly in love with me."

"What does he look like?" he growled.

"He's a gorgeous blond, with big blue eyes, not as dark as yours. He pouts for hours if he doesn't win when we play Go Fish," she said, and wiped a stray tear from her cheek.

Blake chuckled. "He sounds like real competition. How tall is he?"

"Oh, I don't know. About as tall as your average five-year-old, I suppose," she said.

"Well, that's a relief. I suppose I can leave you alone with him for a few more months."

She almost dropped the phone and had to grab the cord before it got away from her completely. Putting it back to her ear, she heard him say, "Are you still there?"

"Yes," she said, and wiped another tear away.

"I've been doing a lot of thinking," he said casually. "You told me over and over again that I didn't love you; you explained in great detail why I couldn't love you. But one thing that you never said was that you don't love me, and it seems to me that should have been your number-one reason for calling off a wedding. Well?"

What did he want? To reassure himself that she was

all right, that she wasn't pining away? She bit her lip, then said weakly, "I don't love you."

"You're lying," he snapped in return, and she could feel his temper rising. "You're so crazy about me that you're standing there crying, aren't you?"

"No," she denied, fiercely dashing the wetness from her face.

"You're lying again. I've got a meeting waiting for me, so I'll let you get back to your patient, but I'm not through with you. If you thought you could end it by getting on a plane, you have a lot to learn about me. I'll be calling you again. Dream about me, honey."

"I will not!" she said fiercely, but she said it to a dial tone, and she *was* lying anyway. She dreamed about him almost every night and woke up with her pillow damp from the tears she'd shed in her sleep.

Thoroughly rattled, she returned to Kevin, and delighted him by losing a game of Go Fish.

Over the next few days her nerves gradually settled down, and she stopped jumping every time the phone rang. A blizzard shut the city down for two days, knocking out phone service and the electricity. The electricity was restored in a matter of hours, keeping them from freezing, but the phone service waited until clear skies had returned. She was out in the snow with Kevin and Amy, building a snowman for them with their inexpert but hilarious help, when Francine called her.

"Dione, you have a call! It's your friend again. Come on in; I'll bring the children in and get them dried off."

"Awww, Mommy," Kevin protested, but Francine was already pushing his little wheelchair inside and Amy followed obediently.

"Hello," Blake said warmly after she stammered out a hesitant greeting. "Are you pregnant?"

This time she was prepared and held on tightly to the receiver. "No. I...I thought about that, too, but everything's all right."

"Good. I didn't mean to get carried away. Serena *is* pregnant. She didn't waste any time when Richard came back. She was so excited at the possibility that she couldn't wait to take one of those early warning tests, or whatever you call them."

"I'm happy for her. How do you feel about being an uncle?"

"It's okay by me, but I'd rather be a father."

She cautiously leaned against the wall. "What do you mean?"

"I mean that when we get married I'm going to throw away my whole supply of—"

"We're not getting married!" she yelped, then glanced around to see if anyone had heard her. No one was in sight, so she guessed that Francine was still occupied with the children.

"Sure we are," he returned calmly. "On the first of May. You set the date yourself. Don't you remember? I was making love to you."

"I remember," she whispered. "But don't you remember? I broke the engagement. I gave your heart back to you."

"That's what you think," he said. "We're getting married if I have to drag you kicking and screaming back to Phoenix."

Again she was left listening to a dial tone.

She couldn't make any sense out of what he was doing. Sleep got harder and harder to attain, and she lay awake going over the possibilities. Why would he insist that they were getting married? Why couldn't he just let it go?

It was a week before he called her again, and Francine had an amused gleam in her eye when she handed her the phone. "It's that dishy guy again," she said as Dione lifted the receiver to her ear.

"Tell her thank you," Blake chuckled. "How are you, honey?"

"Blake, why are you calling me?" she asked in desperation.

"Why shouldn't I call you? Is it against the law for a man to talk to the woman he's going to marry?"

"I'm not going to marry you!" she said, and this time she bellowed it. Francine popped her head out of the kitchen and grinned at her.

Blake was laughing. "Sure you are. You already know all my bad habits and love me anyway; what could be better?"

"Would you listen to reason?" she yelled. "It's out of the question for me to marry you!"

"You're the one who's not listening," he countered. "You love me, and I love you. I don't know why you're so convinced that I can't love you, but you're wrong. Just think of the fun we're going to have while I show you how wrong you are."

"This is crazy," she moaned.

"No, this isn't crazy. You've got some crazy ideas, though, and you're going to get rid of them. You've convinced yourself that no one is going to love you, and you walked away from me, knowing that it was tearing me apart and half killing yourself at the same time. Your mother didn't love you, and Scott didn't love you, but they were only two people. How many people since then have loved you, and you pushed them away because you were afraid of getting hurt again? I'm not going to let you push me away, honey. Think about it."

"Some guy," Francine teased when Dione walked into the kitchen. Then she saw Dione's white face and quickly pushed a chair at her, then poured a cup of coffee. "Is something wrong?"

"Yes. No. I don't know." Dazed, she drank the coffee, then raised stunned golden eyes to the other woman. "He wants to marry me."

"So I gathered. What's so surprising about that? I imagine a lot of men have wanted to marry you."

"He won't take no for an answer," she said abstractedly.

"If he looks as great as he sounds, why would you want him to take no for an answer?" Francine asked practically. "Unless he's a bum."

"No, he's not a bum. He's...even greater than he sounds."

"Do you love him?"

Dione buried her face in her hands. "So much that I've been about to die without him."

"Then marry him!" Francine sat down beside her. "Marry him, and whatever problem is keeping you apart will be settled later. You'd be surprised how many problems people can settle when they're sleeping in the same bed every night and they wake up to the same face every morning. Don't be afraid to take the chance; every marriage is a gamble, but then so is walking across the street. If you didn't take the chance you'd never get to the other side."

Words tumbled around in Dione's mind that night as she lay sleeplessly in bed. Blake had said that she was afraid of getting hurt again, and it was the truth. But was she so afraid of getting hurt that she had deliberately turned her back on a man who loved her?

No one had ever loved her before. No one had worried about her, held her when she cried, comforted her when she was upset....

Except Blake. He had done all those things. Even Richard had thought she was strong and confident, but Blake had seen beneath the act, had realized how vulnerable she was, how easily hurt. Blake had replaced the memories of violence with the memories of love. When she dreamed of a man's touch now it was his touch she dreamed of, and it filled her with aching need.

Blake loved her! It was incredible, but she had to believe it. She had set him free, expecting him to forget her, but it hadn't happened like that. It wasn't a case of "out of sight, out of mind." He had gone to the trouble of finding out where she was, and he had given her time to think about a life without him before he called. He hadn't given up.

As the days passed she went through her routine with Kevin with a smile on her face, humming constantly. He was so willing to do anything she asked that it was a pleasure to work with him, and she knew that soon he wouldn't need her any longer. That automobile accident that had injured him was long forgotten, and all he was concerned with now was if he would be able to play ball by the time summer came.

"How's your patient doing?" Blake asked the next time he called, and Dione smiled at the sound of his voice.

"He's doing great. I'm about ready to graduate him to a walker."

"That's good news, and not just for him. That means you'll be able to take a long honeymoon."

She didn't say anything, just stood there smiling. No, Blake Remington didn't give up. Any other man would have thrown up his hands in disgust, but when Blake decided that he wanted something, he went after it.

"Have you fainted?" he asked warily.

"No," she said, and burst into tears. "It's just that I love you so much, and I miss you."

He drew a long, shuddering breath. "Well, thank God," he muttered. "I was beginning to think I really would have to kidnap you. Lady, it's going to take a lifetime of massages to make up for what you've put me through."

"I'll even sign a contract, if you want," she said, swiping at the tears.

"Oh, I want, all right. An ironclad contract. What day can I fetch you? If I know you, you have Kevin's schedule mapped out to the very day you kiss him good-bye and walk away, and I'm going to be there to meet you when you walk out the door. You're not getting out of my sight until you're Mrs. Remington."

"April twelfth," she said, laughing and crying at the same time.

"I'll be there."

He *was* there, leaning on the doorbell at nine o'clock sharp that morning, while a spring snowstorm dumped its white load on his unprotected head. When Francine opened the door he grinned at her. "I've come for Dione," Blake said. "Is she awake yet?"

Francine opened the door wider, smiling at the tall man with the slight limp who entered her house. There was a reckless air about him; he was the sort of man who didn't let the woman he loved walk away from him.

"She's trying to get everything packed, but the children are helping her and it could take a while," Francine explained. "I imagine they're both wrapped around her legs and crying."

"I understand the feeling," he muttered, and at Francine's questioning look he grinned again. "I'm one of her ex-patients," he explained.

"Take good care of her," Francine pleaded. "She's been so good to Kevin, keeping his spirits up, not letting him get bored. She's special."

"I know," he said gently.

Dione came around the turn of the stairs with two tearful children in her arms. She stopped when she saw Blake, and her entire face lighted up. "You came," she breathed, as if she hadn't dared to let herself really believe it.

"With bells on," he said, going up the steps in a graceful leap that made a mockery of the remaining limp. There was no way to get his arms around her without including the children, so he pulled all three of them to him and kissed her. Amy stuck her finger between their mouths and giggled.

Blake drew back and gave the little girl a rueful look, which she returned with wide-eyed innocence. "Are you the man who's taking Dee away?" Kevin asked tearfully, lifting his wet face from Dione's neck.

"Yes, I am," Blake replied gravely, "but I promise to take good care of her if you'll let me have her. I was her patient, too, and I need her a lot. My leg still hurts me at night, and she has to rub it."

Kevin could understand that, and after a moment he nodded. "All right," he sighed. "She's real good at rubbing legs."

"Kevin, let Dione put you down," Francine directed. When both of the children were on the floor, Amy wrapped her plump little arms around Blake's leg and looked up a long, long way to his face. He looked down at her, then lifted his eyes to Dione's face. "At least two," he said. "And maybe even three, if you don't give me a daughter on your first two tries."

"I'm thirty years old, remember," she said cautiously. "Almost thirty-one."

"So? You have the body of an eighteen-year-old, only in better shape. I should know," he murmured, the hot light in his eyes making her cheeks turn pink. In a normal voice he said, "Are you packed?"

"Yes, I'll bring my suitcases down. You wait right here," she said hurriedly, turning and sprinting up the stairs. Her heart was galloping in her chest, and it wasn't from the stairs. Just seeing him again had been like getting kicked, except that it didn't hurt. She felt alive, truly alive; even her fingertips were tingling with joy. In eighteen days she would be getting married!

"Hurry it up!" he called, and she shivered with delight. Picking up her two suitcases she ran down the stairs.

When they were in the car he sat for a long moment just looking at her. Francine and the children had said their last good-byes in the house, not coming out into the snow, so they were all alone. The snow had already covered the windows of the car, encasing them in a white cocoon.

"I have something for you," he murmured, reaching into his pocket. He withdrew the ruby heart and dangled it before her eyes. "You might as well keep it," he said as he clasped it around her neck. "It never did work right after you tried to give it back, anyway."

Tears burned her eyes as the ruby heart slid down to its resting place between her breasts. "I love you," she said unsteadily.

"I know. I had some bad moments when you first gave the heart back to me, but after I thought about it, I realized how frightened you were. I had to let you go to convince you that I loved you. Lady, that was the hardest thing I've ever done in my life, letting you get on the plane without me. Learning how to walk again was child's play compared to that."

"I'll make it up to you," she whispered, going into his arms. His familiar scent teased her senses, and she inhaled it delightedly. The smell of him brought back hot, sunny days and the echo of laughter.

"Starting tonight," he threatened. "Or better yet, as soon as we can get to the hotel room I've booked for us."

"Aren't we flying back to Phoenix today?" she asked, lifting her head in surprise.

"In case you haven't noticed, we're in the middle of a snowstorm." He grinned. "All flights are grounded until it clears, which could be days and days. How would you like to spend days and days in bed with me?"

"I'll try to bear it," she sighed.

"Do you spell that b-a-r-e?" he asked, nuzzling her neck. Then, slowly, as if he had waited as long as he could, he closed his lips over hers. He kissed her for a long time, savoring the taste and feel of her, then pulled himself away with a visible effort.

"I'm able to drive now," he said unnecessarily as he put the car into gear.

"So I see."

"And I'm flying again. I tested a new engine last week—"

"Are you going to keep doing the dangerous stuff?" she interrupted.

He eyed her. "I've been thinking about that. I don't think I'll be taking as many chances as I used to. There's too much excitement going on at home for me to risk missing any of it."

She was swimming laps, the hot May desert sun beating down on her head. The exercise felt good to her body, stretching muscles that had felt cramped. She had missed the pool and the well-equipped little gym where she and Blake had played out so many of their crises. That morning she had gone to a Phoenix hospital and been hired on the spot; she would miss the intensity of a one-on-one therapeutic relationship, but the regular hours would permit her to be with Blake at night and still keep doing the work she loved.

"Hey!" a deep voice called. "Are you in training for the Olympics?"

She began treading water. "What are you doing home so early?" she asked, pushing her hair out of her eyes.

"That's a fine welcome," her husband of two weeks grumbled. He shed his coat and draped it over one of the chairs, then pulled his tie loose. Dione watched as he systematically undressed, dropping his clothes on the chair until he stood as naked as the day he was born. He came into the water in a neat, shallow dive, and reached her with a few powerful strokes of his arms.

"If you get caught like that, don't blame me," she warned.

"It's too hot for clothes," he complained. "Did you get the job?"

"Of course I got the job," she sniffed.

"Conceited." He put his hand on top of her head and ducked her, which didn't bother her at all. She was as good a swimmer under water as she was on top of it, and she kicked her graceful legs, darting away from him. He caught up with her when she reached the edge.

"You never did say why you're home so early," she said, turning to face him.

"I came home to make love to my wife," he replied. "I couldn't keep my mind on what I was doing; I kept thinking about last night," he said, and watched in fascination as her eyes grew heavy-lidded with memory.

He moved in closer to her and pressed his mouth to hers, his hand going to the back of her head and slanting her mouth across his. Their tongues met in mutual desire, and Dione quivered, letting her body float against his. Her legs twined with his and found them steady.

"You're standing," she said, lifting her mouth away.

"I know." His hand moved purposefully up her back and deftly unclipped her bikini top. He pulled it way from her and tossed it out of the pool. It landed on the tiles with a sodden plop. His fingers touched her breasts, cupping them together as he leaned forward and took another kiss.

With a moan she twined her arms around his neck; then she was wrapped around him like a vine. No matter how often he made love to her, it kept getting better and better as her body learned new ways of responding to him. The cool water lapped around them, but it didn't cool their hot skin. The fires within burned too brightly to be dampened by a little water.

He lifted her out of the water until her breasts were on a level with his mouth; then he feasted on the ripe curves that thrust so beguilingly at him. "I love you," he groaned, pulling at the ties that held the minuscule bikini bottom on her hips.

"Blake! Not here," she protested, but her body lay

against his in sweet abandon. "Someone will see. Miguel...Alberta..."

"Miguel isn't here," he whispered, sliding her down the length of his body. "And no one can see what we're doing. The glare of the sun on the water takes care of that. Put your legs around my hips," he directed.

Suddenly she laughed aloud, throwing her head back and lifting her face to the hot Phoenix sun. "You're still a daredevil," she crooned, catching her breath as he took her with a long, delicious slide of skin against skin. "You love to take chances."

She clung to his shoulders, her senses dazzled, drenched in the beauty of the day. He watched her face, watched the wonderful play of emotions in her exotic eyes, watched them grow slumbrous, watching her teeth catch that full, passionate lower lip as she quivered with the desire he was carefully building in her. "Lady," he chanted. "Woman. You're all mine, aren't you?"

She laughed again, drunk with pleasure. She lifted her arms to the sun. "For as long as you want me," she promised.

"Then you'll go to your grave as my lady," he said. "And even that won't be the end of it."

**New York Times
Bestselling Author**

LINDA
MACKENZIE'S
MOUNTAIN
HOWARD

Wolf Mackenzie is an outsider, a loner who chooses to live with
his son on top of a Wyoming mountain rather than face the
scorn of a town that dismisses him as a half-breed criminal.
Until Mary Elizabeth Potter comes storming up his mountain.
The proper, naive schoolteacher couldn't care less about the
townspeople's distrust—she's just determined to give Wolf's
son the education he deserves. But when Mary meets Wolf,
an education of another kind begins. Now Mary and Wolf
are teaching each other—and learning—about passion,
forgiveness and even love.

"Howard's writing is compelling." —*Publishers Weekly*

Available mid-March 2000 wherever paperbacks are sold!

MIRA

HE COULDN'T FORGET.
SHE COULDN'T REMEMBER.

SHARON
SALA
remember me

Clay LeGrand's life is shattered the day his wife, Frankie, disappears without a trace. It seems as though his questions will never be answered...until the day he comes home to find Frankie, safe, in his bed.

But Frankie remembers nothing of the two years she was away. Not where she was, or how she got the strange tattoo on her neck, the needle marks on her arms. She has no answers...but someone does, and he's willing to stop at nothing to keep Frankie's secrets—and her life—for himself.

Sharon Sala has a "rare ability to bring powerful and emotionally wrenching stories to life."
—*Romantic Times*

On sale mid-November 1999
wherever paperbacks are sold.

LINDA HOWARD

66457	LOVING EVANGELINE	___ $5.50 U.S.	___ $6.50 CAN.
66480	DIAMOND BAY	___ $5.99 U.S.	___ $6.99 CAN.
66432	ALL THAT GLITTERS	___ $5.50 U.S.	___ $6.50 CAN.
66479	DUNCAN'S BRIDE	___ $5.99 U.S.	___ $6.99 CAN.
66153	MIDNIGHT RAINBOW	___ $5.50 U.S.	___ $6.50 CAN.
66478	THE CUTTING EDGE	___ $5.99 U.S.	___ $6.99 CAN.
66274	WHITE LIES	___ $5.50 U.S.	___ $6.50 CAN.

(limited quantities available)

TOTAL AMOUNT $_____
POSTAGE & HANDLING $_____
($1.00 for one book; 50¢ for each additional)
APPLICABLE TAXES* $_____
<u>TOTAL PAYABLE</u> $_____
(check or money order—please do not send cash)

To order, complete this form and send it, along with a check or money order for the total above, payable to MIRA Books®, to: **In the U.S.:** 3010 Walden Avenue, P.O. Box 9077, Buffalo, NY 14269-9077; **In Canada:** P.O. Box 636, Fort Erie, Ontario, L2A 5X3.

Name:_____
Address:_____ City:_____
State/Prov.:_____ Zip/Postal Code:_____
Account Number (if applicable):_____
075 CSAS

*New York residents remit applicable sales taxes.
 Canadian residents remit applicable GST and provincial taxes.

MIRA